PROLOGUE

Rusty

There weren't a lot of jobs in Rocky Point, Maine, especially after the lumber mill shut down. And custodial services didn't exactly pay a mint, even at a fancy school like Blackbrook Academy. But Rusty Nayler knew the secret of success:

Rich folk played by a different set of rules.

In that way, Rusty could still be a part of the game. He held the keys to every lock in the school. With Rusty on their side, a desperate student could find their way into the labs after hours. They might even get late-night access to the contents of their teacher's desk drawers.

For a price.

And then there were the . . . extracurriculars. Blackbrook had a curfew, and strict policies about drinking and private shenanigans in the dorms. As a member of the staff, Rusty was tasked with upholding those policies.

But he could also be convinced to look the other way, or even help hide the evidence. It was extraordinary, the things that money could buy.

Over the years, Rusty had amassed quite a tidy sum from Blackbrook students with too much money and not enough sense. It was a nice gig. Certainly, the perks made it easier to ignore the jeers of students when he was mopping up their messes or emptying their trash cans. He never responded, but he did keep it in mind when he set his fees.

That was part of the game. He never could understand the locals who wouldn't play along. Those like Linda White, who knew the rules as well as he did but rejected every chance to take advantage of them. Those like young Vaughn Green, who refused to even believe the game existed and that he was part of it . . . whether he liked it or not.

Or so Rusty had always thought. He'd given Green a job when the boy first came to Blackbrook, scholarship in hand, eyes shining with delusions Rusty didn't have the heart to dispel. Green might be a Blackbrook student, but he wasn't really one of them. For two years, he'd watched the poor kid working himself to death, trying to play the game against those who'd already bought themselves a winning hand.

But then, the storm had come. Green had shown a different side of himself that day.

It took a murder for him to get a clue.

And in the weeks that followed, Rusty saw how Green was sneaking around and taking advantage of the chaos that had followed the storm. Little wonder. Ever since the headmaster's murder, Blackbrook was in free fall. Parents had yanked their precious youngsters' enrollment. The administration was forced to cut back on staff hours and even terminate a few jobs. Everyone had to look out for themselves.

That's what Rusty was doing out here, at midnight, forcing a stubborn old lock buried in a tangle of knotty vines. He should have charged more for this task. But some deserved favors. Those who had weathered the storm by Rusty's side definitely counted.

The student had remained silent the whole time Rusty struggled with the lock. Usually, they never stopped talking, always ready to explain in great detail how they weren't really a cheater or a degenerate or a thief but that *this* was a special circumstance.

Not this time. Maybe his companion knew there was no point in lying.

Rusty hacked away at the vines until the creaky door budged. No one had used this tunnel since Prohibition. Lord only knew what might be hidden away down there.

He cast a careful glance at the kid. "Okay. We're in."

His companion nodded once and climbed past him into the hole in the vines. Rusty eased in, too, casting the weak yellow beam from his flashlight around the dirty stone walls riddled with invading roots, mold, and creepy-crawlies.

"What are you looking for again?" he asked skeptically.

"I didn't tell you the first time."

Fair enough. But Rusty was sticking around, anyway. There'd be hell to pay if something happened in this death trap and got traced back to him. Blackbrook was under enough scrutiny, and the interim headmaster wasn't about to let things slide.

But it was all Rusty could do to keep up. The kid wasn't even using a flashlight. He turned a corner, then another, and all of a sudden, Rusty knew exactly where they were headed.

"Wait a minute—"

But Rusty was the only one who stopped. He shone the beam up over the familiar walls.

"You never said this was where we were going."

Rusty turned, but the kid had vanished.

"Hey!" he hissed, suddenly *very* conscious of who else might be listening. "Where'd you go?"

His flashlight beam flickered as he cast it about the dank space, illuminating mossy walls and detritus washed up in the flood. Generations' worth of odds and ends.

"Get back here!" Rusty whispered into the shadows. But the kid was gone.

His light faltered again. Rusty tapped at the base of the flashlight. He should have put in new batteries before this little outing. In the darkness he thought he heard some shuffling, and when the light came up again, it shone on more junk. Decades old, by the look of it. Rusty had no idea how the papers and pictures and boxes and blankets had survived the flood. He peered closer. A hobo's hideout? But then he saw the school crest, and the name on the papers.

Oh. *Him.*

Just another enterprising young Blackbrook cheat. Fifty-odd years of thieves and degenerates. Rich folk with their own sets of rules.

He heard footsteps at his back. At last, they could get out of there.

His flashlight flickered again, but not before he saw the face of the person approaching.

"It's you," blurted Rusty Nayler.

They were the last words he would ever speak.

1

Orchid

Class was over, but the bell didn't ring. The intercom system was still a bit spotty since the flood. Their teacher, Dr. Olverson, went on about Planck's constant for another few minutes, then stopped and looked sheepishly at the clock.

"Oh," she said. "I guess . . . you're all dismissed? Don't forget chapter four for homework! Do the first six questions in the back of the text."

They "all" consisted of six students, each of whom was silent as they scraped back their lab stools and packed up. Orchid McKee watched them cluster into groups as they left class for lunch or their dorm. She was used to not being invited to join. What she wasn't used to were the stares. She hated being watched.

But now, as part of the Murder Crew, it was nearly as constant as Planck's.

Yikes. Orchid. On second thought, maybe it was a good thing she didn't have friends to whom she might say dorky stuff like that out loud.

She finished wrapping her scarf around her face and headed out into the frigid cold. The scars of the flood were still evident everywhere on campus. Yellow bands of caution tape stretched across the quad, guarding against the endless slicks of mud and black ice. Most of the buildings had boards and warning signs over doors and windows. Blackbrook was in session, but it still felt abandoned. Most of the student body had not returned in the wake of the murder. The ones who did said it was creepy.

Orchid and the rest of the Murder Crew were the creepiest part.

Speaking of the Murder Crew . . . Vaughn Green bounded down the stairs of the administration building and met her on the walk. "Hey!"

"Hey," she replied warily. Which Vaughn would meet her this time?

"I thought I might run into you."

"Chances are good. There's only a hundred kids left on campus."

"Where are you headed?"

"Home to Tudor House." She nodded in the direction of the imposing stone edifice at the edge of the campus.

If his steps faltered, he covered it well. "Can I walk with you?"

"Sure." *It's a free country, Vaughn. You can be my BFF today and then totally blow me off the next time we're in history class together.*

They walked in silence for a few steps, but then Vaughn got a few feet in front of her and turned. Orchid stopped.

"Can I—um—carry your books?"

"What?"

"I just feel like a jerk, you know? You're all weighed down, and I'm a guy, and—"

"You want to *carry my books*?" Orchid replied, her eyebrows disappearing into her bangs. "What is this, a Victorian novel?"

Vaughn held out his hands, smiling. What nerve. This was too much. Okay, he wanted to have it out? Fine by her.

"You know when you were a jerk?" she said. "When you went ahead and picked Violet Vandergraf as a partner for the 1920s poster project in history class. I told you I was coming back to Blackbrook."

Vaughn's face fell. "You did."

"And now I get back and everyone is all partnered up without me, and all the good topics are taken."

"Yeah . . ."

"*And* Violet is a moron," she added as she swept by him. "So, you know, good luck with that."

"Wait, Orchid!" He skipped to keep up with her. "I—I didn't mean to pick Violet—"

"What?" she snapped, not deigning to look at him. "You got confused by which girl named after a flower you survived a flood and a murderous rampage with?"

"Yeah, that sounds exactly like something I'd do," Vaughn mumbled.

She rolled her eyes. It was exactly what he *had* done, though.

He cast about, as if looking for an excuse. "I—I didn't think you'd want to be my partner."

Now she stopped. "After all the time we spent texting over break?"

Vaughn didn't respond. Typical.

"I kind of figured you'd have my back, you know? After everything." She started walking again. She could tell he was still keeping pace beside her. "And, not to harp on it or anything, but the only posters left are some crap about the Teapot Dome scandal and then an argument in *favor* of Prohibition."

"I'll fix this," Vaughn replied. "Violet and I are . . . my topic is . . ."

"Rumrunners," Orchid finished. Did he not even remember that? There were only eleven people left in the class. "Lucky you, in attendance the day topics were being handed out."

"So then you pick temperance," he said. "We'll do a huge group project, for and against. There'll be lots of stuff in the historical society to help us out. Rocky Point saw a fair bit of action smuggling liquor in from Canada. I'm going to be doing my poster mostly by myself anyway. We'll share the load."

She looked at him. "That sounds like a lot of extra work for you."

"It is," he admitted, then quickly added, "but I don't mind."

"And testing's in, like, a week." Vaughn was a scholarship student. If he didn't ace his standardized tests, all kinds of collegiate doors would be closed to him, even with a Blackbrook diploma.

Or maybe more accurately, *despite* one. The school's storied reputation was as trashed as its campus at present. Murder tended to have that effect on a pricey private school.

"Let me make this right."

Orchid took a deep breath. She wanted to believe him. And standing here on the quad, staring up into his adorably hopeful expression, she almost did. This was the easy Vaughn, the open Vaughn. The one she'd gotten to know through texts back and forth between Maine and California.

Every time things had gotten hard over break, every time she'd been reminded just how much she risked by remaining Orchid, Vaughn was there with a text—a snippet of new song lyrics, a description of the ice floating in the slate-gray sea—a reminder of what she'd lose if she decided not to come back to Blackbrook.

You'd think after all those years in Hollywood, she'd be over boys with pretty faces. But that was precisely it. Orchid had never been interested in boys her age, and she'd never been into anyone at all during her time at Blackbrook. Not like that. It was too dangerous.

Until Vaughn had caught her alone in the firelight on the night of the storm. When he'd seen past her disguise to notice the *real* Orchid. Even in the bloodshed and terror that followed, Orchid had not forgotten that moment.

But maybe Vaughn had.

"I'm really not interested in playing games," she said at last.

"Me neither. I'm sick of them." As always, his words sounded heartfelt. Was it another game?

"Well, I don't know what to think when you act like this—"

"I'm sorry. It won't happen again. I just—I didn't want to assume. Everyone has been really weird since coming back. You know what they're calling us?"

Orchid pursed her lips. "The Murder Crew."

"Yeah." Vaughn shrugged. "It's not like Scarlett wants to be seen with me. And I know you two are hanging out a lot more, or whatever . . ."

"Yeah," Orchid admitted. "Want to trade? *You* can be Scarlett's new BFF." She was obligated now. Not just because of the whole Murder Crew thing, but also because Scarlett was the only person on campus who knew Orchid's real name.

"I'd rather be with you."

That was all he said, but it still made Orchid catch her breath. No one had said they wanted to be with her and not been a creep in . . . well, possibly ever. She looked at him. Vaughn just stood there, waiting, with an expression on his face like he was more than prepared for her to say no.

But she didn't want to say no.

She shoved her textbooks and test-prep binder at him. "Fine. You can carry my books."

Vaughn broke into a smile like she'd just handed him a puppy. He really was awfully cute. Tall and lanky, with that big, stupid grin and those unusual, golden-brown eyes. When they started walking again, they were a full foot closer to each other on the sidewalk. Their arms brushed. Even through all the layers of their parkas it was . . . nice.

"I'm glad you're back," he said. "Even though you said you were returning, when term started and you were still gone, I thought you'd pulled a Karlee. Or a Kayla."

Orchid didn't blame Karlee Silverman or Kayla Gould *or* their parents for staying far away from Blackbrook this term. They'd been attacked and drugged by a murderer. For all Orchid knew, the pending lawsuit was massive.

If the parents on Orchid's student-enrollment forms weren't entirely fictional, she was sure they'd be keeping her away as well. Real live parents tended to act concerned when their children were held captive by a murderer in a secret passage under their dorm room. But, as it was, she got to make the decision herself.

And she'd promised Vaughn that she'd return.

She just had to make sure she was safe here. Ironically, the murder was not the biggest threat Orchid had faced last term. Orchid's stalker wasn't new, but for three years she thought she'd escaped his detection. She hadn't.

"I had stuff to take care of back home," she said with a shrug.

Stuff like making sure all her accounts were securely locked down and her protection order was still in place. Stuff like figuring out how her stalker had gotten access to her private information and making sure it never happened again. Stuff like seriously weighing whether or not she could afford to keep being Orchid McKee or if she was going to be forced to erase her and vanish once again.

The problem was, she *liked* the person she'd created at

Blackbrook. The scholar, the scientist. Orchid had spent her childhood being told she was worthwhile solely because her face could make money for other people. She was beloved by strangers who had never seen her for real. Here, her teachers liked her mind. Here, she felt like a whole person.

Blackbrook, and Orchid McKee, were worth saving.

"Stuff like what?" Vaughn asked.

"Dealing with everything," Orchid said. "Therapy." That wasn't a lie. She had been to see her therapist a lot. They'd talked about the murder and about Mrs. White. All those months that Orchid had been living with Mrs. White, she'd never dreamed that the woman was capable of murdering someone. Even when Orchid had confronted her in the secret passage below the kitchen, it was hard to wrap her mind around the idea. Mrs. White had been an aged hippie, not a killer. The older woman herself seemed shocked that she'd done it when she confessed everything.

"Oh."

She looked at him. She hoped he wasn't one of those guys who got weird about therapy. Especially since she and her therapist had spent a fair bit of time talking about Vaughn, too. Her therapist thought this crush was "good for her," whatever *that* was supposed to mean.

"Did *you* talk to anyone? It's a lot to take in."

He gave her a wry smile. "Not a lot of shrinks in Rocky Point."

Of course. "What about the new school counselor?"

"I'm sure he's fully booked. Don't know if you're aware

of this, but there was a murder on campus last term. A lot of people are struggling with grief."

"Didn't you get that message from him? We Murder Crew members take priority for appointments." Orchid had already gotten two voicemails from the guy—a Mr. Winkle—about setting up a meeting, and Scarlett had mentioned seeing him.

But Orchid already had a therapist she could trust. If Mr. Winkle was so busy, she'd rather he focus on people who needed him, like Vaughn.

Vaughn frowned and was quiet. "The counselor's from away. I don't think he'd understand."

But Orchid did. This town was very, very small. However close to Mrs. White she had been from living with her in Tudor House, it was nothing compared to Vaughn's bond with the woman. He'd known her since childhood. She was once a resident of the girls' reform school that Tudor House had been before it was rolled into Blackbrook Academy. During the storm, Orchid had gotten the sense that they knew each other very well, indeed.

"You don't know until you try," she said.

"Yeah. Maybe."

"Well, you can always talk to me." She placed a gloved hand on his parka sleeve. "No one should be alone in this."

That was the decision she and her therapist had come to. Orchid had been too much alone. Murder aside, she was safer at Blackbrook, away from her old life. Besides, the killer was behind bars, and her stalker was sequestered and had been given stern warnings. Nothing else was going to happen here.

The sound he made was too grim for a laugh. "I'm not alone."

"Orchid!" someone called. They both looked up to see Scarlett Mistry bounding over, her crimson wool coat trailing out behind her like a cape. Where Orchid dressed to blend in, Scarlett liked to stand out. As she approached, she caught sight of Vaughn. "Oh. You."

Vaughn nodded brusquely. "Hello to you, too."

"How was your break or whatever?" Scarlett asked him.

"Busy. We had a lot of work to do on campus to get it ready for you to enjoy when you came back."

She gazed dismissively over the mud slicks and yellow caution tape. "Guess you have a lot more to do."

"Ouch," Orchid said, getting between them. "Give it a rest, will you?"

Vaughn straightened and handed her back her books. "I think we've reached Murder Crew critical mass. I'd better make myself scarce. I've got stuff to do back home, anyway."

"Okay, bye!" Scarlett trilled.

Orchid shot her a look, then turned to Vaughn. "I'll see you later, though, right? We have to talk about the history project. And . . . stuff."

He smiled again. "Yeah. And stuff."

Orchid watched him head off toward the bridge to Rocky Point. And Scarlett watched Orchid watch Vaughn.

"Eww," she said at last. "Do you *like him* like him?"

Orchid sighed. "Little bit." Lot bit.

Scarlett rolled her eyes. "But why, though? Look who you

are, and look who he is. You should be dating someone in a boy band, or a pro athlete."

"I'm *seventeen.*"

"The son of a president?" Scarlett suggested.

"Now that's just gross."

"I'm just saying. Famous people don't date nobodies from nowhere."

"*I'm* nobody from nowhere," Orchid reminded her. "I'm Orchid McKee. I have no family, no home—" No past. No support, except what she paid for. And as for friends . . .

Well, there was Vaughn. And Scarlett, when she wasn't driving Orchid nuts.

Scarlett was the only person at Blackbrook who knew Orchid's secret. Last term, during the storm, Orchid had confided in her, fearing that Headmaster Boddy's killer was the stalker who had sent Orchid a threatening letter and meddled in her tuition payments. It hadn't been, but the truth was out, anyway. And now, Scarlett had decided that they had to be best friends.

Perhaps it had been a mistake. It wasn't that Scarlett was untrustworthy . . . exactly. She just wasn't precisely trustworthy out of the goodness of her heart.

If Scarlett Mistry even *had* a heart.

"Nobody . . . for now," Scarlett pointed out. "I'm not ready to close the door on Emily Pryce just yet."

Especially if she could find a way to make Orchid's erstwhile fame work in her own favor.

"Think of how awesome it would be for you to make a triumphant return to celebrity."

Orchid shook her head. Hard. "I don't want to return. Not to Hollywood." Being a child star was hell. Being a grown-up star sounded even worse.

"Well, you say that now. But after you get a degree at some fancy Ivy League school . . . People get super impressed by all that. Natalie Portman. Emma Watson."

Now Orchid just laughed. "I'm so glad you aren't the one making decisions for me, Scarlett."

"For now," Scarlett repeated darkly. She hugged herself. "Let's get back to the house before we freeze."

They headed up the steps of Tudor House and went inside. Orchid kept her eyes averted from the floor of the hall. She never even went into the conservatory anymore. Couldn't, without picturing Headmaster Boddy's lifeless body and gray face.

Scarlett, however, appeared unaffected. They hung their coats on the rack and toed off their boots. Dr. Brown, the interim headmaster and new resident coordinator, was super strict about mud, especially given the reduced staff.

Orchid had been stunned to learn that they were keeping Tudor House open for dorm space, but then again, most of the other buildings on campus had been damaged in the storm. Not that any of the girls they'd moved in were happy about staying in the Murder House . . . or with the Murder Crew.

"Did you do those practice tests?" Scarlett asked her, gesturing to her binder.

Orchid nodded. "I feel pretty good about everything. Ten wrong answers in verbal—"

"Ten!" Scarlett exclaimed. "We have to run them again, tonight!"

"Ten isn't the end of the world—"

"I reject that premise."

Again, Orchid shook her head. One would think, after what they'd been through in the storm, that Scarlett would have gained a little perspective. But that was, perhaps, underestimating the place her friend held in her own worldview.

"I think there's the real possibility of diminishing returns with these practice tests," Orchid said. She wouldn't mention the two blanks she'd left in the math section. "I don't want to wear myself out before the real one."

"And I don't want you to miss answers you know you should have gotten. Think about it. We're up against child geniuses who have been running drills since they were in diapers and movie stars' children who have hired ringers to take the test for them—"

"And you want me back in Hollywood?" Orchid cried.

"We're up against *Finn.*"

Ah, there it was. Scarlett couldn't bear to be beaten by her ex–best friend, Finn Plum. If there was any chink to be found in her blood-red armor, that would be it.

She looked at her friend—since that was what Scarlett was. When Orchid had been scared during the storm, Scarlett had listened. When she'd confronted Mrs. White in the secret passage, it had been Scarlett who broke down the door.

"Okay," Orchid said. "*One* more practice test."

Scarlett beamed and pulled out her stopwatch. It was crimson, of course. "Grab your number two pencils! I'll meet you in the study."

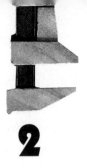

2

Green

Vaughn Green never had enough—money, food, sleep, time. For years, he'd been running on the fumes of the future. All he had to do was get through the winter, get through the term, get through Blackbrook, and then get out. Away from Rocky Point. Away from Oliver. Away from everything that had made up his not-enough childhood.

The storm had changed all that. Or, at least, he thought it had. For the first time ever, he'd gotten emails and texts over winter break. The Murder Crew had been through something together, and they felt almost like real friends. Peacock had apologized for anything she might have done to hurt him and added what seemed like a genuine invitation to hang out when she got back to school. Finn Plum kept in touch and commiserated with Vaughn over how the cleanup was proceeding and whether or not Tudor House would be sealed due to its being a crime scene. Mustard asked if they might be hiring on the janitorial staff. Karlee and Kayla had emailed to tell him about their folks pulling them out of school. Scarlett had pretended he didn't exist, of course. But he didn't care, because there was also . . .

Orchid.

He and Orchid had kept up a steady stream of texts all those long weeks. Every morning at dawn he'd see her responses from the previous evening, and he would send her things he knew she wouldn't see until she woke up, many hours later, on the West Coast. It had become a ritual of sorts, a lifeline he clung to in the dark, gray days, working to shore up the ruin of the Blackbrook campus, of Rocky Point.

Of any semblance of a relationship with Oliver.

The gloves had come off in the storm. They'd fought all their lives—with words, with fists—but something had changed in the wake of Boddy's murder. He'd like to say it was him, that Vaughn had finally realized what his brother was capable of. In a way, he'd known for years, even if he'd tried to deny it. After all, Oliver was the only family that Vaughn had left.

But that wasn't it at all. It wasn't that Vaughn knew.

It was that Oliver *knew* he knew.

It didn't matter that, in the end, Oliver hadn't murdered the headmaster. Once Vaughn had been willing to admit to himself that his twin brother was in fact *capable* of murder, there was no looking back. Not for either of them.

The porch creaked, the door squealed on its hinges, and Oliver looked up from the couch, where he was playing the latest video game they shouldn't have been able to afford, gunning down insurgents via remote control.

Vaughn knew his lines. He was supposed to ask, *Don't you have a custodial shift?* And then Oliver was supposed to sneer and say that if Vaughn's precious work-study was so important, he could cover it himself.

By now, they could do it all in a look.

But then Oliver surprised him. "I did go in. Rusty's office is all locked up. No one's seen him all day."

Vaughn frowned. Rusty had been working a lot of overtime lately, given all the damage the campus had sustained in the storm. "Think I ought to go over to his place, make sure he's all right?"

Oliver turned back to his game. "No. I do not think that."

Of course he wouldn't.

Vaughn went to the kitchen for a snack. The cupboard held ramen. As usual. Oliver could drop sixty bucks on a new video game but balked at spending money on groceries. As Vaughn set the hot pot on, he turned over approaches in his mind. Finally, he decided on direct. "Why did you partner with Violet Vandergraf for the poster project in history?"

"Because she's an idiot," Oliver responded, eyes glued to the screen. "Closest thing to getting to do it my own way." After a minute, he went on. "How did you know? Did she ask you to meet up?"

"No." He had to be careful. "I saw Orchid McKee. You know, from Tudor? She thought maybe we should have partnered up."

"Yes!" Oliver shouted as he blew a tank to smithereens. Fake blood fake spattered the TV screen. "Murder Crew back in business!"

Vaughn grimaced as he poured the hot water into the bowl. "Something like that."

"Well, I don't care. Tell her you'll ditch the other chick as long as she stays out of your way. I don't need her help or her glitter pens or whatever."

Orchid did not seem the glitter pen type. "That hardly seems fair to Violet."

Oliver paused his game. "I'm getting them confused right now. Which one is in the Murder Crew?"

"Orchid."

"Orchid, Violet, Petunia, Pansy . . . I don't care who my partner is. Let them do it together, and I'll be the odd man out. That works better for me anyway."

That would have been Oliver's suggestion, if he'd been the one to run into Orchid. And maybe Vaughn should have let the chips fall that way.

But Orchid wanted to be *his* partner. To spend time with Vaughn.

"I'll do it," he blurted.

Oliver blinked at him in disbelief. "Our history homework?"

"Yeah."

"You don't take history."

"Right."

"And you've got our testing next week."

Vaughn was done with this little interrogation. "Do you want me to do your homework for you or not?"

Oliver's expression went cold. "*Our* homework, brother. And fine. Not like you were so thrilled with my B-plus last term.

Let's see if you can do any better." Oliver returned to his game. More droplets of blood spattered on the screen.

Vaughn turned away to eat. That game was so ridiculous. Dead bodies made a lot more blood than that.

And then there was the other thing. The one Vaughn didn't even want to think about.

It took a ferry, four buses, and a long, long wait on a folding chair in a grimy hallway masquerading as a reception area, but finally, Vaughn was admitted. They hadn't blinked twice at the ID he presented them. He supposed he shouldn't be surprised anymore. No one at Blackbrook had sniffed them out in three years. But somehow, when it was a law enforcement officer, Vaughn thought they should be . . . more observant.

Everyone was polite to him, at least. He'd visited half a dozen times since the storm, helping her meet with a lawyer, making sure she had everything she needed. They probably recognized him by now.

Both of him.

He was already sitting in the visiting room when they brought her in. It wasn't like the movies, with old-fashioned phone receivers and bulletproof glass. Just a little window with a metal grate.

Vaughn kept his features neutral when she sat down. It was his best shot at convincing the only person who might notice the difference.

"Hello," said Mrs. White.

"Hi." Was he capable of more than single syllables? They'd see.

"What do you want?"

What did he want? "More information." That was true.

"Did you find the things?"

Vaughn swallowed. *What things? How far did this conspiracy go?* Beneath the desk, his hands tightened into fists.

"You should have found the place," she went on in hushed tones. "It's overgrown, true, but not that hard to find."

"I—I didn't." His heart pounded. Oliver had been out nights, coming home muddy and frustrated. Usually, he spent his free time with his hoard in the old boathouse, but obviously, he'd found a different place to skulk lately. Vaughn hadn't been able to bring himself to ask what he'd been doing.

She frowned. "I wish they hadn't sealed . . ." She stared at him through the smeared glass pane, and her eyes widened in horror. "Vaughn," she whispered. "Oh God, Vaughny—"

His jaw clenched. *He knew it.* "What are you telling him? What are you getting him to do for you?"

"Nothing!"

"Don't lie to me again!"

Mrs. White narrowed her eyes. "You're one to talk, Vaughn Green. You've never tried to be Oliver before."

He'd never needed to. Never wanted to. In all their years of pretending, it had always been Oliver trying to be Vaughn, and only doing marginally better than Vaughn was doing now.

Tears came into her eyes. She looked so old now. So lost. "I'm just trying to help—"

"Don't you think you've helped enough?" He'd spent weeks pretending she hadn't kidnapped his classmates. Hadn't stuck a knife into the chest of his headmaster. This was Linda White. His grandmother's best friend. His godmother.

She'd confessed to all of it, which he supposed saved some money when it came to the lawyers. Now they were just awaiting sentencing. The lawyers had pushed for minimum security. They'd talked about her spotless record, the stress she'd been under from the storm, and the fact that she had lived in the house since she'd been a child . . . but Vaughn didn't hold out much hope. Karlee and Kayla had delivered victim impact statements. Blackbrook wanted her head on a pike. They were lucky Maine didn't believe in the death penalty.

She'd still spend the rest of her life in prison.

"I thought you didn't want to be involved," Mrs. White sniffed.

"I don't think I get a choice in the matter. Oliver's seen to that."

Mrs. White said nothing.

"You can't play both sides. I helped you with your lawyers, I brought you books, and you acted like a remorseful, broken, little old lady. But this whole time, you and Oliver are secretly plotting . . . what?"

She cast her eyes about, as if searching for cameras. "Nothing."

"No more games. My grandmother did this to me, too. I'm not going to be saved by you all keeping me in the dark."

She laughed mirthlessly. "Ah, yes. You're the good twin, and he's the bad twin. What a helpful fiction."

He'd spent years thinking it was just a fiction, too. Some joke Gemma used to make when they'd been little that had somehow become stuck in their psyches. Hating himself because he was the golden child. The Blackbrook kid—the one who was going to get out while Oliver stayed mired in his resentment and delusions of glory.

It was a big reason why he agreed to Oliver's lunatic plan.

If Oliver went to Blackbrook, too, they'd be the same.

But then, in the storm, he wondered if there was a nugget of truth to the idea. Maybe Oliver *was* bad. Really, really bad. Because he couldn't shake the idea that his brother *could* have killed Headmaster Boddy.

His own brother, a murderer.

Orchid acted like Vaughn should be traumatized to learn that Mrs. White was a killer, the way she herself was traumatized. But Vaughn was actually relieved.

At least it wasn't Oliver.

He couldn't tell Orchid that, though. Or explain that going to a therapist—especially that stupid school counselor with his stupid, gentle voicemails—would open up a huge can of worms.

Hello, sir. Well, I'd say my major source of stress is the fact that I have to secretly share half my life with my twin brother. Who hates me. Also, it's possible he conspired to murder the headmaster. So maybe there is something irretrievably . . . broken inside of him? How do you know if your only family member is a sociopath? And how much time have we got?

"I don't know what you and Oliver are up to," he said, "but you need to give it a rest. You're already in so much trouble—"

"Then I have nothing to lose."

"But Oliver does!" Vaughn leaned forward. "He's got to let this all go. Finish school. Get out." Get out, too.

"Oh, so he's going to be Vaughn Green in college, too?"

"We'll get two scholarships. Different schools. No one will know."

"You don't think you'll get caught?"

"No one's caught us yet. I don't think this is the kind of thing anyone is looking to catch." Unlike, say, *murder.* But he didn't twist the knife any further. "And when he's in school, he can just . . . start going by Oliver. People change their names in college all the time."

Now Mrs. White leaned forward. "You think you're so smart, Vaughny. You and your Blackbrook scholarship."

Vaughn blinked but kept his jaw tight. This was right out of the Oliver playbook.

"But you know what? All Blackbrook kids are stupid in the exact same way. I know that better than anyone."

"I don't want to—"

"You think you're so special. So perfect. You're so full of yourself, you can't see the obvious truth."

Vaughn rolled his eyes. "Yeah, yeah, yeah. I know this story. Dick Fain stole everything from Gemma. Gemma was the one to invent the glue that had made him and Blackbrook millions. The fortune should be hers." And Oliver's. And . . . his.

"That's not what I'm talking about."

For once.

"I mean the whole good twin/bad twin fantasy," she said, her tone poison. "You think we kept everything from you because we wanted to *protect* you? Not even remotely. We wanted to protect *ourselves*. You can't be trusted to keep our secrets. To do what needs to be done."

"You *needed* to murder your boss? You *needed* to kidnap those kids?"

She looked away. "I made a lot of mistakes. I got scared. Oliver won't have that problem."

"Oliver's not a killer," he said. But his tongue felt heavy afterward, as if there were more words to come.

Not yet.

I hope.

Mrs. White looked as if she could finish his thought as well.

But then again, she *was* a murderer. Vaughn hated to think they could spot their own kind. He also hated that these were the categories he had to put people in now: *murderer or not, capable of murder or not.*

Mrs. White didn't get any other visitors. He was quite certain Scarlett Mistry wasn't braving the prison's grimy folding chairs, even though she'd liked her old residence proctor well enough when they'd all lived happily together in Tudor House. You didn't stand by the murderer. Everyone knew that.

And yet here Vaughn sat. Maybe he *was* stupid, after all.

"It doesn't matter," she said at last, crossing her arms. "Oliver's going to go through with his plan, whether or not I help him."

"Okay, then help me," Vaughn begged. "Help me so he doesn't hurt anyone. So he doesn't make the same mistakes you did."

"Still playing good twin?" she mocked.

"Still playing brother." Vaughn was done with games, just like he'd told Orchid. "He's the only family I have, Mrs. White. My parents are gone. Gemma is gone. I can't lose him, too."

This seemed to get through to her. Vaughn remembered all the afternoons at Gemma's kitchen table. He remembered his grandmother's experiments, turning pennies green and making hot ice. Always, Mrs. White had been there, too.

"I should have helped Olivia when she was still alive," Mrs. White said at last. "We shouldn't have waited so long. When Dick died, I should have . . ."

She didn't finish. There was little enough to be done then. At least, that's what Gemma had thought. Oliver believed differently and was determined to stop at nothing to reveal the truth.

Vaughn had never been sure exactly what that meant. Lawsuits, he supposed. And those were won by whoever could pay the lawyers the most. That certainly wasn't Oliver.

So what was left? Once Oliver had set the record straight but gained nothing in the process?

Vaughn wasn't naive enough to think his brother would be satisfied. When they'd first come up with the plan of the two of them attending Blackbrook as one student, Oliver had thought he could get into the labs and quickly prove his mettle. But he couldn't even keep up with the other students, let alone recreate his grandmother's work without her notes.

Vaughn had thrived at Blackbrook, but all Oliver had seen was the gulf that separated him from the other kids there. And that's when his plans had turned from justice to revenge.

"If you tell me what he's looking for, I can help him stay on track and out of trouble."

He hoped.

Mrs. White was quiet for a long time. Vaughn felt hot. He wasn't a fool. And he wasn't a sap, either.

"He's my brother. I would never do anything to get in his way. I just want—I don't want anyone else to get hurt. I'd like to think that after all that's happened, you care about that."

She looked down. "Okay," she whispered at last. "But you aren't going to like it."

3

Scarlett

Time's up!" Scarlett said, and threw her pencil down. "Let's see how you did."

Orchid didn't put up a fight when Scarlett whisked her test sheet out of her hands and lined it up with her own.

"I'll just check the answers."

The blanks on her own form seemed to stick out like blinking hazard lights to Scarlett. She wondered if Orchid could see them. Quickly, she flipped to the solution page of their test-prep binder and started to score the tests.

It . . . went about as well as she'd been expecting. Orchid had improved. Only eight wrong answers this time. Down from ten.

Ten! That number had been floating in her head the entire time they'd taken the test. She was lucky they weren't doing the math portion. Only ten wrong! And Orchid was supposed to be the math and science genius of their little duo. Verbal was supposed to be Scarlett's strength. That's how it had worked with her and Finn. If Orchid was a double threat, it changed the calculus.

Actually, given Orchid's past, she was maybe a quintuple threat? Some girls had all the luck.

Scarlett totaled the scores, then gave herself an extra 150 points for good measure.

"So much better!" she announced. "You're up to a 740."

Orchid smiled. "That's great. What did you get?"

"780," Scarlett said with a shrug. She was so screwed. And there was no one to help.

The great thing about Orchid McKee was that she was totally trustworthy. The terrible thing about Orchid was that she was totally trustworthy. If Orchid were Finn, they could come up with some scheme. But she wasn't Finn.

Last term, when there'd been a dead body in the conservatory and secrets around every corner, Orchid was the only person in Tudor House that Scarlett could say with one hundred percent certainty was *not* a murderer. And when she'd come to Scarlett to confide her biggest secret, Scarlett knew for sure that she was safer with the ex–movie star than with her former best friend, Finn. Who, it turned out, had been lying to her for months.

But that didn't mean Scarlett didn't miss Finn's particular talents for creative—if not entirely ethical—problem-solving.

Although maybe this wasn't something they could cheat their way out of. And maybe a 630 was fine. Even if it was in verbal. On a practice test. Where she was far less nervous and mistake-prone than she'd be on the actual day . . . ugh!

This couldn't be happening to her. Not Scarlett Mistry, who was fated for Blackbrook humanities valedictorian—as long as that townie Vaughn Green remembered his place. And if he did beat her, she needed to ace these tests even more. Her parents would kill her if she didn't get at least a 1400. Actually kill her.

Blackbrook couldn't take any more bloodshed.

"Are you okay?" Orchid asked.

"Fine," she snapped. "Should we try math?"

"Tonight?" Orchid fairly leaped away from the desk. "I have homework."

"Right." Scarlett did not. Half of her classes were being taught by subs. They'd watched a Shakespeare adaptation on television in English today. And not even a good one.

Scarlett had no idea what her parents' tuition money was presently going toward. Probably shoveling the muck out of the girls' dorm. Or the lawsuits. There must be a ton of lawsuits. Scarlett had figured her own parents would mount one, but they'd chosen a "wait and see" approach. As in, wait and see if what happened had any bearing on her grades or her college prospects.

Or her test scores. She looked down at the 780-that-was-really-630.

If she didn't get into the Ivy of all their dreams, maybe then they'd sue. But in order to get the ball rolling on all that, she'd have to actually tell them that she wasn't scoring 800. Even in verbal.

And the last time she'd admitted that to anyone hadn't gone so great.

It was Scarlett's own fault, really. That new school counselor,

Perry Winkle, had been so adamant that everyone in the Murder Crew meet with him to discuss the "traumatic events" of last fall.

Never show weakness. Scarlett was supposed to know that better than anyone. But one tiny mention of a less-than-impressive showing on a practice test, and the man had suggested getting a tutor.

"A tutor?" Scarlett had sneered. "I don't *get* tutors. I *am* a tutor. I'm actually the head of the Student Tutor Alliance, so . . ."

"Everybody needs help sometimes," Mr. Winkle had said.

Not Scarlett Mistry. And if this pathetic counselor couldn't understand something as fundamental as that, then there really was nothing he could do for her.

She'd just have to find another answer.

"Hey," she said to Orchid. "Did you go talk to that counselor yet?"

"Winkle?" Orchid was already packing up her supplies. "Not yet. I was just talking to Vaughn about him."

Now, there was a boy who needed actual help.

"And, you know, I did go to my therapist in California over the break."

"You have a therapist at home?" Scarlett asked. "One who . . . knows the truth about you?"

"Of course," said Orchid. "I needed someone I could talk to. Everyone needs a little help sometimes."

Scarlett snapped her pencil in two. "Oh God, not you, too."

Orchid seemed to realize that she'd crossed a line. "Let's go get dinner."

"You mean the latest microwaved feast?" Scarlett rolled her eyes. That was another thing that had deteriorated since the storm. The new interim headmaster, Dr. Brown, had decreed that one kitchen was more than sufficient to feed all remaining students, including those at Tudor House. So instead of Mrs. White's delicious, vegetarian, home-cooked meals, Scarlett was left picking through a limp salad bar at Blackbrook's main dining hall.

The trade-off, she supposed, was that she wasn't being fed by a murderer. But it was a pain in the butt to hike down to campus through the frigid Maine evenings. Most nights, she just made herself a frozen dinner in the Tudor House kitchen.

But Mrs. White seemed to haunt every corner of that space.

It was strange, Scarlett thought as they exited into the hall and she saw Orchid do her usual move of averting her eyes. Most of the students hated the hall—the spot where Headmaster Boddy had died. And the administration had sealed off the conservatory, where his corpse had been stored that long, awful day, as well as all four entrances to the secret passages they'd discovered as they searched for the head-master's killer.

But it wasn't the memory of Mr. Boddy's lifeless form that bothered Scarlett. The headmaster was dead. There were no such things as ghosts, and the house had been thoroughly cleaned. No, it was everything else. The storm and its after-math had revealed all sorts of problems to Scarlett.

Her best friend was a liar. Her housemate was hiding a huge secret. Her resident proctor was a murderer. And, somehow, she hadn't picked up on any of it. She'd tried to track down the killer and hadn't come close. Her instincts were way off.

Scarlett feared that she didn't have a clue.

She wasn't making the right choices, and that was evident long before she had a number two pencil in her hands. Maybe the bad test scores had nothing at all to do with the trauma of the storm and the murder and the stress of being back on this wreck of a campus.

Maybe Scarlett was just doomed to fail.

The kitchen was already occupied by two of the other girls—both new to Tudor. Though Scarlett's friends and former housemates Nisha and Atherton had transferred to schools *without* murderers on staff, the school had managed to fill not only their rooms but even half the downstairs rooms, which had formerly been common areas, due to the current lack of non-flooded residential options. Scarlett and Orchid's new housemates included interim headmaster Dr. Brown; Rosa Navarro, a new transfer student who mightn't have known about the house's history; and one of the Murder Crew's own: Beth "Peacock" Picach.

Peacock stood at the counter now, six feet tall but seeming even larger, the dyed streaks in her blond hair faded somewhat from her signature teal blue to a pale mint. She wore yoga pants and a cutoff sweatshirt emblazoned with a bright blue mandala and was chopping kale to add to a suspicious-looking collection in the pitcher of the house blender.

"Scarlett! Orchid!" Peacock called as she scooped the kale into the blender. "You're just in time. Do you want to try some of this energy smoothie? It's a new formula my life coach, Ash, made up for me. Rosa's having one."

They looked over at the new girl, who was in a chair by the tiny kitchen table, reading a textbook and watching the others with wary eyes. Maybe she'd finally gotten the download on who her housemates were. "I said I'd *taste* it."

"What's in it?" Orchid asked.

"Kale"—Peacock was adding more as she spoke—"apple, pineapple, some ginger, and this new protein powder Ash got for me. He's from California. You can tell me how authentic it is." She slopped in some milk, popped on the top of the blender, and revved the engine.

"If it's got kale," said Orchid dryly, "that's pretty authentic. Any avocados on hand?"

Peacock frowned. "It's not in the recipe . . ."

"I was joking," Orchid said, sliding into the spare kitchen chair across from Rosa. "I long ago gave up on finding avocados in Rocky Point."

Peacock started pouring her concoction, which was a dark green color, into glasses. "It's supposed to help me with my Ayurvedic detox. I'm trying to incorporate more plant-based meals into my diet. We're working on unlocking my energy from my solar plexus chakra." She presented a glass to Scarlett. "You can tell me how I'm doing."

Scarlett blinked at her. "I can tell you that nothing that just came out of your mouth made the remotest bit of sense. That's not how any of this works."

"Well, I'm still really new," Peacock said, looking sheepish. She pressed the smoothie into Scarlett's hands. "But how does it taste?"

Scarlett sipped. Pretty good, actually. And way better than the salad bar. She'd work out Peacock's butchering of millennia-old cultural and religious traditions after standardized tests were done. "Yum, thanks."

Peacock passed the rest out, but Rosa waved hers off. "You used almond milk. I'm allergic to nuts."

"Oh no!" Peacock said. "My bad. I'll make it with soy next time. Can you have soy?"

Rosa nodded. And just like that, Scarlett now knew one hundred percent more about the new girl.

She was woefully behind. There had been a time, back in the glory days, during which all newcomers to Blackbrook would be subjected to Scarlett for orientation. It was a great opportunity for everyone involved: The new kid would have a chance to learn from Scarlett, the student body president, all about the school and its culture, and Scarlett would get an opportunity to size up the competition.

But Dr. Brown hadn't even told her about Rosa, and the new girl kept so much to herself that she'd been in the house two full days before Scarlett even knew of her existence.

Maybe she could make up for the delay now. They sat down to drink their smoothies, crowding around the tiny table.

"So, Rosa," Scarlett asked, "how are you liking Blackbrook?"

"It's fine."

"Where did you transfer from?"

"Overseas."

This girl was giving her very little to work with. "What's the name of your old school?"

"I had . . . tutors. School is kind of a new thing for me."

A perfect opening! "If that's the case, then you should let me show you around. I don't know if Dr. Brown mentioned it, but I'm the student body president. I take it upon myself to orient all the newcomers to Blackbrook."

Rosa glanced from Scarlett to Orchid and back again. "Is it required?"

"No, not as such, but—"

"Then no thank you."

Scarlett's fingers tightened so hard around the smoothie glass, she was shocked it didn't crack.

"Peacock!" Orchid said at once. "How's training going?"

"Okay," she replied. "Especially since Dr. Brown talked Coach Lungelo out of quitting. But the team has basically fallen apart. We've got no chance for team placement this season, and I don't have a decent practice partner to—"

"Why didn't you transfer?" Rosa asked abruptly.

"She wouldn't do that," Scarlett said. "Blackbrook loves her."

Peacock took a long drink of her smoothie, saying nothing. Weird.

"Well, actually, I did try to transfer," she said at last. "But there were some complications. They wouldn't let me play for a year, and—"

"You tried to transfer?" Scarlett asked. She felt . . . personally hurt. Mostly because she'd had no idea.

"They wanted to redshirt you?" asked Rosa.

"Yes," Peacock said to Rosa.

"Sucks," the new girl replied.

Scarlett wasn't sure how some homeschooled kid from overseas was down with all the sports lingo. "So, Rosa, do you play tennis?" The new girl was tall. Maybe she'd be a ringer, or at least help Peacock round out the team.

"I'm not joining the team, if that's what you're asking."

But Scarlett was not to be deterred. "What activities *do* you want to get involved with here at Blackbrook?"

"Oh," she drawled, "so we're doing the new-student orientation after all?"

Orchid giggled into her smoothie.

"I'll tell you the truth, Scarlett," said Rosa. "I've been here for a week now, and all I see are problems. The campus is a disaster area, security is practically nonexistent, especially given the school's recent history, and there's a total leadership vacuum. It is beyond me why any of you came back here. It's like you have a death wish."

Orchid looked at her lap.

Scarlett narrowed her eyes. "There aren't going to be any more deaths here. The killer is in jail."

"Oh, that's how it works?" Rosa replied. "There are people

who are killers and people who aren't, and now you've sorted it all out?"

"Well, what do you suggest?" Scarlett said. "We just go ahead and advance-imprison anyone who we suspect has sociopathic tendencies?"

"No," Rosa said. "I'm just saying that anyone can kill, given the appropriate motivation."

"That's not true!" Scarlett exclaimed. She looked at Orchid. "You don't support this, do you?"

Orchid pursed her lips. "I think a lot of people could be driven to taking a life. Or . . . trained into it. Like soldiers."

"That's different than Mrs. White knifing the headmaster in the middle of the night over an argument."

Peacock, who had been drinking her smoothie in silence, piped up. "I think she got angry and lost control. It's not so different than what happened to me, right? I was so angry at Mustard, I punched him. And then he cracked his head on the tile. He could have died. I could have killed him without meaning to." She shuddered. "After what happened, I knew I had to make a change. I don't want to be the kind of person who could kill anyone or . . . hurt anyone. And I definitely don't want to be the kind of person someone thinks is *capable* of killing. It hurt so much to think that anyone might call me a killer, like what happened last term."

Scarlett frowned. That had mostly been Vaughn's doing. And then he'd convinced Mustard, who hadn't known any of them enough to judge properly.

"I didn't realize I had all this latent anger in me," Peacock continued. "That's why my parents and I hired the life coach. Ash is helping me channel my anger into tennis and release it through—"

"Please do not say 'chakra' again," Scarlett mumbled.

"Meditation," Peacock finished. "And diet. I don't necessarily understand it all, but Ash does. He's trained." She finished her smoothie. "I want to be a better person. Not just a better tennis player. Isn't that what we all want?"

Was it? Right now, Scarlett would settle for a better test score.

"I love Blackbrook," Orchid said. "I found a home here. I don't want to give up on it just because something bad happened here. I did that once already. I can't spend my whole life running."

Rosa seemed satisfied with this answer.

"What she said," added Scarlett. "Some of us have invested a lot in this school, though I can understand how that would be hard for a new person to understand."

"I understand," Rosa said, "even if I don't agree."

"Then what are you doing here, if it's murder central?" Scarlett snapped.

The new girl just smiled. "Relax, Scarlett. I'm here to learn, like everyone else. Now, if you'll excuse me, I have work to do."

After she left, Scarlett could not shake her annoyance. "I don't like that girl."

"You don't like anyone," Orchid pointed out.

"That's not true!" She looked at her friend in dismay. "I like you."

"Sorry." But Orchid didn't look sorry. She looked amused. "I meant to say you don't like anyone you don't find useful in some way or another."

Peacock laughed as she stood up to go wash out the glasses. "That's so true."

Scarlett crossed her arms over her chest. "That's . . ." *Huh.* "Okay, that's accurate, in the sense that it's better to spend time with people you enjoy spending time with, or have something in common with. That's just . . . friendship, though. That's not using them. No one is just nice to people for no reason at all."

Orchid stared at her in wide-eyed disbelief. "I mean . . . nice people are. That's kind of how it works."

"I was being nice to her!"

"Were you, though?"

Scarlett rubbed her temples. Someone bring her back to her practice tests, where she only had to choose between A, B, C, and D.

There was a pressure on her shoulder. Orchid's hand. "Hey. I'm sorry. I know you were only trying to help."

"Do you think we're just friends because now I know who you really are?"

Orchid shot a quick look over at Peacock, who was grinding up kale stalks in the garbage disposal loudly enough that Scarlett could have screamed her words and the tennis star wouldn't have heard.

And she hadn't screamed them. She wasn't stupid. She was keeping Orchid's secret.

But not—ugh—because she thought it was useful! Or not *only* because of that, at least.

"Look what we survived together," Scarlett said. "We were living in a house with a murderer. It could have been *us* she went after next, not Karlee and Kayla. We're all that's left, Orchid. We have to stick together."

If she'd wanted to befriend someone *really* useful, she'd be finding out who was going to proctor their tests this weekend.

"So we're really the Murder Crew, huh?" Orchid said.

"Yeah." Scarlett nodded. "Only, we're definitely all done with murders."

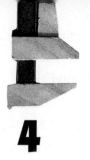

4

Peacock

From: *ash@phoenixmanagement.org*
To: *elizabeth.picach@BlackbrookAcademy.edu*
Subj: *Re: Not Sleeping*

I'm sorry to hear you've been having problems sleeping in your new residential quarters, but, given all you've told me about your history in the house, I can't say I'm surprised.

First, I'll ask you: have you had any gluten today?

Remember: houses aren't haunted—people are haunted. The unease you feel is actually your own energy being reflected back onto you. The memory of what happened there last term is living in your mind, and, if you aren't careful, it will start to have an effect on your body as well. We would not want it to impact your game.

One method that I think might be impactful for you here is to do a bodily inventory as you tour each room in the house. Go into each room and sit with your feelings, then report back to me what is happening there—what you remember about that room, what it's being used for now, who is living there, and how you feel about all of that.

I look forward to reading your thoughts. Remember: you are stronger than what happened last term. We are making you the architect of your own house of success!

I am honored to share with you the illumination within,
Ash

From: *elizabeth.picach@BlackbrookAcademy.edu*
To: *ash@phoenixmanagement.org*
Subj: *Re: Not Sleeping*

Dear Ash,

No, I haven't had any gluten at all! I've been sticking pretty firmly to the smoothie cleanse you gave me. I even got some of the girls in the house to share with me tonight. (Well, not the new girl, Rosa. She's apparently allergic to nuts.) So it can't be that.

Letting this sleep issue affect my game is exactly what I'm scared of. I'm already having that shoulder rotation issue, and Coach doesn't seem to take it seriously. What do you suggest?

Okay. I did the house tour. Here's what I ended up with.

TUDOR HOUSE TOUR

Ballroom: The last time I was in here was for the freshman winter whirl. I came with my ex, Finn. That's what I think of when I'm in here. I remember I had on a pink dress. It was before all that "Peacock" stuff really got started. Right now they are using it for music classes, which gets kind of annoying for the people living here, but the arts building was damaged in the flood so ¯_(ツ)_/¯.

Conservatory: Can't go inside. Big padlocks on the doors. Something about it being a crime scene, but everyone knows Mr.

Boddy died in the hall. Finn told me there was a secret passage here, but I don't think it was the one where . . . well, you know.

Library and billiards room: I couldn't go inside these. They are being used as bedrooms right now, since the girls' dorm was so badly damaged by the flood. Dr. Brown, our interim headmaster, is staying in the library, and the new girl, Rosa, is in the billiards room. I guess they had a hard time getting volunteers, because of the murder. The rest of us are all sleeping upstairs.

Study: Dr. Brown has started mandatory study hours in here every night for the Tudor House residents, so I spend a lot of time in here. It's really cozy, with the fireplace and all. They said there's an entry to a secret passage in here. I don't know where, though—maybe behind one of the bookshelves?

Kitchen: That study passage comes out here. The entrance is in the back of the pantry. It's where Mrs. White kept the people she kidnapped. I can't believe all of that was going on during the storm. I can't believe people blamed ME! They've sealed it off too, now.

Dining room: No one uses this room as much now, because if we want to eat here, we have to do the cooking ourselves. When I stand in this room, all I think is that this is where they all started blaming me. I think I still hold some anger at Finn. I know he came after me and all that, but . . . I don't know. Also, it makes me think I should try to talk to Mustard again, too. I reached out to him like you said, but he never answered me. I'm really, really sorry I punched him. I don't want people to think of me as violent. I don't think I am violent. I've never even broken a racket. It just makes me think of how angry I was about that letter the other players sent to Boddy, about me lying about the tournament faults. I'm not a cheater. I'm not!

At least that appears to have gone away. Dr. Brown hasn't said a word about it.

Lounge: This is where Headmaster Boddy spent his last night. I used to be a lot more freaked out in here, but we've been watching movies and stuff here at night, so I'm getting used to it. The fireplace still doesn't work, though. Scarlett said it's because of how they sealed off the entrance to that secret passage. Isn't it wild that they were here all these years and no one but Mrs. White knew about them?

Hall: It's a lot brighter here, now that they have the new window that's just plain glass. It doesn't look at all like it used to. Which is good, I guess. Harder to remember that this was the place Boddy died. That this was the place I almost killed Mustard.

I almost killed someone. That should scare me more, but what mainly scares me is the idea that everyone else on campus knows. They call us the Murder Crew. They used to cheer for Peacock, and now it's, like—I don't know. I'm scared I'm finished before I've even gotten a chance to get started. I need to get ahead of this thing. I want to get back to my game. I want everyone else to get back to the game, too. But how can I do it while I'm still here?

Let me know if I did it right!

I am honored to share with you the illumination within,
Beth

From: *ash@phoenixmanagement.org*
To: *elizabeth.picach@BlackbrookAcademy.edu*
Subj: *Re: Not Sleeping*

You did it perfectly. Keep up the good work.

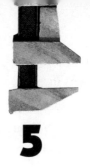

5

Plum

Finn Plum stood on the front steps of Tudor House. He puffed his breath out into the dark, frigid air and raised his hand to ring the bell. Then he put it back down again. Another deep breath. Another swing and a miss.

Come on, Plum. What's the worst that could happen?

But he knew what Scarlett could be like, if she wanted. Once upon a time, he'd helped her be exactly like that.

So, then, maybe not Scarlett. Beth owed him now, after he'd helped her out with that whole cheating letter situation. And hadn't she proved that she could be every bit as underhanded as he could?

He raised his hand toward the bell again.

The door opened. Dr. Brown, the interim headmaster, stood on the threshold, frowning. Once more, Finn wondered if she'd also been tipped off about Finn's secret project. He'd deleted Boddy's notes on the subject, along with the letter all those tennis players had sent the old headmaster about their suspicions about Beth, but that had been the last time he'd had access to administrative files.

Or other items of great importance to him.

"Mr. Plum," Dr. Brown said dryly. "Coed visiting hours end at seven."

"Oh, I'll be out by seven, Doctor," Finn said, smiling broadly. Either way, he had no intention of lingering in the Murder House. It was bad enough what the kids on campus were calling them.

And even worse that, to a good half of the Murder Crew, he was persona non grata.

"Who are you here to see?"

"Beth Picach?"

"She's at the gym."

Of course she was. "I meant Scarlett Mistry." *Here goes nothing.*

"You meant?" Dr. Brown's eyebrows shot toward her hairline. "As in, you mixed up their phenomenally different names or as in, you find them completely interchangeable?"

"Well, ma'am," Finn said. She was a tough one. "What I really meant is that I had a question about a project. For class. And they're both in my class, so . . . I mean . . ." He shrugged.

"So you meant that those two female students are interchangeable in your mind."

"Not remotely!" Finn exclaimed. "Only that either one could help me, in this particular instance."

Dr. Brown blinked at him.

"It's for class," he repeated.

She blinked again.

Those were usually the magic words when it came to sweet-talking the faculty. But Dr. Brown wasn't a teacher.

Not really. She was a board member, assigned to fill in at the school until the board of directors appointed a new headmaster. As far as Finn could tell, she hated the students at Blackbrook only slightly less than she hated the school's "culture of sloppiness."

Otherwise known as the main reason Finn and Scarlett used to be able to get away with the things they did. Dr. Brown had quickly sealed up the secret passages and reset all the passwords and firewalls in the administration's computer system. Strategically, she was a brick wall.

Maybe that would be Finn's in with Scarlett. She'd probably be dying for someone to commiserate with. Somehow, he doubted Orchid was devious enough to scratch Scarlett's itch.

Finally, Dr. Brown sighed and opened the door wider. "She's in the study. Working. Be quick."

He dashed inside, then stopped flat in the hall. It looked . . . different. He was used to a soft, golden glow highlighting the glossy wood carvings and rich parquet. The last time he'd been here, there was less than that—the light of a few candles, leaving dark, shadowy corners that well hid the smears of Headmaster Boddy's blood that Mrs. White hadn't quite cleaned up.

He supposed it made sense to install brighter lighting. Dr. Brown wouldn't want anyone to think that they were still hiding something in this house. But it did detract some from the atmosphere. Under the harsh new lights, you could see every scratch in the paneling, every scuff mark along the floor. He averted his eyes and headed for the study.

Scarlett was sitting at the desk, bent over a test prep book, scrubbing furiously with her eraser on an answer sheet. Of course she'd be taking the tests extremely seriously. Finn felt differently. If he got what he needed, no one would care about his test scores.

She was so intent on her work, she hadn't even noticed him entering. He cleared his throat.

She whirled, dark hair flipping over her shoulder, and fixed him with a determined glare. "Oh. You."

"Hey, Scar," he began.

"What are you doing here?"

"I'm here to see you?" Oops. That wasn't supposed to come out as a question.

"What for?"

He chuckled. "Why does it have to be for anything?"

She didn't respond. Just stared at him.

"Okay, fine," he admitted. "I need your help."

"Of course you do." She rolled her eyes. "Well, I'm sorry, but I don't have time for anything but test prep right now."

He glanced at the pile of workbooks on the desk. She was really making herself crazy with this stuff. "I could help you study—"

"I already have a study partner, thanks."

"Oh. Orchid?"

"If you must know," she sniffed.

A pale comparison if you asked Finn, but pointing that out would not be the move to make right now. Scarlett would get defensive, and he wanted those famed defenses down.

He toed the thick oriental rug. "You know, Scarlett, I

thought after everything we went through, during the storm . . . I thought maybe we'd made up."

"I thought that, too, Phineas Plum," she replied brightly. Too brightly. Plus, she'd used his full name. "But then, even after I braved a freaking blizzard, and a murderer, to rescue your sorry ass, in the middle of the night—even after all that—I somehow wasn't cool enough to be told your super confidential exciting secret. Unlike Peacock, who, I'd like to point out, is a sweet girl but maybe a bit too trusting that this whole Murder Crew thing means we're all real-life BFFs."

"What's that supposed to mean?"

"It means that all I had to do was tell your ex-girlfriend that I knew what you were up to, and she talked to me about it. Very wise choice you made, confiding in her."

He put his hand over his brow. Of course Beth would assume that Scarlett knew. She'd always been too trusting. That's why the whole idea that she might cheat at tennis was laughable. It was just a way for her rivals to shut her down.

But Finn's ex-girlfriend's tennis career wasn't his problem at the moment. His experiment was.

"So you know?"

"Everything," she spat. Her big dark eyes radiated deep hurt.

He sighed. There were few options left. He had to throw himself at her mercy. "I'm so sorry, Scar. But now that you know, I know you understand."

"Understand what?"

"Why I had to keep it a secret!"

"No, I don't, actually." She crossed her arms and leaned back against the desk. "Enlighten me."

"Well . . ." he fumbled. "You know. Because of the school rules about who owns any inventions or discoveries made here. I had to keep my project on the down-low. If they found out, it would ruin everything. And if you decided you hated me and wanted to use it as ammunition . . ."

"You think I'd do something like that?" she scoffed.

"I've seen you do it, Scar. Lots." He'd been part of every one of their ruthless plans to obliterate their academic competition. But this was bigger than school. This was his whole future.

She shook her head, glaring at him as if he were something you'd scrape off your boots at the door. "Peacock didn't tell me anything."

Wait . . . what?

He gaped at her as she turned and started straightening up her books. "I—what did you just say?" he sputtered.

"I can't believe you fell for that. You aren't as smart as you think you are." She gathered her test prep into her arms and turned. "And, I'd like to point out, I am offended to my core that you told Peacock. Peacock, and not me?" She snorted in indignation. "Are you still into her?"

No. Yes. Maybe. "So wait. Beth didn't—"

"Of course not!" Scarlett looked disgusted. Worse, she looked disappointed.

Finn had to admit he was a little disappointed in himself, too, for falling for it. The move was a Scarlett classic: make her victim agree with her on the reason you were about to believe in her lie. They both knew Beth could be a touch . . . gullible. So of course he'd buy Scarlett's story that she'd tricked Beth into spilling everything.

Scarlett was on a roll. "You're going to tell me everything, and you're going to do it right now, and then—maybe—I'll decide whether or not to help you."

He shook his head. Figured. She was always after an angle. "And you wonder why I never told you before."

"Well, right now, I've already got enough to go on to rat you out to Dr. Brown and—"

He held up his hands in capitulation. "Wait a second before—"

"—which is good, because I needed an in with her anyway."

"Scarlett!" he hissed.

She gave him her most innocent expression. It was not very innocent, if you knew her.

"There's nothing to rat out anyway, if you don't help me," he said. "I was hiding my stuff in the secret passage during the storm, and in all the chaos when the cops came, I never got a chance to retrieve it. And now they've locked up the conservatory, and I can't get in."

"So what do you want me to do about that?"

"Help me," he said, flabbergasted. "You live here. Surely you can think of something."

"Like helping you break into the conservatory?"

No. That lock was hard-core. And all the windows to the conservatory had been boarded up—Finn had checked—the better to prevent people trying to catch a glimpse of the blood-stained floor within.

"Or into the other entrance to that passage—"

"The entrances have been sealed," said Scarlett with a shrug. "It was one of the almost comically paltry ways the school tried to reassure parents that it was safe for us to return."

"Yeah, by, like, Rusty or some other janitor," Finn pointed out. That's what they decided was an important repair needed at this school, ignoring the fact that half the dorms and the entire chem lab were wrecked by the storm. "I can handle that part."

"Then what do you need me for?"

"To provide cover. Look, the last thing I need is anyone catching me. And this house is so crowded now. I need an inside man—er—woman."

He needed Scarlett. That's where this had all started to go wrong—when he hadn't trusted his best friend. He needed her quick, clever mind to catch all his absentminded mistakes. Stuff like hiding his experiment underground. In a flood. It was supposed to be for a few hours, not weeks! Who knew what was happening to it down there?

Scarlett pursed her lips. "And you think I want to get caught in your scheme? All I want to do is . . ." She looked down at the practice tests in her arms and took a deep breath. "Okay, fine."

"Really?" He practically hopped up and down.

"But this better not take very long."

"Would I lie to you?" he asked, then caught the look on her face. "Don't answer that."

Together, they crossed the hall toward the lounge. But the second Scarlett opened the door, he realized his mistake.

Several pairs of eyes looked up from the TV screen.

"Oops, sorry," said Scarlett, and they shut the door. She turned to him. "It's a pretty full house here these days. We can try again tomorrow . . ."

Finn clenched his jaw and looked down at the floor. Somewhere under there was his entire future. He was so close. He just wanted to take a jackhammer to the tile.

Scarlett was looking at him with the first glint of sympathy he'd seen on her face. "So, this passage—you say it goes from the conservatory to the lounge?"

"Yeah."

Her brow furrowed. "Well, the one in the kitchen apparently connects to the study. Curious, don't you think?"

He shook his head. "Why?"

She rolled her eyes. "Because they have to cross one another, don't they?" She made an X with her forearms. "Underground."

Finn's eyes widened.

"Maybe they connect somehow!" A door opened at the top of the stairs, and Scarlett tugged on his arm and led him back into the study. She stood next to the fireplace. "Okay. Do your thing."

"My thing?"

"Your whole 'let me handle unsealing the passage' thing." She gestured to the wall with the fireplace on it. "Handle it. Quick, before Dr. Brown comes to kick you out."

Right. That. He went over to the fireplace, looking for the

seams that might open, like the hidden switch he'd found in the conservatory, like what Mustard had told him he'd found on the lounge's mantel. But he didn't see anything.

Scarlett watched him. "What are you doing?"

"I'm looking for the switch . . ."

She shook her head. "They removed the switches. That's what I told you." She pointed at the bookshelf behind her. "Orchid told me it used to be in a fake book up there."

Sure enough, just above Scarlett's head, he saw a shelf with a conspicuous gap between the volumes, and what looked like a hastily nailed down piece of a two-by-four instead of the study's usual bronze busts and other Blackbrook-appropriate bookends.

"Can you get that off and hot-wire it or whatever?"

He'd see. He opened up his backpack and removed his tool kit. The two-by-four was easy to pry off, but underneath the piece of wood, he found . . . nothing. No switch, no wires, nothing to indicate that anything like that had ever been there.

"Rusty was a bit more thorough than I'd expected," he mumbled. He couldn't get thwarted by the janitor again.

Scarlett cast a glance at the door. "Whatever you're going to do, be quick about it. Remember, Dr. Brown knows you're here."

He was so close. He would not let his poor project spend one more day in that dank old passage. "Where did Orchid say the passage entrance was?"

"Behind the bookshelf," said Scarlett, wringing her hands.

Okay, time for the blunt approach. He studied the shelves, examining the decades-old layers of varnish for anything that looked like a recent application. There—bright as a copper penny, a line far too straight even for New England maple. He dug the tip of his crowbar into the varnish and— *CRRRRRRRAAAAACK.* The line split into two neat halves. An opening! He pulled harder on the edge of the crowbar. The bookcase shifted.

Scarlett let out a small squeal. "How are we supposed to hide that from Dr. Brown?" she hissed under her breath.

They'd figure it out. They always did. He opened the entrance. "Hurry. We still need to figure out how to get in and get to the other passage."

"You want me to come with you?" She shook her head. "I thought I was just a lookout."

He handed her a flashlight. "Yeah, and right now, I need you to look out for whatever door leads into the other passage."

She seemed dubious.

"It'll go faster with both of us," he promised.

Scarlett had apparently done the same calculation. She took the flashlight and followed him down into the passage.

This one was deeper than the one where he'd hidden his work. Finn noticed that right away. He supposed it made sense for one to go over the other, since they had to cross some-where. Also, that root cellar or whatever was at the kitchen end of this one—where Mrs. White had dragged Karlee and Kayla—was pretty far underground.

The stairs ended, and the passage curved around to a

straightaway. Scarlett shone the flashlight on the rough stone walls and grimy ceiling.

"I'm not going to be happy if I get spiderwebs in my hair. Or spiders," she added after a second.

"And I am?"

"What is this project, anyway?"

"A dye," he said. "A very, very black dye."

"Wait," Scarlett said, unamused. "I'm risking spiders and the wrath of Dr. Brown for a dye? I thought at least whatever you'd invented was worth money."

Finn rolled his eyes, though he knew she couldn't see that in the dark. "I wonder if Dick Fain had people telling him that his invention was 'just a glue.' Trust me, this is going to be big. Electronics, military—"

"Okay! You've convinced me." Scarlett was quiet for a few steps, as if thinking it over. "Black dye from Blackbrook, huh?"

Not from Blackbrook, if he had his way.

"Why were you hiding it here, anyway?"

"Well, I was hiding it in the lab at school, but someone must have found out about it before the storm last year. They tattled on me to Headmaster Boddy. It's terrible that he died, but it does mean that I'm safe."

"Why does it mean that? Only Boddy is dead, not whoever tattled on you."

Finn didn't answer that.

"Well, it had better be worth millions," Scarlett grumbled from behind him. "And you'd better be prepared to be very generous with me for helping you."

That sounded like his best friend. He looked back at her, grinning. "Come on. Admit you missed our schemes."

She bit her lip. "Okay, just a little." She shot her beam of light behind him. "What's that?"

He followed the direction of the light. It was a metal latch in the ceiling. "The trapdoor! You were right!"

"It must lead to the other passage!" Scarlett exclaimed. She hopped up and down. "Open it!"

He handed her the flashlight and gripped the crowbar in both hands. Carefully inserting the tip in the crack in the trapdoor, he pulled.

The door fell open.

And a body dropped out and onto their heads.

6

Mustard

Mustard opened the door to his dorm room and found his roommate making out with a girl. Again.

"Dude!" Tanner Curry exclaimed as his girlfriend rushed to cover herself and Mustard backed quickly out into the hall.

While he waited, Mustard examined the whiteboard affixed to their door for the coded markings they'd worked out last week. A red mark in the upper right corner of the board meant "stay out." The board was clear.

"You forgot the code," he called through the door.

"Tanner!" Amber complained, exasperated.

"Sorry, baby!" his roommate said to her. "I'm not used to roommates. You know that." He called out through the door. "You can come in, soldier."

Tanner always called him that, with a cocky grin. Mustard didn't mind, if he was being honest with himself. It reminded him that this banishment, this school—it was all temporary.

They'd had the usual "call me Mustard" conversation when he'd first moved in. Mustard, of course, had started out calling his new roommate by his last name, which was what the boys always did back at Farthing Military Academy. But Tanner had said that was weird, and he already had enough trouble living up to his family's reputation.

Mustard supposed he of all people should call others by the names they preferred.

He entered to find Amber—Tanner's girlfriend—yanking her sweater back down and rearranging herself on the couch. Their hair was mussed.

"Hey, Mustard," she said sheepishly.

"Hey." Mustard walked over to his side of the room, where the sheets on his bed still had perfect hospital corners, pulled so tight you could bounce a quarter off of them.

At least they'd stayed off his bed this time. He took off his coat and hung it in the closet, then sat down at his desk. Tanner ran a hand through his hair and picked up the controller for his video game console. The familiar strains of the game's theme song rang out of the top-of-the-line speakers installed at strategic points in the room. Amber sighed and grabbed her cell phone.

"Want to play?" he asked Mustard.

"Nah, I've got homework," said Mustard. Besides, he'd just spent the past half hour giving one-syllable answers to the world's perkiest guidance counselor. Perry Winkle had wanted to "touch base" with all the students who'd been on campus during the murder of Headmaster Boddy, but Mustard didn't have much to say about that night.

Everything traumatic had come afterward, anyway.

Tanner shrugged and picked single player. "Probably better, anyway. You kick my ass at this game."

Tanner never seemed to have homework. Mustard wasn't sure what that was all about. Most of the kids he'd met at Blackbrook last term were nuts about their academics. Finn Plum certainly was. But Tanner seemed to view the whole thing as just another checkmark in his family's plan for him, and he kept his commitments as light as possible. He rowed crew and played a game Mustard had never heard of before called squash. Neither seemed to be something Tanner cared much about in his off hours. It was just part of the routine: diploma from the right kind of upper-crust New England prep school, followed by a degree from the right Ivy League college, followed by a position at the right Wall Street hedge fund and the right seat on the right kind of boards, like his father and his grandfather and every other ancestor had enjoyed, all the way back to the *Mayflower*, probably.

Mustard used to know what it had been like to have your life on rails. Before he'd screwed it all up.

"Hey," Amber asked without looking up from her phone, "did you notice if they cleaned out the bathroom down the hall yet? It was *nasty* in there."

"They didn't," Mustard replied.

"Ugh, what is *with* janitorial this week?" Amber groaned, still texting.

Mustard said nothing.

"You can always go home and use the bathroom at the

Murder House," Tanner teased her as he killed enemy combatants on-screen.

"No thank you." Amber shuddered. "Bad enough I have to sleep there." She cast a quick glance at Mustard, who pretended to be fascinated by his biology notes. He knew what people said about those folks who'd been in Tudor House during the storm. The Murder House, the Murder Crew.

Not much of a crew. He'd only spoken to two of them since school resumed. Most of his time was spent studying at the library, trying desperately to catch up on the kind of academia that all the Blackbrook kids took as a matter of course. He could shoot guns and survive in the wilderness, but the basics of cellular respiration still eluded him. He could rattle off hours of American military history, but he knew next to nothing about Maine during Prohibition.

There was a knock at the door. "Trash collection!"

"Oh, thank God," said Amber.

Mustard opened the door to find none other than Vaughn Green on the threshold, wheeling a giant rubbish bin.

"Oh," he said.

"Hi," said Mustard. Well, this was awkward.

"Are you doing the bathrooms next?" Amber asked from the couch as Green dumped out their little trash can into his large one. "The one down the hall is disgusting."

"Um . . . yeah, we're a little short-staffed at the moment." He gave Mustard a curious glance, and when he walked out the door, Mustard followed.

"Did you talk to Rusty?" Green asked. "About that janitorial job? You can see how much needs being done."

Mustard looked away and stuck his hands into his pockets. "Yeah. I don't think it's for me."

Green's mouth went into a line. "Oh. Don't want to get your hands dirty?"

No, your boss is a creep. But Mustard didn't say that. He didn't like the way Green was looking at him, either, as if he'd been in on it, too. As if Mustard disgusted him.

Mustard recalled, in the storm, how difficult Green had been at lunch, taunting them all about the murderer being in the house. He'd been right then—it was his own godmother. He also remembered how Green and Rusty Nayler had gone together into town. How close they'd been.

Maybe they were all in on it together.

"Hey, janitor-guy!" Amber called from inside the room. "Don't forget the recycling! Lot of soda cans this week."

"My name is Vaughn," Green mumbled under his breath, then headed back inside to collect the cans. Mustard followed, warily.

Vaughn was pointing at the pyramid of cans Tanner had erected on the coffee table. "This isn't my job. I'm not a maid."

Tanner paused the game and looked at him. "Hey, Vaughn! Wow, man, I haven't seen you since freshman music! Still playing the guitar?"

Instantly, Vaughn's demeanor softened. "Yeah."

"Cool. I didn't know you still went here."

Mustard rolled his eyes. Tanner wasn't a bad guy. Just kind of a blockhead.

"Duh," said Amber. "He's in Violet's history class and"— she dropped her voice to a whisper, though everyone in the room could still hear her fine—"the *Murder Crew*?"

Tanner looked from Green to Mustard and back again. "Cool," he repeated. He gestured to the other controller. "Want to play?" It was his roommate's version of a peace offering. Like how the first day Mustard moved in, Tanner had pointed to the fridge stocked with pizza bagels and said "mi casa es su casa" in such a genial tone that Mustard never did determine if he meant it as a microaggression. Still, he ate the pizza bagels.

Besides, Tanner's cluelessness definitely worked in his favor. Mustard didn't need a roommate who was too observant.

Green appeared confused. "I'm working."

Tanner snorted. "Whatever, dude. You guys are so far behind, what's another half an hour? You ever play this?"

Green picked up the controller. "My brother has this game."

"Good, then I won't have to explain." Tanner flicked over to the two-player version. "As long as you aren't a ringer like soldier boy, here."

Green was not a ringer. In fact, he sucked. He died right away. And then again. And again.

Tanner tried explaining.

"It's really violent, isn't it?" Green asked.

Tanner blinked. "Well, yeah. It's about soldiers rooting out insurgents in a war zone?"

Green glanced down at the controller and then at the

screen. "Do you think it's true, what they say about violent video games desensitizing people to real-life violence?"

"Oh, is that what they say?" Tanner asked wryly. He looked at Mustard over Green's head as if to ask, *Is this kid for real?*

Mustard didn't know. He felt like he was waiting for the other shoe to drop when it came to Vaughn Green. The whole janitorial staff had to be wondering, by now.

"They say that," said Amber. "But Tanner plays all the time, and he's the biggest teddy bear I know."

Tanner shot his girlfriend a grin. Mustard had almost forgotten she was still there, on her phone. That was one of the weirdest things to get used to at Blackbrook. They hadn't been allowed devices at Farthing, unless they were being used for exercises. But here, everyone was glued to a screen.

"I think it's a thing they say to make excuses as to why some people commit violence," said Mustard.

Green shot him a look. "Why do *you* think they do?"

He affected a shrug. "Lots of reasons. Any reason. Greed, jealousy, hatred, self-defense, anger"—they both flinched a little bit at that one—"war, cruelty . . . sometimes just because you were told to do it by a person of authority."

"Really?" Tanner asked.

"Yeah, they did this whole experiment once. Had men in white coats tell volunteers to electrocute someone they couldn't see. And a lot of people did."

"They did not," Tanner said, incredulous.

"They did," Mustard replied. "Milgram Experiment. Look it up."

Tanner searched for "Milgram" on his phone, and Green seemed deep in thought. "You'd kill someone because someone else told you to?"

Mustard didn't know what to say. It was sort of the whole point of soldiers. "I mean, yeah. If it was the right thing to do." This *was* something they'd studied at Farthing. Unlawful orders. War crimes. "War is complicated." He nodded at the video game. "But the game isn't. You can tell who you're supposed to shoot because they have red targets on them."

"Easy to tell who the bad guy is," said Green. "I don't know. I'm no better at that in the game than I am in real life."

"OH MY GOD!" Amber shouted all of a sudden. She was staring at her phone screen, eyes wide and jaw open. "Violet just texted me. They found another body in Tudor House."

There was a moment in which everyone in the room seemed to be frozen. And then, almost in unison, they grabbed their coats and bolted for the door.

The biting winter wind whipped across the barren greens of the Blackbrook campus. There was already a sizable crowd of students gathered on the muddy front lawn of Tudor House.

There were also several cop cars. Mustard's steps faltered.

"This look familiar?" Tanner called to him and Green.

Mustard didn't have too many memories of the cops. He didn't think they'd come by car the last time, though. The bridge had been washed out.

Now there was an ambulance as well as police, and also as a bunch of teachers trying desperately to get the students to disperse. No one was dispersing.

"Hey!" Amber called. "Can I go in my house?"

"Soon enough," replied Dr. Brown. She was a Blackbrook board member standing in for the headmaster this term. Tanner had told Mustard she was a big executive at Curry Chemical, like half the board, including his father and two uncles.

Dr. Brown stood with her arms spread wide, as if she could single-handedly block out the image of the house and the emergency vehicles from the students' insistent gaze and, worse, phone cameras. She herded them away from the porch and cop cars. "Right now, I want all you students to follow me to the dining hall."

There was a mass sigh of complaint. Mustard started to follow the rest of the group but then caught sight of Vaughn Green, who seemed to be hanging back. Their eyes met, and Green cocked his head toward the back of the house.

They fell into step and slid around the back while the others dutifully marched off. Mustard had almost been one of them.

"Guess you were right about most people following the orders of authority figures," said Green.

"Yeah, but you didn't do that."

"Does that make me a rebel?" He smiled. He had a nice smile. Mustard wished he knew what the other boy's deal was. Sometimes he seemed all right, like when Mustard had approached him about the job. But other times . . .

"I think it means you think for yourself."

Green's eyebrows went up in approval. "Don't hear that often. I'll keep it in mind. Come on. Let's try the kitchen door."

The kitchen door was locked, but Green produced a key from a hollow space at the top of the doorjamb.

"Come here a lot?" he asked Green.

"All the time in childhood."

Right. Mrs. White. Long-time family friend of a murderer. Another reason to be a bit wary.

Green pushed the door open and they found Orchid and Peacock sitting at the kitchen table, looking as if they'd seen a ghost. Orchid jumped up and rushed toward them.

"Vaughn!" she cried. For a second, Mustard thought she'd throw her arms around him, but she stopped short. "You won't believe it!"

"What happened?" he asked. He seemed to be standing taller than he had a few seconds ago. "What is it? Did Lin— Mrs. White . . .?"

"I don't know!" Orchid gasped. "He was in the secret passage, and—"

"The passages are sealed," Mustard blurted. "I thought," he added quickly.

"Not anymore, I guess," said Orchid. "Scarlett and Finn found him, in the passage—"

"Finn!" Mustard broke in. Oh, crap. What had Plum gotten himself into now?

"Found who?" Green asked.

Mustard felt cold.

"Rusty Nayler," Peacock broke in. She was watching Mustard carefully, her hands clasped tightly in front of her, as if indicating that she wouldn't punch him again.

Mustard kind of wished she would punch him again.

This couldn't be. This couldn't be.

Green was silent. Mustard had nothing to say, either.

"Oh, Vaughn," said Orchid. And now she did hug him. Were those two a thing? "Oh, Vaughn, I'm so sorry."

"I don't understand," Green whispered after a long time. "Mrs. White is in jail. I saw—"

"You saw her?" Orchid pulled away, her expression a mix of confusion and disgust.

"I saw the police take her away," he corrected. "And Rusty—I saw him . . . a few days ago . . . I think." He put a hand to his forehead.

This was getting into dangerous territory.

"Sit down," Orchid said quickly, and led him over to the kitchen table. Mustard supposed he should be grateful for that.

The door to the kitchen opened, and in walked Scarlett and Plum. They saw the others and stopped dead.

"Oh," said Plum. "Guess the gang's all here."

He looked good, Mustard thought. Considering that he'd just ruined everything.

"What are you two doing in here?" Scarlett asked. "Don't you think we have enough to deal with? A second dead body and all? *This* is the time for a Murder Crew reunion?"

"What were you guys doing in the secret passages?" Orchid asked. "They're supposed to be sealed."

Scarlett pursed her lips and shot an unreadable glance at Plum. Were those two still a thing? Mustard could not keep track.

"I'm actually really glad we have the opportunity to join together," said Peacock brightly. Her hands were still clasped before her. "I think we left a lot of unfinished business here last term, and this will give us the opportunity to get some closure and really clear the air. My life coach says that the resonance from conflict between people in our lives can contribute to lingering—"

There was a bang from the front of the house, and the whoosh of Maine wind. "Scarlett Mistry and Phineas Plum!" shouted the voice of Dr. Brown from the hall. "Where did you run off to?"

"Crap," said Scarlett. She looked at Green and Mustard. "You two better get out of here. Now."

Green shook his head. "I want to know what happened to Rusty."

"He died." Scarlett's tone was sharp.

"Scarlett!" cried Orchid. She looked about the room, then crossed to the pantry that had once been the entrance to the room's secret passage. "Here. Get in the closet."

"No way," say Mustard.

"Just for a minute. It's not like she's going to search the place."

Moments later, he and Green were shoved unceremoniously in with cans of soup and bags of flour. Darkness closed around them. He smelled stale air and old food and then, after a moment, Green, who might have spilled someone's trash on his clothes.

Great. He inched away.

"Don't like being in the closet with me?" Green asked.

"What's that supposed to mean?" Mustard snapped.

What little he could see of Green's face in the sliver of light from the door looked confused. "Because I smell like a janitor?"

"Oh," said Mustard. "Right." He peered through the crack at the others, outside in the kitchen. No, Green was not the member of the Murder Crew he'd choose to get trapped in a small dark space with. And the last place he wanted to be in general was in this house while Dr. Brown investigated the death of Rusty Nayler.

"There you are." He heard Dr. Brown's voice. "And I should have known you'd find these two. What did I tell you all about congregating? The rumor mill will be working overtime as it is."

"We *live* here." That was Orchid.

"Then I suggest you find your bedroom."

"But, Dr. Brown . . ." Peacock. "I have to finish my smoothie. I'm on a cleanse—"

"And I need to speak to Miss Mistry and Mr. Plum."

"Um, let's go, Peacock," Orchid said. "We can come back . . . *later*." He saw her cast a glance toward their closet.

And they must have left, because after a minute, he heard a chair scraping and then Dr. Brown's weary sigh.

He was about to find out how very bad this was. He really should have left.

He heard Scarlett clear her throat. "Is everything . . . all right, Dr. Brown?"

A bitter laugh. "Of course, Miss Mistry. We just dragged two corpses out of this house in the past month. Everything's *fine*." Another pregnant pause. "And I'm supposed to run this madhouse of a school, despite the fact that our top students— the ones who keep telling me I should trust them with actual aspects of this administration—are breaking rules every time I turn around."

"But—" Scarlett began, then was quickly shushed by Dr. Brown.

"You're supposed to be the smartest kids in school. I want you to help me find one reason why I shouldn't expel you right this minute."

"My parents give a lot of money to this school," Scarlett said bluntly.

Beside him, he heard Green give a quiet little snort.

"And they sent me back here, when a lot of their friends transferred their kids to Deerfield or Choate. How many more Blackbrook students can you afford to lose?"

Dr. Brown said nothing for a long moment. "I regret to admit that you are correct. The school's charter requires a minimum enrollment to remain operational. And I am here to ensure that no further incidents occur to endanger that." She sighed. "The official story is that Mr. Nayler unfortunately succumbed to exposure."

Mustard forgot to breathe entirely.

Not so Green, who seemed to be fighting some inner battle. His breath was going in angry puffs as he stood tensely at Mustard's side.

Oh, no. He put his hand on the other boy's shoulder.

It wasn't enough.

"The 'official' story?" Green shouted. "Then what *really* happened to Rusty?"

And before Mustard could stop him, he shoved the closet door open, and they both tumbled out.

7

Scarlett

Scarlett's first mistake had been listening to Finn. Well, maybe not her first. The *majority* of her mistakes, seen as a continuum, might come down to having listened to Finn. And this most recent time had possibly been the worst of all.

Though, she thought, as she stared at the two boys lying on the tiled floor in a heap, allowing Orchid to stick her boyfriend in the kitchen pantry five minutes ago was right up there, too.

Dr. Brown did not start at the commotion. She did not jump up from her seat when two more Blackbrook students came bursting out of the closet. She merely lifted her eyebrows, then fixed Scarlett with a look.

"Do these boys' parents also give a lot of money to Blackbrook?"

Not exactly. Vaughn was a scholarship student, and an eternal pain in her butt. Dr. Brown would be doing Scarlett a major favor if she expelled him.

Maybe Orchid had delivered a blessing in disguise.

Vaughn and Mustard were scrambling to their feet.

Vaughn's face was a mask of anger. Mustard looked—well, he looked a little sick.

Vaughn pointed an accusing finger at Dr. Brown. "Rusty has friends in Rocky Point. He's lived here his whole life. People will care about what happened to him, and—"

"Calm down, Mr. Green," said Dr. Brown, annoyed. "I'm not concocting a cover-up. The paramedics said that Rusty did appear to die of an exposure-related incident, I'm sorry to say. Whether there were extenuating circumstances—well, no one can tell that at this point. But what I do not want spread as gossip among the very *precarious* student body is that his body lay undetected for what appears to be several days in the unused corridors under this house."

Vaughn's arm dropped to his side. His expression was pained. "I've been so busy, I didn't notice how many shifts he was gone for. I—"

"I'm sure you can understand that privacy is necessary," Dr. Brown went on. "You would not want to see the school put into a bad situation, were you to be less than discreet."

"But—"

"For I cannot imagine that Deerfield or Choate have scholarships available for you."

Vaughn stopped speaking.

"And you, Mr. Maestor," she went on, "I don't believe Farthing Military Academy will have you back, will they?"

Mustard clenched his jaw. Interesting, thought Scarlett. In another era, she might have done something with that information. But right now, her hands were more than full.

Dr. Brown sighed and shook her head, looking at all four of them in utter exasperation. "I don't know what I'm supposed to do with you. Disciplining teenagers is not my strong suit. When employees at Curry act up, I just fire them. What can I do to you all? Detention? Does detention even work at a boarding school?"

Scarlett wondered what in the world the board of directors had been thinking, placing Dr. Brown here.

"Maybe I should send you to Winkle. That's what we brought him here for—crisis counseling. And you're definitely all in crisis . . ." She trailed off, as if considering her options.

Scarlett frowned. Wait, Winkle was a crisis counselor? She thought he'd been a normal guidance counselor. No wonder he had no more academic advice to give her than "get a tutor."

"You have all been to see him, right?"

Scarlett, Mustard, and Finn nodded obediently. Vaughn said, "I'm getting to it."

"Get to it faster," said Dr. Brown. Vaughn blinked at her in surprise, and even Scarlett felt ready to jump to his defense.

"I'd like to check that off my list, and it's very clear you all could use some guidance right about now. Guidance I am not equipped to deliver."

Yeah, no kidding, lady. What kind of clown show was the Blackbrook board running here? Scarlett was utterly appalled. Headmaster Boddy had been kind and caring. A little lenient, maybe—which had worked to Scarlett's advantage— but she could never imagine him snapping at the students this way.

For the first time, Scarlett wondered if staying at this school meant going down with the ship.

At last, Dr. Brown stood. "Here is the situation as I see it. You four remain here at this school for your own reasons. Which means you need Blackbrook. And I need to salvage what remains of this fine institute's reputation. So why don't you all stop skulking around the private dark spaces of this house doing heaven knows what and concentrate on your *actual* schoolwork?"

Beside her, Finn started to say. "Dr. Brown, we were trying to—"

"I know *precisely* what you were doing. In closets, in secret passages . . ." She gestured vaguely toward the pantry.

"No!" said Mustard quickly, looking horrified. "You don't—"

"I read your file, young man," she snapped. "And I may not have much experience dealing with teenagers, but I was one once. I know what teenagers like to do if given the opportunity, and I also know that it will *not* be happening on my watch."

No one thought it worthwhile to contradict her again.

"And now, I think it's time for the gentlemen to depart these premises, once and for all. I will be escorting each of you back to your rooms—and, Mr. Green, you to the edge of campus. And I don't want any more *shenanigans*, or any further discussion about what you saw or heard here today, or I *will* be forced to hand down consequences. Do I make myself clear?"

They all agreed. And then, without further ado, Dr. Brown marched the boys right out of the house. Scarlett barely even got a backward glance from Finn, let alone either of the other two. Each of the boys appeared traumatized, though possibly for their own reasons.

Approximately a minute later, Orchid made her way back downstairs. She met Scarlett in the hall.

"What happened?"

All kinds of things, but Scarlett figured Orchid would want the most relevant first. "Vaughn didn't stay in the pantry. Busted out and started confronting Dr. Brown about Rusty."

You could never trust him for a scheme. Scarlett could have told Orchid that ages ago.

"I can't imagine what he must be feeling," said Orchid, who seemed determined to miss the point. "First Mrs. White, now Rusty . . . I think they were very close. Working together, and having that connection from Rocky Point? He must be devastated."

Scarlett imagined he was, and the berating they'd all received from Dr. Brown hadn't really helped matters. They were all suffering, and the best the interim headmaster had managed was to be annoyed that a single visit to the school's guidance counselor hadn't sorted them out.

Perry Winkle certainly hadn't helped her with her little SAT problems, and Vaughn was in far more need of professional help than she was.

She hoped. Or else Scarlett was in real trouble.

"At least Vaughn didn't have a dead body fall on top of him tonight," she grumbled.

"Oh, right! I'm sorry!" Orchid cried. "Are you okay? You

seem okay. I remember when I found the headmaster—I nearly fainted. Is there anything I can do?"

Scarlett had *not* nearly fainted when Rusty's corpse had fallen down. Then again, she'd hardly seen it. She'd been hit in the shoulder with some part of his body, but it wasn't like they'd gotten a good look at his face. She'd screamed and rushed toward the exit, not even waiting for Finn. She hadn't even made it out of the study when Dr. Brown intercepted her and Finn, coming up the stairs from the secret passage. And Dr. Brown hadn't let them leave the room or even speak to each other during the endless hour it took the paramedics to get out to Tudor House.

"I'm fine," she told Orchid. Not really, though. She was fine about being one of the people who had found Rusty, but not about anything else that had happened that evening. Dr. Brown had left her with too many unanswered questions. "But . . . maybe Finn and Vaughn aren't. Do you want to go after them?"

Orchid nodded.

"I don't think so," said a voice from behind them.

The girls turned to find Rosa standing in the doorway to the billiards room—which had been converted into her bedroom—her arms crossed over her chest.

"Excuse me?" Scarlett put her hands on her hips. "No one asked you."

"I believe Dr. Brown said no one leaves the house tonight. You should be up in your rooms."

The nerve! "Who died and made you our proctor?"

"*Who died?*" Rosa mocked, raising her eyebrows. "You're seriously trying that line on me? Where should I start?"

Orchid put her hand out. "Maybe she's right, Scarlett. Dr. Brown sounded pretty mad. You don't want to push it with her."

"Dr. Brown as good as said she can't afford to kick any of us out of school right now. What is she going to do to us?" She turned to Orchid. "Come on. Don't you want to check on Vaughn?" Scarlett sure as hell wanted to have it out with Plum. He could have gotten them expelled tonight. *Expelled!*

Orchid pulled her phone out of her pocket and cast a guilty glance at Rosa. "You know what? I'll just text him."

Scarlett rolled her eyes, but Rosa nodded and disappeared into her bedroom again.

"Are you serious?" Scarlett asked. "You're going to let the new girl boss you around?"

"What, you'd prefer I let you boss me around?"

Yes. Obviously.

"Whatever." Scarlett turned on her heel and marched up the stairs. No one ever listened to her. Finn hadn't, and now he'd lost his project in the corpse-infested basement. Dr. Brown hadn't, and now she was dealing with another scandal. Orchid hadn't, and now she wasn't going to get to see Vaughn tonight.

Which probably wasn't a bad thing, if Scarlett really thought about it. Orchid could do way better than some Rocky Point nobody.

In her room, Scarlett turned to her computer. Her stats were way down this month. She hadn't been posting much.

First because it was hard to concentrate after the storm, and these past few weeks, because of stress over her test scores. It was tough to watch everyone abandoning her, though, or, worse, making up reasons why she was absent.

Because that's what people did. Jumped to crazy conclusions if they weren't given utterly reasonable alternative explanations. Dr. Brown was right to make sure the story was clear about Rusty's death. You had to give people a story they found easy to accept. That's why she hadn't said anything to disabuse the headmaster from her opinion that she and Finn had been down in the secret passage because they'd been looking for a place to hook up.

Mustard, however, had been very quick to deny it when it came to him and Vaughn in the closet. Boys and their fragile egos! It would be just like some macho military kid to prefer expulsion to the mere suggestion that he might have been making out with another guy. Scarlett shook her head.

She looked down at her sweater. It had gotten grimy and dusty down in the passage, but when she went to strip it off, she felt her hair flop against her face, clammy and sticky. She touched a hank of the black tresses, and her hand came away red.

Scarlett's breath caught in her throat. Was she bleeding? She rushed to the mirror to check out her head and neck but saw no injury there. And nothing hurt, at any rate. Well, maybe her shoulder was a bit sore from where Rusty's body had slammed down on it in the passage . . .

Rusty.

People who died of exposure didn't bleed. People who had heart attacks didn't bleed either.

Whether there were extenuating circumstances—well, no one can tell that at this point.

Scarlett stared at her reflection in newfound terror. But the murderer was in jail! Mrs. White was in jail!

There had to be another explanation. Maybe dead bodies just . . . bled? Scarlett wondered if that was the kind of thing you could look up on the internet.

Her phone buzzed on her desk. She picked it up and turned on the screen.

Finn

We need to talk.

She snorted and typed back.

Sure do. Do you know I have Rusty's blood in my HAIR?

Finn

Do you really think that's important right now?

Uh, yeah. Because people who freeze to death don't bleed.

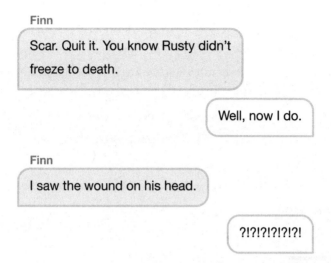

Finn

Scar. Quit it. You know Rusty didn't freeze to death.

Well, now I do.

Finn

I saw the wound on his head.

?!?!?!?!?!?!

Finn didn't type anything. Scarlett practically screamed at the phone.

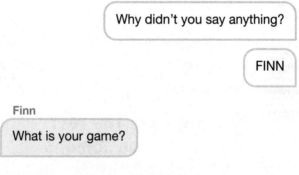

Why didn't you say anything?

FINN

Finn

What is your game?

Scarlett blinked at the phone.

I have no idea what you're talking about.

Finn

Yes, you do.

Phineas Plum, I swear on my life, I haven't the foggiest clue what you are implying. Explain yourself.

Three little dots. For what seemed like an eternity. And then:

Finn

Explain this. I found it on the body.

A picture popped up on the text screen.

For a second, she had no idea what she was looking at. And then, it hit her. A wad of twenty-dollar bills, smeared with blood, and a scrap of paper with a message scrawled across it in her signature crimson ink.

You can have the rest when I see you tonight.

S.M.

8

Peacock

From: *elizabeth.picach@BlackbrookAcademy.edu*
To: *ash@phoenixmanagement.org*
Subj: *Another body!!!*

Ash, I don't know what to do! They found another body in my dorm. Well, Scarlett and Finn did. They broke into the study's secret passage, even though it was supposed to be sealed or whatever, and it turns out the janitor was in there. Dead! No one knows how long. No one knows what happened. Everyone is totally freaking out.

I guess it was some horrible accident or whatever, but what if everyone starts blaming it on me again? What am I going to do? I'm afraid to even go to class tomorrow. I'm afraid to talk to anyone. I tried to talk to the others tonight, but Dr. Brown just sent us all to our rooms.

I'm not going to sleep all night. And I'm supposed to give an oral report in history tomorrow.

Beth

From: *elizabeth.picach@BlackbrookAcademy.edu*
To: *ash@phoenixmanagement.org*
Subj: *Re: Another body!!!*

P.S. I am honored to share with you the illumination within.

From: *ash@phoenixmanagement.org*
To: *elizabeth.picach@BlackbrookAcademy.edu*
Subj: *Re: Another body!!!*

Hey, Beth,

I'm so sorry to hear this! First things first—just breathe. Just take a minute right now to close your eyes, breathe in, and just feel your body. All your muscles and tendons and bones. The air moving through your lungs. The blood moving through your veins.

You're safe. No one thinks you're a murderer. I'm sure whatever happened to that poor man, it's just like your headmaster said—a terrible accident.

Look, I've been doing this a long time. I've worked with lots of talented young people who are like you—who are scared that they're going to make some move, some mistake, and their fans will turn against them. But you didn't do anything. You were in the wrong place at the wrong time when your old headmaster was murdered and, once again, now. You did nothing wrong—you were just in the same house as this guy. But so were a dozen other girls. So was your friend Orchid. So was Scarlett. So was Rosa.

They're all feeling this same fear. Rosa especially, I bet, because she's new. She doesn't have the bonds that you've built up with the rest of your friends at school. Reach out to her.

I'm overnighting you some melatonin to help you with the sleeping thing, as well as a special concoction. Forget the smoothie cleanse. This is for stress relief, which I think you and your friends are going to need a lot of going forward.

I am honored to share with you the illumination within,

Ash

9

Orchid

Orchid woke gasping for breath. It was not unusual.

She stared at the ceiling and went through the steps.

Step one: Acknowledge it. She was having a panic attack. What was happening to her was only a panic attack.

Step two: Breathe. Breathe in. Breathe out.

Step three: Be present. She was safe, in bed, in her room at Blackbrook.

Step four: The countdown trick. Five things she could see: one, the window over her bed; two, the curtains hanging from the rod; three, her coat hanging on the back of her desk chair; four, the lamp in the corner; five, her phone charging on her nightstand. Four things she could touch: one, her thick fleece duvet cover; two, her fluffy down pillow; three, the silk cord on her pajamas; four, her old teddy bear, Bobo—

Wait. Where was Bobo? She dug around under the covers but could not feel the bear. She sat up, her heart still pounding wildly, and checked the floor around her bed. No bear.

Bizarre. She never went to bed without him.

But she'd been distracted last night. Up late texting with Vaughn, drifting off, only to be woken by the persistent little buzz in her hand that meant another message from him was coming through. They'd finally convinced each other to put down their phones and go to sleep. She hadn't minded. He'd needed it. Vaughn was shaken by Rusty's death and lost as to what to say to his neighbors. Blackbrook was becoming a very dangerous place for the folks from Rocky Point.

But not for Vaughn. That's what she'd tried to tell him last night. *You're not alone in this,* she'd texted him.

> **Vaughn**
> Oh, I know that part. Believe me.

He must mean the other people in the village with connections to the school.

> Come to campus for breakfast tomorrow. I promise it won't be one of Peacock's gross smoothies.

> **Vaughn**
> Those actually didn't sound half bad.

> Depends how you feel about drinking sand.

Vaughn

> I grew up digging clams on the beach. I've eaten plenty of sand.

Orchid was shaking out her sheets in search of the stuffed animal before she realized that her anxiety had faded away.

"Well, good," she said aloud. Her therapist advised her to acknowledge the end of a panic attack, just like she was supposed to acknowledge its onset. All it meant was that her strategies to survive these episodes were working. The attacks might never go away completely, but at least she was able to manage them.

Her dreams had been a step beyond their usual level of unpleasantness last night. She hadn't been able to avoid imagining that Rusty Nayler's death was connected to her own troubles.

Rationally, Orchid knew better. She'd spent time and money making sure that Keith would never be able to hurt her again. Her restraining order was up to date. Her accounts were all locked down. And, of course, there was her insurance policy.

Tudor House was safe. Blackbrook was safe. *Orchid* was safe.

She checked her phone for new messages, but there was nothing more from Vaughn. She did, however, have an email from the school counselor.

From: *perry.winkle@BlackbrookAcademy.edu*
To: *orchid.mckee@BlackbrookAcademy.edu*
Subj: *Evaluation*

> *Dear Miss McKee,*
> *I've been trying to get in contact with you for a week now. While we are all very sorry for your trouble, the administration is eager to put the events of last term to rest. We want to make sure that you are concentrating on what is most important: your studies. Please come to my office at your earliest possible convenience to discuss these matters.*
> *Sincerely,*
> *Perry Winkle*
> *Guidance Counselor*

Wow, what a gentle bedside manner he had! Clearly, Mr. Winkle was cut from the same cloth as Dr. Brown. Neither of them seemed to have the first clue how to deal with kids in trauma, or maybe kids at all. Orchid no longer felt guilty for blowing this dude off in favor of her regular therapist. She should warn Vaughn to keep clear, too.

Orchid had quite enough of older men telling her what to do.

She slid out of bed and checked for Bobo underneath. Nothing. So weird. But she'd worry about it later. Vaughn would be by soon enough.

After Orchid visited the bathroom, brushed her teeth,

and got dressed, she spent a few more minutes searching for her stuffed animal, to no avail. It was very curious. She never took it out of the room. Maybe it had somehow made it into the laundry?

She brushed her shaggy hair. She'd had it freshly dyed in her preferred mousy brown while in California, much to Scarlett's dismay. Orchid wasn't sure what the other girl's plans were for her. Sometimes she regretted telling Scarlett her secret, but there was nothing she could really do about it now.

She reached for her glasses where she usually kept them, on the nightstand.

But there was nothing there.

Orchid frowned. She looked on her desk. No glasses. A jolt of adrenaline coursed through her system.

Breathe. Breathe. She went through her countdown.

Bobo being missing was odd enough. But she *knew* she'd had her glasses last night. They were as fake as her hair color and just as vital a piece of her disguise.

She crossed to her chest of drawers and examined the surface. The usual menagerie of pens, loose change, barrettes, and paper clips were scattered around. No glasses. The lid of her jewelry box was open.

Orchid didn't usually wear much jewelry anymore, but she kept a few pieces from the old days. She glanced inside. Everything seemed to be in order, except . . . She dug through necklaces and bangles, her breath hitching in her throat. Where was her orchid ring? The ones the twins had given her? She didn't see it at all.

Panic rose within her again, and she tried to step back and use her strategies . . . to no avail. There was no reason at all for these things to be gone. She was safe here. She was safe here.

She needed to get out. Now.

Orchid stepped into the hall and ran right into Scarlett. The other girl seemed as shaken as she was, with shadows under her eyes and a haunted expression.

"What's wrong?" they both said to each other.

"I'm—missing things from my room," Orchid said.

"Me too," said Scarlett.

Orchid stopped. This was unexpected. And possibly very good news. Orchid would much rather the idea that they were dealing with a common thief. "You are?"

"Yeah, I think. I have this pen. Or I used to. And I don't know where it is. But it's my red pen. You know the one."

Orchid most certainly did. She'd seen its work on dozens of little passive-aggressive notes since she'd first become Scarlett's housemate. Her initials, scrawled on jars of tahini in the fridge. Her reservation of the study in the evening for private tutoring sessions. "When did you last see it?"

Scarlett shook her head. "I don't know. I've been sticking to number two pencils this week."

"So maybe we just have a garden variety thief," Orchid said. Funny how much of a relief that was! "All the new people who have moved in this term—"

" 'New people' is right," Scarlett snapped. "Like that Rosa girl. She's always watching everyone. What if she's been casing the place?"

"It's not Rosa," said Orchid.

"How do you know?"

Orchid rolled her eyes. She did not have time to get into it with Scarlett Mistry today. It would turn into a Whole Thing. "We'll figure it out. I have to go. I'm supposed to meet Vaughn for breakfast."

As if on cue, her phone buzzed in her pocket. She reached for it.

Vaughn

Sorry, can't make it today. Custodial staff frantic.

Orchid swallowed her disappointment. She imagined that every janitor on campus was freaking out. She texted back.

Totally understand. Talk later.

One good bit of news. If Vaughn was busy with the other janitors, he wouldn't have time to talk to Mr. Winkle, either. Orchid doubted a conversation with him would do Vaughn the slightest bit of good right now.

She looked at Scarlett. "I'll talk to Rosa." No, that wasn't good enough. "I mean, feel her out. Try to get to the bottom of this." That should satisfy Scarlett. And Orchid should talk to Rosa, anyway. If someone was breaking into their rooms at Tudor, Rosa should know about it.

Scarlett didn't look convinced. Time for a change in subject.

"You have English soon, right?" Orchid asked her.

Scarlett nodded, still looking distracted.

"Don't worry," said Orchid, as if someone saying "don't worry" had ever helped her stop. "It's just a pen."

It's just a teddy bear. It's just a pair of glasses. It's just a ring . . .

Yeah, she needed to talk to Rosa and figure out what was going on.

Somehow she managed to bundle Scarlett off to class. Then she steeled her nerves and knocked on the billiards room door.

Classes were pretty much a blur. By the time Orchid was done for the afternoon, she barely remembered what her teachers had been talking about. On the plus side, there was a break in the ever-present cloud cover, bathing the campus in a wan golden light. The sun hung low on the horizon, and the wind had died down, making the frigid temperature feel—well, slightly less frigid than usual.

Instead of heading straight back to Tudor House, Orchid decided to take a little walk and clear her head. It shouldn't have surprised her at all that her path wandered toward the edge of campus and the bridge that led across the ravine into Rocky Point. The ravine was beautiful in the late-afternoon sunlight—all rocky crags and a ruined but picturesque old boathouse.

She hadn't heard from Vaughn again, though she couldn't say she was surprised. The janitors on campus had already been having a rough time of it before the head of their department was found dead. Everyone at school was whispering about it—despite Dr. Brown's insistence that it was just a terrible accident.

All a campus needed was a single murder, and anything else that happened would automatically look suspicious. It wasn't that different, Orchid thought, than her own situation.

Everyone assured her that Keith was contained. Twelve months on house arrest. It was the most they could ask for, given what his lawyers had called the "circumstantial" nature of her underage testimony. It was a miracle, they said, that they'd managed that much.

Her team and law enforcement had communicated the contents of the letter she'd received right before the storm last term. The response from what she assumed was his lawyer was swift and decisive.

Mr. Grayson has no knowledge of this letter, or of Emily Pryce's whereabouts. Thanks to her unfounded attacks on his character, he is not even in the entertainment industry anymore. He suggests that perhaps this letter was sent by one of the millions of fans that Miss Pryce, with Mr. Grayson's dedicated help as her manager, cultivated over their years of partnership. He is very sorry for her trouble.

What a prick. With distance, Orchid could say that. If he were rotting in a jail cell, where he belonged, she could have screamed it.

He was no more "sorry for her trouble" than Mr. Winkle

was. They were both just trying to cover their own asses. And she was done letting anyone walk all over her.

She was a different girl now, at seventeen, than she'd been all those years ago. She'd faced down a murderer when she'd confronted Mrs. White in the secret passage. If she'd had that strength back when she was fourteen, would she have somehow been able to prove that Keith Grayson was a murderer, too?

Because he'd killed the twins—Jen and Kate Steelman. He'd killed them as much as if he'd stuck knives into their hearts.

Orchid swallowed thickly, thinking of the missing ring. They'd each had one. Hers had been rose gold, Jen's had been platinum, and Kate's yellow gold. They'd bought them to commemorate the last film they'd done together, *Three Orchids*, a beautiful, artsy, coming-of-age movie. So different from the all the schlock they'd done before. For the first time, Jen and Kate had even been able to play separate roles instead of sharing the screen as one character, as they had since infancy. For the first time, they'd defied their manager and done what they wanted to do.

The film hadn't been released. The studio shelved it after the Steelmans' tragic deaths. And Orchid had run as far as she could get. But still, every time something scared her, her mind instantly went to Keith, as if she'd never truly be free.

She picked her way across the rocks at the edge of the ravine, then looked up to see a familiar face exit the old boathouse. She broke into a smile. Enough obsessing over the twins. There were more pleasant things to think about.

"Vaughn!" she cried, and waved.

He came closer. "Orchid?"

"Duh!" She laughed and beckoned to him. Sunset on a cliff overlooking the sea with a cute boy? Talk about self-care!

"What are you doing out here?" He came toward her.

The breeze lifted the ends of her hair and the fringe on her scarf. She felt a bit like a Jane Austen heroine. "What are you doing? Cleaning the old boathouse?"

"Yeah," he said. His hands were in his pockets, and he was keeping his distance. She skirted around a few boulders until they were face-to-face.

"I'm sorry we couldn't do breakfast this morning."

"Oh. Yeah."

Why was he like this? Over text, he was so warm and charming, and then in person, sometimes, so awkward and distant. Was he just shy? He wasn't shy when he was singing. He hadn't been shy when he'd found her after chemistry class. "Are you feeling better?" She reached out a gloved hand and touched his arm.

He stared down at her hand as if it was a specimen in a jar, curious and strange. "I feel fine."

She forced a laugh. "Really? You look kind of out of it."

He met her eyes. She loved the color of his eyes. A sort of light greenish brown. Like old pennies. "Sorry. Long day. Though, honestly, I don't remember much of it."

"Me neither," she admitted. "I just want things to go back to normal around here."

Vaughn snorted. "What's normal?"

"Okay. Good point. Are you feeling better about Rusty? Have you talked to other people in town? How are they taking it?"

"There was a meeting this morning. I don't really want to talk about it."

"I understand. I'm glad I saw you, though. I've been thinking about you all day."

He blinked, and his eyes softened. "You have?"

She bit her lip and looked away, her cheeks heating. "Yes. Sorry, am I not supposed to say that?"

"No," he said quickly. "You can say anything you want to." Now it was Vaughn's turn to come forward, his expression awash in some kind of sudden realization. "You . . . you really like me, don't you?"

Orchid laughed for real, a short bubble of joy that frosted in the cold air between them. Boys were so clueless. "Yes, you idiot. Of course I like you."

"Do I like you?" he asked, as if he was only just considering the question. "Oh wow, I do! Huh . . ."

She gave a little shake of her head. It was kind of cute. Kind of.

He still looked a little overcome. "But . . . *what* do you like about me? Exactly? Is it the puppy dog act?"

"What?"

"The music?" He was nodding. "It's got to be the music, right? Chicks really dig a guy with a guitar."

"Vaughn," Orchid said, confused, "I can't tell if you're messing with me or—"

He took her hand and tugged her closer. "Do you want to kiss me?"

She snatched her hand back. "Not like this."

"What's wrong?" he pressed.

She took two steps back. How did he go from sweet to creepy so quickly? "It's just . . . It's not how I pictured our first kiss."

That wasn't entirely true. Kissing on a cliff at sunset would have been kind of perfect. But then Vaughn had to go and ruin it.

"*Our first kiss*," Vaughn repeated mockingly. "Jeez, do I move slow!"

"Eww," Orchid said. "Stop it!"

At once, he straightened. "You're right. I'm a better person than this. Your first kiss should be . . . right."

She eyed him, warily.

He raised his hands in surrender. "I am not going to touch you."

Her mouth opened. But didn't she want him to touch her? Hadn't that been what she'd gone to sleep thinking about last night? "Vaughn—"

"No," he shot back. "I gotta go. But thank you, Orchid. You've given me a very precious gift."

And then he turned and headed across the bridge.

Orchid watched him go, her emotions roiling from baffled to annoyed and then right on to angry. What had happened to the guy who'd insisted he didn't want to play games?

She marched back toward campus, her mood dark. Vaughn was half the reason she'd come back to Blackbrook. He was the only thing that had helped her get through this bizarre day. And then to mess with her emotions like that—she hadn't stayed up comforting him over text message for him to turn around and ridicule her this evening for admitting she had feelings for him. If she wanted to be jerked around, she could go back to Hollywood.

Maybe Scarlett was right. She *could* do better.

She pulled out her phone and looked over last night's texts. He'd been vulnerable with her then, open and honest about how much the whole Mrs. White thing was still bothering him. Mrs, White was Vaughn's godmother, a close friend of his own grandmother's. He felt like an out-sider at Blackbrook, and fellow townies like Mrs. White and Rusty Nayler helped him feel more at home. And now they were both gone. Orchid's heart had ached at those confessions.

Is it the puppy dog act?

Was that all it had been? An act, to get her to feel bad for him?

Her jaw was tight as she stabbed out a text to him.

> What the hell WAS that?

After a moment, she saw three little dots appear, then vanish, then appear again.

Orchid rolled her eyes. She actually didn't want an excuse. He could make any excuse he wanted over text. Clearly, they were all lies.

> You know what, Vaughn? Don't bother trying to explain yourself. I just want to know one thing: Who do you think you are?

This time, there was no response at all.

10

Green

Who *do you think you are?*

The message felt like a bleeding wound that Vaughn ignored, hoping it would go away. The phone festered on his coffee table, facedown, taunting him. But he wouldn't answer Orchid. Couldn't.

Not until he heard what Oliver had to say.

He hadn't been able to hack school today—and Vaughn never skipped classes, no matter that Oliver might. This morning, at the custodial services meeting with Dr. Brown, where she'd informed the staff of Rusty's death, he'd felt sick. Not the usual, slow-burning nausea of his life, but a deep, agonizing pain. As if everything were so twisted up, inside and out, that there was no escape. Afterward, he'd asked Dr. Brown if he could go home. To his surprise, especially after her behavior to him yesterday, she'd agreed.

"Rest," she said. "I looked at your file, Mr. Green. You're one of our most promising students."

"Thank you."

"We're counting on you to get top scores on your standardized tests this weekend. So you do what you need to do today. I will get in touch with your teachers. And please, don't forget to make an appointment with the guidance counselor."

He went home, but all he could think was, *What if I don't get top scores on my standardized tests?*

Dr. Brown was paying too much attention to all of them. Looking in everyone's files, keeping track of what they were all still doing at this school. For years, he had been able to fly under the radar. No one was correlating his work-study schedule with his classes. No one was asking questions about how he found time to take all the classes he took and work custodial and, you know, study and eat and sleep.

But now there were so few kids at Blackbrook, and Dr. Brown appeared determined to figure out what made each one tick. Vaughn couldn't afford that.

When Oliver came in, Vaughn was poking halfheartedly at his brother's favorite video game, the one where you shot anyone who was getting in your way.

"I thought you found this game too *violent*," Oliver sneered at him. "Didn't you say it would rot our brains?"

"Yeah, well, I needed to get some aggression out," Vaughn said, and promptly got shot in the face. Man, he sucked at this.

"Man, you suck at this," said Oliver. He perched on the arm of the couch.

Vaughn tossed the controller aside. "What did you do to Orchid?"

He'd never understand. Oliver had the same smile he did, but, somehow, he made it so *awful.* "Oh, yeah. Why didn't you tell me you had a girlfriend, brother?"

God forbid he have anything left that belonged only to him. "She's not my girlfriend."

"She seems to think she is."

For a moment, the bottom dropped out, and Vaughn was left dangling over some deep, black abyss. "What did you do to her?"

"Come on, man, I don't kiss and tell."

Vaughn clenched his jaw. "What. Did. You. Do."

Oliver was silent for several seconds. "Do you really want to know how far she let me get with her?"

The next thing he knew, he was on the ground, Oliver beneath him, one fist filled with Oliver's shirt, the other raised to strike. His brother was laughing in his face.

"You're right, Vaughn. Those games do turn a person violent. Look at yourself."

He raised his fist higher. "Tell me the truth."

"I didn't touch her." Oliver was capable of looking a person in the eye and lying like he was reciting the weather, but this statement had the ring of truth. "I swear." He shrugged underneath Vaughn, who let him up. Vaughn was breathing heavily, his heart pounding, but Oliver just looked amused. Delighted, even.

Vaughn realized his mistake. Oliver didn't want Orchid.

He wanted leverage.

Oliver dusted himself off. "No, I wouldn't do that to my

brother. He finally decides he likes a girl, why would I be the person to wreck his big romantic moment?"

"Shut up."

"And it *was* romantic," Oliver went on. "Sunset, big cliff. Like something out of a movie."

"I said, *shut up*."

"If it helps, she really, really wanted to kiss you." He could ruin even that. He could ruin everything, any time he wanted. Vaughn thought about her texts.

What the hell was that?

Who do you think you are?

He was no one. He couldn't afford to be Vaughn Green, to be anyone. The second he tried, Oliver would be along to smash it to pieces.

"So I'm going to let you have this," said Oliver, leaning in, "if you behave."

"Whatever," he replied. "You overplayed your hand. Whatever you did to her, she hates us now."

"Come on, lover boy. If she hates you, it's just because you didn't kiss her when you had the chance. Go serenade her outside her window tonight. She'll be putty in your hands. Chicks dig dudes with guitars."

Vaughn wouldn't dignify that with a response. Wouldn't give his twin any more ammunition.

"It's nice to see you in love," Oliver went on.

Vaughn cursed under his breath.

"Why are you in such a bad mood?" Oliver said. "I'm sorry. I was just teasing you. I really am very happy for you."

There was a time Vaughn would have believed that. There was a time he would have believed that happiness was an emotion his brother was capable of. That his apologies were real.

"It's important that someone cares about you, you know," Oliver said. "Because you've convinced yourself that no one else does. That the whole world hates you. That your own brother hates you and is out to destroy your life."

Vaughn still said nothing.

"Imagine how I feel! I don't even *have* a girlfriend. My brother hates me, too, and I don't even have a pretty Blackbrook girl to kiss me and make it all better."

"What do you want?" Vaughn ground out.

Oliver sat back on his heels. Was he surprised that Vaughn wasn't denying that he hated him? Or was he just pleased they no longer had to pretend? "The same thing I've always wanted. Revenge. And I want you to help me."

Vaughn sighed.

"You owe me. You owe Gemma."

Vaughn thought he was just about done owing Oliver anything. He'd already given up half his life. More than half . . .

"If there was anything to prove, don't you think Gemma would have proved it years ago?" He didn't disbelieve his grandmother. Not exactly. But he didn't understand why she had let it go. Why she'd spent all those years being bitter instead of fighting back.

He knew Oliver did, though. Oliver felt it the way everyone in Rocky Point felt it as their tiny island slipped into the sea and there was nothing anyone there could do to stem the tide.

Power didn't reside in their hands, and no one—no one—was getting out.

Well, except for the Blackbrook kids. Once, it had been a boys-only boarding school, just as Tudor House had been a reform academy for wayward girls. All those young men with bright and glorious futures that deserved to be protected, and all those girls with no futures at all. Tudor House itself had been swallowed by Blackbrook, the same way Olivia Vaughn's invention had been co-opted by Dick Fain.

"Gemma—she just didn't have that fight in her. She wasn't ready to take on the whole world."

"And you are?"

"*We* are," Oliver said. "The two of us. Me, because I don't care what people think. And you—because you really, really do."

Vaughn was silent. Oliver loved to give him grief about getting into Blackbrook, about the scholarship that had marked him forever as the "smart one." The "good twin," as Linda White had said.

But Oliver was plenty smart, too. This whole rotten plan had been Oliver's. And he wasn't going to stop without seeing it through.

"I went to see Mrs. White," Vaughn said at last. "I made her tell me what you guys are doing."

"Oh, good," his brother replied. "Saves me having to explain. So, what do you think?"

Vaughn shook his head. "I told you. I don't think there's anything down there." If there were, Mrs. White would have taken Oliver down ages ago, instead of concocting some jail-bird confession.

"There's a ton of stuff down there. But I couldn't get into the places I needed to. Now, thanks to your little friends on the Murder Crew, we know the entrances to the secret passages. We have a chance."

"Wait," Vaughn scoffed. "You want to break into Tudor House and go into the passages through the entrance in the study or the kitchen?"

"Yes."

"No."

"No?" Oliver raised his eyebrows at Vaughn.

"Can't be done. Too much security."

"Please, I heard Finn Plum managed in about five minutes. And he's clueless."

"Yeah, well, clueless enough to get caught," Vaughn replied. "Now Dr. Brown has every entrance on lockdown. It was all-hands-on-deck for the custodial staff today. I was there at the meeting, don't forget."

"You'd never let me forget." Oliver rolled his eyes. Their argument about who was doing most of the work portion of the work-study requirement for their scholarship was not a new one.

"She's not taking any more chances, after what happened to Rusty. She's having an expert in to make sure the staircase behind the bookshelf in the study is permanently sealed, and in the meantime she's nailed the bookcase to the wall."

"And the kitchen?"

Vaughn shrugged. "Boarded up this morning. Besides, she already threatened to expel me last night. I don't think sneaking back into Tudor House is the answer."

Oliver frowned. "I spent weeks looking for the entrance in the woods that Linda told me about."

Vaughn had to tread carefully. "Did you find it?"

Oliver's eyes narrowed. "What kind of question is that?"

"A straightforward one. Did you find the entrance?"

"What, exactly, are you asking me?"

It was horrible, to think evil things about your brother. Dreadful to imagine that he might commit unthinkable atrocities, unforgivable sins. But that's what Vaughn had been doing ever since the storm. Maybe for longer than that.

When he and Oliver were little and their parents went on the road, Gemma used to put them in the bath together. She said it saved the water heater. And every single time, Oliver would contrive a way to get soap in Vaughn's eyes. When his eyes would water, Oliver would laugh and say Vaughn was crying.

When Vaughn actually cried at the teasing, Oliver would laugh even harder. Everything was a trap, and the more Vaughn fought to escape, the more he got entangled.

Vaughn didn't know if Mrs. White had been correct about him, about how believing he was the good twin meant there must be an evil twin, too. If she was, then maybe it meant that by pushing Oliver away, he was giving whatever tendencies his brother had room to grow. Neither of them had anyone else. Not anymore. Even Orchid was just a fantasy. He couldn't be with her.

He couldn't even be with himself.

Vaughn took a deep breath. "You know what I'm asking you. Rusty was found dead in the secret passage."

Oliver stared at him in shock. "I don't want to kill anyone!"

"Don't want to, or won't?"

"Especially not anyone from Rocky Point."

"Don't want to, or won't?"

"Vaughn—"

"Don't want to, or *didn't*?" He was screaming it now.

"Didn't!" Oliver screamed back, right in his face. "What's wrong with you! You think just because Linda killed Boddy in a fit of anger, that I'm going to do something that dumb?" Oliver shoved himself to his feet and crossed the room. "You're the one with the anger problem, you know. Not me."

Vaughn stood, too. His hands clenched automatically into fists, and as soon as he realized it, he forced himself to release them. "Not true."

Oliver snorted. "You gave me a black eye last month because I took your place for three extra hours during the storm."

"And *you* gave me a bloody nose—"

"You just tackled me to the floor at the very suggestion that I might have touched Orchid without your permission."

"It wasn't about *permission*," Vaughn said. He wasn't even sure how consent worked in their situation. If Orchid kissed Oliver, thinking he was Vaughn . . . *this* was why he couldn't be with her.

"You just accused me of murdering our boss."

Vaughn didn't have anything to say to that.

"Do you have any idea how that makes me feel? That you think I'm capable of doing . . . whatever?" He spat the last word, as if unwilling to elucidate what he included in that *whatever.*

"Do you have any idea how it makes me feel," Vaughn shot back, "knowing that you *are* capable of it?"

Again, there was no denial. Oliver's tone was dark when he spoke again. "I didn't murder Rusty. Believe what you like."

"Promise me—"

"I promise I didn't."

Vaughn wasn't done. "Promise me you won't kill anyone."

Silence reigned in their little house. Ice cracked. Radiators dripped. Rocky Point slid farther into oblivion.

"I only want what's ours," Oliver said at last. "Help me, and you can decide how that happens. If you really think—" He stopped, and the next words came out as if chipped, one by one, from the granite of the island itself. "If you really think that there's something *wrong* with me, then you have to help me. You have to keep me on the straight and narrow."

Vaughn clenched his jaw so hard, he thought his teeth might shatter. There was no one else left. No one who really knew him. Only Oliver.

"I know where the entrance to the passage is," he said softly. "In the woods."

Oliver leaned forward, the spark of the chase back in his eyes. "You do? How?"

Vaughn closed his eyes, and when he opened him, he saw his own face, reflected back at him. "Because I was Rusty's friend."

11

Plum

It wasn't fair. Finn didn't think he was asking for too much. All he wanted was to claim full ownership of his own invention, the one he'd created, all by himself, on his own time. Sure, he'd done his work in the school labs, using the school's equipment, and under the agreement that he'd made with Blackbrook . . . but *still*.

Was that any reason that he should have to share what was rightfully his?

And Scarlett! Pretending she wanted nothing to do with him, claiming that she had no idea what he was after, and all along, she'd been bribing Rusty Nayler to get her hands on Finn's work. He'd always known she was manipulative, ruthless, and a markedly good liar. But, it turned out, she was better than he'd ever suspected.

It had taken him the whole evening to work out what had really happened and how skillfully she'd manipulated the situation to get him exactly where she wanted him.

First: she must have heard about his project and, more, divined where he'd hidden it during the storm.

Second: she'd bribed Rusty to go retrieve his work out of the secret passage.

Why that hadn't worked was a thought exercise to which Finn did not want to devote too much time. Maybe Rusty had banged his head on a pipe, passed out, and frozen to death. Maybe his corpse had been chewed on by rats. Finn didn't know. Biology wasn't his chosen field.

But he didn't think Scarlett had *killed* the man.

Probably.

However it happened, Rusty had not made it out of the passages with Finn's stuff. So the third step of Scarlett's plan must have been: when Finn approached her with an offer to team up, she played the innocent and let him unseal the passages all by himself.

That made sense. Didn't it?

It was the only explanation he could think of. Unless there was something else that Scarlett wanted from Rusty, and the fact that he was in the secret passage was nothing more than a red herring.

Either way, one thing was perfectly clear: Finn could not trust Scarlett. She had some nerve being so upset that he had lied to her last term. That he'd kept secrets from *her*. Scarlett obviously had plenty of secrets of her own.

He wouldn't let her outmaneuver him this time. He had the evidence—the money she'd given Rusty. He just didn't know what to do with it. Turning it in to Dr. Brown would be counterproductive, for certain. One thing he was sure of after his observation today, Scarlett had not been able to get back into the passages to steal his work. The word on the street was that Dr. Brown had engaged every person with a hammer on Rocky Point to lock those passages down.

And that left Finn back at square one. He wished he'd thought of bribing Rusty when he'd had the chance. But the passages had been secret for so long, it had never even occurred to him that his invention would be unsafe there.

Securing his work had to be priority one. Getting revenge on Scarlett . . . he'd worry about that later.

After classes, he headed straight to the gym. Finn might not be able to trust anyone, but that didn't mean that he had to work alone. He needed an in at Tudor House, and the best option left to him could almost certainly be found working out.

They'd finally erected the new winter dome over the tennis courts. It glowed in the darkness. Finn let himself inside.

Beth was there, beating the pants off an entire stable of freshmen. Her previous victims were slumped on the benches, dripping with sweat and watching her destroy the latest contender. The coach stood by the net, frowning.

"Okay, Picach," he said at last. "Let's take ten."

Beth did not look like she wanted to take even two, but as she was trotting obediently off the court, she saw Finn. Her whole demeanor changed, a broad smile breaking out across her face. Peacock, the terror of the tennis courts, vanished, and Beth reappeared. She turned to the coach.

"Actually, maybe some of the others want extra practice time? I'm happy to give up my place."

Coach Lungelo looked surprised. "Really? Okay, then. I'll run some drills for the underclassmen."

"Wonderful," she said. She clasped her hands before her. "Thank you so much for sharing with me the privilege of your time and expertise." She turned toward her victims—um, opponents. "I am honored to have played on the other side of your net. Stay radiant."

The other players exchanged bewildered glances. Finn didn't blame them.

"Hey!" she greeted him. "I'm so glad to see you. Did you come to the courts looking for me?"

"Um, yeah." He gestured to the rest of the team. "What was that?"

She cast them one backward glance. "They're hopeless. Everyone good went to Newark Academy. But I'm trying to hold more gratitude for the things I have, rather than get frustrated about what I don't. My life coach says that positive aspecting will help potentiate my flow state."

"I'm sorry, what?" Finn asked. "Are those tennis terms?"

"Basically, I shouldn't trash the team just because they suck and I don't. It's not helpful to their game or my state of mind."

Finn considered this. On one hand, it sounded like nonsense. On the other hand, the old Beth threw candlesticks and punched people. So maybe this was better. "Well, you look good."

"Thank you. I feel good." They'd reached her bag. She grabbed a bottle of water and took a healthy slug. "I think it's my cleanse. My life coach has me on this cleanse—"

"Oh, yeah." He'd heard about the smoothies from Scarlett. "But when I'm working out, I stick to alkaline water."

"What?" Why would anyone mess with the pH balance of water?

She held out the bottle. "It reduces the acidity level in my body and helps prevent free radicals."

"Does it, though?" he asked skeptically.

"Here, want to try it? I don't love the taste, but if I squeeze some lemon into it, it's fine."

Finn blinked at her in disbelief. This was probably not the time to get into an argument with his ex-girlfriend, but had she forgotten everything from their freshman chemistry class? "You're adding lemon juice to alkaline water?"

"Yeah." She took a huge swig.

"Doesn't the citric acid from the lemon—I don't know— *neutralize* the alkalinity?"

Slowly, Beth lowered the bottle, frowning. "Um . . ." Her brow furrowed. "My coach told me to . . ."

"Coach Lungelo?"

"No," she said. "My new coach—my life coach. He's out of California."

Finn was pretty sure acids and bases worked just the same in California as in Maine. "Is he . . . um, *charging* you for this special water?"

She glared at him. "Make fun all you want. Since I've been working with Ash, I've knocked half a minute off my mile and added six inches to my box jump. I don't know how it works, but I know that it does."

"Sure," said Finn, amicably. Placebo was a hell of a drug.

"Anyway, I'm so glad I got a chance to see you. I've been worried about you, Finn." She reached over and touched his arm. "And I want to make sure that I've reached out to both you and Scarlett today. We need to support one another. I think that's part of the reason that things got so . . . mixed up last time."

"Last time we found a dead body?"

"I know, right?" Beth shook her head. "This is too much for us to handle. On top of school and extracurriculars and those stupid tests? I talked to Mr. Winkle at the guidance office. He wants us all to get tutors, but I don't know if it's too late for that. I think they should be giving us extra time on the exam or something, don't you? Because of stress?"

There was an idea. Not that Finn cared about the standardized tests. But Scarlett did. Scarlett could probably make something like that happen, too. He'd mention it to her, if he weren't so furious at her.

"This stress is overwhelming. It makes us turn on each other when we should really be sticking together."

No—*betrayal* made them turn on each other.

"I know none of us would do anything to hurt Rusty," Beth was saying. "You and I, Finn, we've had our differences, but that doesn't make you a murderer."

"Wait, what?" Finn shook his head. "You think *I* had something to do with this?"

"Of course not!" Beth exclaimed. "And I would never insinuate something like that, even as a way to get back at you for doing it to me last term." She smiled at him. "Because we're friends, right?"

He eyed her with some suspicion. Maybe all that acidic alkaline water was going to her head.

"We need to stick together!" Beth went on. "Not let our energies drag each other down. You, me, Scarlett—all the Murder Crew." She thought for a moment. "Also, we might need a better name."

"About Scarlett," he began. "I'm not so sure she's completely innocent this time around. I have evidence—"

"Is this real evidence or like that time you told everyone I killed Headmaster Boddy because you heard us fighting in his office?" Beth grinned at him and shouldered her bag. "Walk me back to Tudor?"

What choice did he have? Beth's long strides might have reflected her extra energy or just a desire to get through the chilly night air as quickly as possible, and Finn hurried to keep up. It was hard to imagine, sometimes, that they'd once dated. He'd been enamored of her skill on the tennis court. As a player, Beth was ruthless, bloodthirsty. It was very hot.

Until she'd turned some of that rage on him. Maybe he'd deserved it, but their breakup had been far from pretty. And now, here she was, serving up platitudes about teamwork and brotherly love.

"My emotional labor has been pretty tied up these past few weeks," she said. "I've had to cope with the return to Tudor House, to my routine, all without losing the inner peace that I fought so hard for over break. There's a real danger of backsliding into the angry, suspicious person I don't want to be anymore. I have to devote myself wholeheartedly to freeing my spirit and allowing myself to be happy."

"Maybe some suspicion is warranted," Finn said. "There *was* a dead body under your house."

"But it has nothing to do with *me*," Beth insisted. "Just like last time. It's the law of attraction. If I let myself get upset about it, other people will start to connect me to this awful thing that happened. If I stay positive, people will see that I'm just living my truth."

Finn hated to admit that she had a point, somewhere under all the woo-woo. Wasn't that how Scarlett had gotten the goods on him? He'd let himself show too much concern over what she knew and how she knew it. He let himself reveal exactly how worried he was about what was in the secret passages.

"Speaking of lingering negative vectors . . ." Beth said, and Finn looked up to see Mustard approaching them on the path. "I guess now's my chance to reverse the energy polarity."

"That doesn't make any—"

"Hey," said Mustard, looking wary as they met him on the walk.

"Mustard!" Beth beamed at him. "I'm so glad to see you. How *are* you?"

"Fine." He gave Finn an unreadable glance.

"I'm sorry we didn't have the chance to talk the other day, in the kitchen," she went on. "I'm so happy to hear that Dr. Brown didn't punish you for sneaking around."

"What are you talking about?" Mustard asked.

"In the closet? Last night? Scarlett said Dr. Brown caught you."

"Oh. Yeah." Mustard looked away. "Green is not exactly sneaky."

"Well, no harm, right?" she said gently. "And how are you doing? With the . . . new death and all?"

"Fine." Mustard shrugged and cast another glance at Finn. "It's not like I really knew him. Green seemed a little upset, though."

"Of course!" Beth exclaimed, as if that had only just occurred to her. "Poor Vaughn. I wonder if I should take him a smoothie. Does anyone know his address in Rocky Point?"

"Scarlett might," Finn said, and immediately regretted it. Beth would probably insist they join forces with her to bring Vaughn a fruit basket or something.

He did not want to be a part of the Murder Crew. He did not want to be part of any crew. All he wanted was to get his dye back.

"Actually, I bet we can get the address from the administration office," Mustard said. "Plum, want to come with me?"

"Pass," said Finn. He didn't need to go to Rocky Point. He needed to get into the secret passage.

"I'll go!" Beth offered.

"Oh," said Mustard, again. He seemed—what?—flustered, every time he looked at them. It was strange, Finn thought. He was generally so unflappable.

Then again, the last time Mustard had spent time with Beth, she'd laid him flat with a single punch.

"I really wanted a chance to hang out with you, Mustard," Beth went on, doing that new hand-clasp thing she'd started. "I think we got off on the wrong foot."

He ran his hand through the short hairs at the nape of his neck. "Or fist."

Then they both kind of laughed at that.

They looked good together, Finn realized. Mustard was as tall as Beth—maybe even taller. Finn remembered picking her up for a formal dance freshman year. She'd been in a pale pink concoction, with a towering pair of heels. He'd thought she looked amazing—like an Amazon. But she'd insisted on changing out of the heels so she didn't loom over him. She said she didn't like bending over to kiss him.

Finn pictured Beth kissing Mustard and frowned.

"Can we finish this discussion inside?" he said, nodding toward Tudor House. Maybe this was best. They could make a plan to hang out there. A plan that would conveniently not include him. He would remain behind and get another crack at those passages. "It's freezing out here."

"Sorry," said Beth. "I'm so warm after practice, I barely noticed."

"Yeah," Mustard agreed. "It's not so bad. At Farthing Military Academy we'd get down to minus-twenty some days."

"Wow!" Beth replied.

Finn scowled, staring at Mustard's annoyingly broad shoulders. When they all started walking again, Beth went in front, and Mustard fell into step at Finn's side. Probably so he could stare at Beth's butt. That's what dude-bros like Mustard did, right?

Peacock and Mustard. They'd go so perfectly together, each with their dumb nicknames.

"Thursday. Are you at the lab?"

"What?" Finn asked.

Mustard was not looking at Beth. He was looking at Finn. His eyebrows were raised, as if he was saying something much more meaningful than "lab."

"Yes." Finn narrowed his eyes. How did Mustard know his schedule?

"I thought I saw you there. Are you free for lunch tomorrow?"

"Why?"

"So we could eat?" Mustard said, as if trying to communicate in a foreign language. "We haven't really talked since—" And now it was Mustard's turn to nod at the creepy mansion looming ahead. "Did the new headmaster follow up on Boddy's threat to you?"

All at once, Finn understood. After Mustard had confronted him in the secret passage last term, he'd confessed to the new kid about his experiment and about how Boddy had discovered that Finn was doing research on the school's dime. At the time, it had seemed to be better than letting Mustard believe what he was likely suspecting—that Finn had killed the old headmaster.

But it was now coming back to bite him. First Scarlett wanted a piece of the action, now Mustard.

However, Finn had taken care to search Boddy's notes at the same time he'd erased the cheating complaints against Beth, in the headmaster's office, during the flood. No one in the Blackbrook administration now knew of his misdeeds, and as long as Scarlett and Mustard kept their traps shut, no one would.

They'd reached Tudor House now, and Beth strode inside as if the place wasn't crawling with corpses. They stood in the brightly lit hall. His skin tingled, the way your flesh does when it remembers it's not supposed to be frozen.

"Let me just shower and change," Beth called, barreling up the stairs. "You guys can wait here."

"Okay," Mustard said. He was still looking at Finn as Beth's blue-tipped ponytail snapped out of sight. "How was it—seeing the dead body?"

"Like the last one."

"The last one didn't fall on top of you."

"Well, maybe I'll get luckier next time." He cocked his head. "Are you playing detective again?"

"No," Mustard said sheepishly. "I don't think it worked out too well."

That was for sure. "Look, why don't you just tell me what you're after?"

Mustard appeared taken aback. "I'm not—"

"You can't squeeze blood from a stone," Finn said. "There's not going to be any money if I can't get my research back, and that whole situation with Rusty just made it a hell of a lot harder."

"What are you two doing in here?"

The boys turned to see a girl standing in the hall, her arms crossed over her parka and her expression disdainful. "Dr. Brown said no guests allowed after last night. Unless you have band rehearsal or an established study hall?"

"Rosa, right?" Finn said. "Hi, I'm Finn Plum, and—"

"I know who you are," Rosa said. "And you, too." She nodded at Mustard, who seemed to have grown another few inches in the last minute.

"Are you new here?" Mustard asked her.

"Yes."

"Where did you transfer from?"

"Abroad."

"Military?"

She clucked her tongue and did not deign to answer. Instead, she said, "So what's it gonna be, boys? Music, study hall, or do I have to ask you to leave?"

Finn made a face. "I'm sorry, are you a hall monitor or something?"

"I'm a resident of Tudor House," she replied, her tone short. "And you almost got expelled last night for sneaking around here. So tell me again how familiar you are with the school rules?"

Mustard laughed at that, but Finn was not amused.

"Okay," Mustard said, raising his hands. "Tell Peacock why we had to leave."

"I'm not your messenger. Besides, I have stuff to do. I was on my way out, myself. Allow me to escort you."

"Hey!" Finn said sharply. "We didn't know the rules, okay? Beth invited us in."

The door to the study opened at all the commotion. Scarlett stood on the threshold. She looked—Finn had to admit—a bit like crap. She was wearing a pair of lounge pants with what appeared to be coffee stains on the thigh, and her hair was tied up in a messy bun. There were dark smudges underneath her eyes.

"What's going on out here?" she cried. "Some of us are trying to *study*."

Finn's gaze went right beyond her to the study—and the bookshelf and the passage to his future. All he could see was plywood. He wondered what she was really doing in there.

"Rosa?" Scarlett asked. "Did you invite these boys in?"

"You know I didn't," the other girl replied. "They said Peacock did. I was just kicking them out."

"Fine by me," said Mustard. "Come on, Plum."

"Wait!" decreed Scarlett. She stared at each of them in turn, but her gaze was on Finn as she said, "Finn can go. Mustard can stay."

"What?"

She glared at him. "You heard me, Phineas. Out of our house."

He clenched his jaw. "Two can play this game, Scarlett."

She laughed mirthlessly. "I haven't the foggiest clue what you mean. I have a planned study session with Mustard." She had nothing of the sort, and every person in the hall knew it. "I don't know what *you're* doing here."

He puffed out his chest. "As I said, Beth invited me."

Scarlett made a show of looking around. "Huh. I don't see her."

"She's in the shower."

"Well, I don't think she invited you *there*," Scarlett said.

Finn scowled, then glanced at Mustard, who was now looking anywhere but at him.

"Now. Get. Out." She turned to Mustard. "Not you. You, I can use."

Finn did not have to stand there and take this. He drew close to Mustard. "Don't believe a word out of her mouth," he breathed to Mustard. "And call me after."

"Okay," said Mustard, then did a double take. "Wait, what?"

"Out!" Scarlett repeated.

With one last, withering glance at his former partner-in-crime, and a stone-faced escort from the new girl, Rosa, Finn left the house.

And Mustard.

In the belly of the beast.

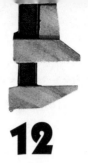

12

Mustard

Mustard almost grabbed Plum's arm as he walked out the door. He almost said, "I'm coming with you." There was no reason he should stay. Everyone else on campus might do what Scarlett Mistry wanted, but that didn't mean he had to.

Girl had the soul of a general, but Mustard was not under her command.

But then Plum had said, "Call me after," and all of Mustard's plans went right out of his head. He was still thinking about how he didn't have Plum's number, and why would Plum think he had his number, and had there been a time when Plum had, in fact, given him his number and maybe he didn't remember because of an unexpected head injury—when Scarlett led him into the study and shut them both inside.

It was then that he began to wonder if flies, too, were distracted upon occasions in which they ended up in spiders' webs.

"Um . . ." he said, because he couldn't think of anything else.

The study looked very different from the last time he'd been there. Then, it was all bookcases and firelight and a murderer tied to a chair. Now, there were half a dozen lamps glowing on end tables and the desk, the fireplace was cleaned out, and giant planks of wood, an open toolbox, and other construction materials lined the back wall.

"You know," said Scarlett, leaning up against the desk and smiling at him, "we've never really gotten the chance to chat."

"We talked plenty during the storm," he replied. He pointed at the tools. "What's all this?"

She shrugged. "Dr. Brown is determined to do something permanent to shut down the secret passages. But I guess it'll take a minute, what with all the other construction on campus. Anyway, *Mustard . . .*"

Call me after, Plum had said. As if he knew what Scarlett had in store for the *during*. And why wouldn't he? Last term, the couple had described themselves to him as a "platonic power couple," though their icy exchange in the hall made Mustard suspect that the "couple" part might not be entirely accurate any longer.

But if he walked out right now, he wouldn't have anything to call Plum about. Aside from the obvious.

"What do you want to talk about?"

"I always make a point of meeting with new kids on campus. Especially students of color. There's so little diversity here—"

"You think we have something in common because we're both brown?" he asked skeptically. "Because we don't." He was nothing like this pampered New York City princess with her little boarding-school fiefdom.

"I am aware that we are very different people," Scarlett said. "For instance, I'm a vegetarian, and according to your intake form, you bagged your first hunting trophy at five years old."

Mustard actually felt his heart speed up. "How did you read my intake form?" he asked quietly.

"Finn got it for me when you transferred in," she said, almost wistfully, given that she was talking about stealing administration documents. "Happier times."

Wait—*Plum* had read his intake form?

Call me after.

"But despite our best attempts, we never did get our hands on your complete file. You know, the one that Dr. Brown referenced yesterday? The one that explained why you are no longer welcome at Farthing?"

Mustard remembered how to breathe out. She had nothing on him. He was safe. "Are we done here?"

"No, *Mustard.* We're not." She stood up straight. Even then, she barely reached his shoulders. "How did you get that nickname, anyway?"

"Wasn't that part in my intake form?" First hunting trophy! He'd bet his father had put that in. Anything to make him sound like a *man.*

"And how quickly we all got used to calling you that!" she said. "Given how bizarre it is."

Back at Farthing, it hadn't been bizarre at all. At least, it hadn't been unusual. They all had dumb nicknames.

It was the one thing he hadn't wanted to lose.

"Besides, I don't want to talk about all the ways we're

different right now. I want to talk about the ways in which we are the same."

"Okay, I'll play," he said, and in the curve of her smile, he immediately realized it was a mistake. But he couldn't retreat now. "How are we the same?"

"Oh, lots of ways. For instance, we each have a keen interest in whatever it was Finn hid in the secret passage during the storm."

That brought him up short, but he did his best to keep his surprise from showing on his face. "I don't know what you're talking about."

"I don't know exactly what I'm talking about, either," Scarlett admitted. "Finn has been remarkably . . . private . . . about his little project. But I've figured out enough to realize that you know a lot more than you're letting on."

"If Finn didn't trust you enough to tell you what he was doing," Mustard scoffed, "what makes you think I'm going to?"

Scarlett stared long and hard at Mustard.

That move might work on some people. But he didn't blink.

"Because," she said at long last, "of all the things we have in common."

He snorted. "Like what?"

"Like our initials. *Samuel Maestor.*" She picked up her phone and showed him the screen.

Mustard felt his heart sink. The picture showed a stack of money with brownish smears of blood on it. And a note—a note he'd hoped was long, long gone.

"What did you bribe Rusty for?"

He swallowed, but his throat had gone dry. "I didn't."

"Liar."

"*I didn't!*" he repeated.

"*Liar,*" she *also* repeated, and she smiled. "And I want to know what you did with my pen, too."

He raised his hands and stepped back. But it was not remotely in surrender. Scarlett had nothing but wild accusations about bribery. Those, he could handle. "You've concocted an entire fantasy here, and I can't imagine why."

"This photograph was taken of what was on the body of Rusty Nayler."

"By you?"

"By Finn."

Mustard closed his eyes. That dum-dum. "I don't know what any of it is. You said that note was written with *your* pen. And it has your initials on it. What do I have to do with any of this?"

But Scarlett wasn't taking the bait. "Well, maybe that'll fly when Finn tries to pin it on me, too. But I happen to know that I didn't write Rusty any note, so it behooves me to find out what the truth is before my former best friend tries to implode my life."

" 'Behooves'?" Mustard said wryly. "You might do better on those standardized tests than you think."

"Tell me what this is, or I'll be forced to go to Dr. Brown with what I know."

"And what's that?"

"That you bribed Rusty . . . to do something . . . on the night he died!"

That was a really . . . inaccurate . . . way to put it. But he was sure that Scarlett was phenomenally talented at putting things in exactly the way she wanted them to be.

This could go very poorly for Mustard.

He was already in trouble with Dr. Brown. And the pushy guidance counselor had seemed mainly concerned over—whether or not Mustard's father planned to mount a lawsuit against the school. Winkle had made several comments about his record at Farthing that convinced Mustard that the dude was not as interested in "guidance" as he was in leverage.

That was the last thing he needed right now.

"Look," she said, "everyone knew Rusty could be bought. There were stories from way back in freshman year that he'd get you liquor from Rocky Point if you asked the right way. Was that what it was? Some hooch for a party?"

" 'Hooch'?" Mustard said. "You've been in Maine too long." He should say yes. But lies had a way of compounding. At least if he stuck with the truth, he wouldn't get tripped up.

"All I want is to close this chapter and get back to studying," Scarlett insisted. "I don't want to be difficult with you. I don't have anything against you. We weathered the storm together. That means something to me."

Funny. That was precisely what Rusty had said. "Murder Crew forever, huh?"

"Something like that," she said. "I mean, as long as you aren't actually a murderer." She eyed him. "But . . . I don't think you are."

"Yeah, I gathered," he replied. "By the way you're so willing to be alone in a room with me and threaten me." He crossed his arms. He knew from experience that it had the effect of making them look especially big and, therefore, intimidating.

Scarlett, however, was not much for being intimidated. "Well," she said slyly, "I have a witness that you came in here with me. If I wind up dead, it won't be much of a mystery."

"I'm sure that will come as a great comfort to your corpse."

Another minute of staring at each other produced no results that either side was pleased with. From what Mustard had learned during his time at Blackbrook, Scarlett Mistry had her fingers in every pot on campus. Nothing happened here without her knowledge, and only slightly less without her explicit say-so. At least, that's how things had been before Headmaster Boddy had been knifed in the hall outside. Now, things were a little different. Scarlett was used to having the upper hand.

But so was Mustard. And so far, Scarlett hadn't given him any indication that she had info on him that might prove . . . problematic. Still, he should endeavor to stay on her good side.

He could make a deal.

"You say your problem is Plum, right? That photo, and Plum's suspicions, and nothing else?"

Her expression turned curious. "Yes . . ."

"I'll get him off your back."

"How?"

"I just will."

Scarlett pursed her lips. "That doesn't sound convincing."

"Plum will find me very convincing, I swear."

Now her eyebrows rose, but she nodded. "Okay. Game recognizes game. You have a deal."

That was sorted. And now he really had an excuse to call Plum.

"You know," she went on, shuffling the papers on her desk, "it's a shame you weren't around before. I think we could have made an excellent team."

"I thought we were a team," he replied. "Murder Crew and all."

"Right, well . . ." She shrugged. "We weren't exactly the world's savviest detectives last term. We were searching the house for intruders while the real murderer was right here with us."

Mustard rubbed the back of his head. He'd been injured by Peacock, but it was Mrs. White who'd nearly killed him when the painkillers she gave him had actually been sleeping pills. By that point in the storm, the old Tudor House proctor had been scared that the students were putting together the facts of Boddy's death.

"I think my sleuthing days are over," he said to Scarlett.

"Really? With bodies falling out of the sky?" She looked skeptical. "Maybe you did kill Rusty. That's the only reason I can figure as to why you're not at least curious about how he died."

Mustard wouldn't characterize himself as incurious. Not exactly.

More like terrified.

But he kept his voice as neutral as possible as he responded. "Dr. Brown said Rusty's death was a freak accident. I don't think there's anything to worry about—"

"Dr. Brown was lying. She can't afford to have another murderer on campus."

He was very close to saying that there was no way for Dr. Brown to know if her campus was completely free of murderers, but that probably wasn't a good thing to point out right then. "What Dr. Brown really can't afford is any situation that would put the students in danger. If she thinks that there's nothing to worry about, then maybe we should believe her."

"That's what she *says*," Scarlett replied. "But does she know? She's not an expert on Blackbrook or on the students here."

Mustard wasn't going to get started on that conversation. "You felt safe before, right? And now there are even fewer kids here. If anyone knows them, it's you."

"I don't know all of them," Scarlett replied. "Like that new girl, Rosa. She lives downstairs from me, and I can't find out anything about her. Not through my usual channels and certainly not from her."

Mustard had also found himself rather curious about Rosa. For all that he'd mocked Scarlett for her obsession with identifying "diversity" at Blackbrook, he and Rosa were probably the only two Latinos in a fifty-mile radius, and she hadn't so much as given him a nod of solidarity when they passed each other on campus. Also, she'd dodged his question about military school, which definitely meant she'd gone to military school. He'd known even before, though. He could tell by the way she stood. Girl had training.

So what was she doing here?

"Well, good luck with your little investigation," he said to Scarlett. He turned to go, but she zipped around and stood in front of him. Scarlett was small but fast.

"She has maps of the campus up in her room," she said as Mustard maneuvered around her toward the door. "I saw them once, from her doorway."

He didn't have time for this. "Maybe she gets lost easily."

"Maybe she's looking for something."

Mustard's hand was on the knob, but that stopped him. "Excuse me?"

"I'm just saying . . . Finn seems to think the little experiment of his is extraordinarily valuable, right?"

He did. At least, he'd been going to extraordinary lengths to keep from having to share the proceeds with the school.

"And someone here—someone other than Boddy—was tipped off to its existence," she went on.

"Yeah, like you and me and probably a half dozen other people. Plum might be some scientific genius, but he's not as sneaky as he thinks he is."

"Okay," admitted Scarlett. "And what if someone who knows what Finn was doing is looking for his work—I mean, if it's worth as much as he says it is? Blackbrook knows the potential of their students—that's why they make them sign that stupid honor code. Half the board is made up of chemical company people, including Dr. Brown. It stands to reason that this place would have industrial spies. Maybe Rosa is working for them."

Mustard thought about that. He thought about his roommate Tanner, whose fortune was thanks to some chemical company in Connecticut, and who never seemed to do any homework at all.

Scarlett gasped. "Or maybe the source of the information was actually Rusty! And the industrial spies bumped him off once he delivered the goods."

"I like your first idea better," Mustard said quickly. "But what do we do about it?"

"Well, maybe while Rosa is out of the house, we can"— Scarlett tilted her head—"break into her room and just, you know, look around."

" 'Look around'?" Mustard asked. " 'Break into her room'? You're really banking a lot on the idea that Dr. Brown can't afford to expel any of us."

"Oh, please, Tex," she shot back, "you think this is my first rodeo?"

"I don't think you know what a rodeo is."

"True," she admitted. "But I do know how to break into rooms in this place without getting caught. We'll just pick the lock. No problem."

If he was going to go to Plum, it was probably best he had all the information. Especially if Scarlett was right, and Rosa really was here to spy on the students and their work. She'd come from somewhere, and transferring to Blackbrook *after* the murder was pretty freaking unlikely.

"Okay."

Together, they left the study and went out again into the abandoned hall. If Peacock had emerged from her shower, she must have realized that the boys had been ejected. Mustard was again struck by the bright lights illuminating every corner of the space. His memory of Tudor House was shadows and candlelight, dark hallways that hid blood spatter, the wail of wind from the broken window. Now it seemed very safe.

But was it?

Silently, they moved down the hall, past the stairs on the left and the library on the right. Scarlett listened at the door. "Dr. Brown isn't in. Thank goodness."

"What about the rest of the girls who live here?"

She gave him a look. "Yeah. We don't even see half of them. Nobody wants to stay in the Murder House."

Amber, Tanner's girlfriend, had said something similar to that.

"Let's hurry, anyway."

They moved on to the door to Rosa's room. Mustard remembered the room well from the storm—the billiards room, in which he'd lain awake on a pile of blankets on the floor, staring at the blackness under the pool table and Finn Plum's slim, pale form beyond. He must have fallen asleep eventually, though. He certainly had never heard the sound of Mrs. White dragging the body of the headmaster down the hall to the conservatory.

Scarlett had her ear pressed up against the door. "I don't hear her."

Mustard glanced back at the front door of Tudor House. "Hurry."

"Yeah," she agreed. "We have to hurry."

They both stood there, staring at each other.

"Well?" she asked him. "Go on."

"Go on what?"

"Pick the lock!"

He shook his head, confused. "You said *you* were going to pick the lock."

"I did not!"

"Yes, you did. You said this wasn't your first rodeo, and you'd broken into the rooms here before."

"Not by lock picking! When I brought it up, you said okay! I thought you had, like, special abilities from military school."

"I didn't take the lock picking elective."

Scarlett gave him a look, like she wasn't certain if he was joking. "Well, can you shoot it off?"

"What makes you think I have a gun on me?"

"The hunting trophy you got at five."

He didn't dignify that with an answer, and instead knelt in front of the door, trying to get a closer look at the latch. Maybe he could stick his ID card in and jiggle the lock. That worked on TV.

Scarlett knelt next to him and peered at the lock, as if she might be able to see through the metal to the mechanism inside. Mustard did not pin his hopes on her suddenly developing

X-ray vision. He pulled his ID card out of his wallet and carefully inserted it in the crack between door and doorjamb.

"So you do have special talents!" Scarlett crowed under her breath.

"Hush." He jiggled. The card went farther in. He wiggled. Was that a click he heard?

Suddenly, the card broke off in his hand. A second later the door flew open.

Rosa Navarro stood above them. He fell back on his heels and looked up at her.

"If you wanted inside," she said wryly, "you should have just knocked."

13

Scarlett

For the second time in as many days, Scarlett sat in the library of Tudor House, on one of the chairs that Dr. Brown must have unearthed from a torture chamber, and marveled about how much her house and school had changed since the last term.

Take this room. Once, it had been a quiet reading room. Now, the book-lined shelves were still there, and the green-shaded reading lamps, but it was otherwise unrecognizable. The comfy armchairs were gone. Dr. Brown had erected a large folding screen to separate what were presumably her sleeping quarters from the rest of the space, which was set up as an office. The administrative offices had been damaged in the storm, and many remained closed.

Dr. Brown stood behind her desk now and glared at Mustard and Scarlett.

"What," she asked them in a tone as dry as the desert, "did I say to you both last night?"

Mustard did not reply. Scarlett, too, thought the question was probably rhetorical.

"Answer me!" She slammed a hand down on the paperwork littering her desk. "Did I not say to concentrate on your schoolwork?"

"Yes, ma'am," they responded obediently and in unison.

"Did I not say to study for your tests?"

"Yes, ma'am." Maybe they should start a spoken-word choir. Scarlett would need more extracurriculars on her college applications to balance out her crummy test scores.

"Did I not say to stop sneaking around this house?"

"Yes, ma'am."

"And what have the two of you been doing?"

"To be fair," Scarlett said, "we were standing openly in the hall. It was hardly sneaking. Anyone could have seen us."

"All the more idiotic, then!" Dr. Brown looked utterly exasperated. Mustard was staring at her with his mouth open.

"I'm just saying." Scarlett sat back in her seat.

This whole week was going from bad to worse. She should not have planned a scheme with Mustard. He was worse, even, than Finn. If only she had a real partner in crime.

Or maybe Orchid was right, and she should just give up on the whole crime thing altogether.

"Why were you bothering Rosa?" Dr. Brown pressed.

"We just wanted to know why she had maps hanging up in her room," said Scarlett. "There's a lot of weird stuff going on here, and a new kid who won't talk to anyone and covers her rooms with diagrams of the buildings on campus is a little suspicious, wouldn't you say?

"No," replied the interim headmaster. "No, I would not say that. I would say that any student who chose, voluntarily, to come to this hellhole at the ends of the earth, despite its being the location of a grisly and sensational murder, and pay our lovely institution a hefty tuition to do so should be respected. I would further say that if I were said student, I, too, would choose not to speak to my fellow students if they called me things like 'suspicious' and utilized their spare time plotting ways to break into the certainly ill-equipped bedroom that this flood-ravaged campus has provided her."

Chastened, Scarlett was silent.

"You, Miss Mistry, are hereby stripped of all leadership roles in campus activities."

Scarlett gasped. "But—"

"You are bullying the new kids!" Dr. Brown said. "How in the world can I trust you to welcome them to this campus?"

Bullying? *Her*? Unthinkable. She was *leading*!

"You can't do this!" she shouted. "I'll leave!"

"Oh, because Choate has all kinds of leadership positions open for a new kid senior year?" Dr. Brown replied.

Scarlett's mouth snapped shut, but her eyes still burned.

"Would you look at that?" the headmaster said with a cruel smile. "It does still feel a bit like I can fire you."

Scarlett swallowed heavily. That was her entire college application—gone. No standardized test score would save her now. Headmaster Boddy would *never* . . .

"We were just . . . concerned, Dr. Brown," Scarlett tried. "We found another dead body in this house yesterday."

"Because of snooping." Dr. Brown waved her hand dismissively in the general direction of the study.

"I'm sorry, is your argument here that we should have left Rusty Nayler's corpse to rot in the secret passage?" Scarlett asked incredulously.

Dr. Brown leveled a glare at her. "You're skating on remarkably thin ice here. Don't push me."

"What if there's another murderer in this house?"

"As I said before, Mr. Nayler died of natural causes. The coroner's office has confirmed it."

Oh. Scarlett hadn't realized that. Maybe the blood and the head wound Finn had mentioned had happened when the body fell out of the ceiling. Maybe this whole thing was one big mistake?

If so, Scarlett was definitely the one paying for it.

"And you have absolutely nothing to worry about when it comes to Rosa Navarro," Dr. Brown concluded. She trained her attention on her next victim. "Now you, Mr. Maestor. What shall we do with you? I think you have far too much time on your hands. You've been remarkably reticent to join any group activities or clubs since you got here."

"No, ma'am," he said, and the Texas drawl was back in his voice. "There just wasn't really the opportunity, what with the deadly storm and, well, the deaths."

"I'm sure our work crews could use an extra pair of hands. They're mucking out seaweed down at Dockery Hall all this week. That should keep you occupied. And it's all the way across campus from any further troublemaking in Tudor."

"Yes, ma'am."

"I'm sure another expulsion would not look good on your record."

"No, ma'am."

Another expulsion, huh? Well, there was the confirmation Scarlett had been looking for. The one that—once upon a time—she and Finn would have methodically rooted out, then used to their own advantage.

But she didn't want to now. Now, much as she hated to say it, all the Murder Crew stuff seemed almost to fit. She and Mustard were in this together.

Which made Dr. Brown their mutual enemy.

"I will repeat myself, since last time it did not sink in. No more schemes. No more sneaking. No more shenanigans. Step another foot out of line and I will find another creative way to make your lives here miserable. Am I understood?"

With one final "Yes, ma'am," they were dismissed, with firm admonitions that Scarlett was to spend the rest of the evening in her room and that Mustard was to head directly to the nearest exit. They were not to confer.

Do Not Pass Go. Do Not Collect $200.

Another boy might have hung his head and shuffled to the door. Mustard didn't precisely march, but he didn't skulk, either. Scarlett was impressed; she could admit that much. And she'd much rather have someone like him on her side than otherwise. Murder Crew 4-Evah and all that.

"Adults always say stuff like that," said Scarlett when they'd reached the base of the stairs. "Like we can't just text each other if we want to. By the way, what is your number?"

Mustard told her.

As she was inputting it into her phone, she said, "Sorry about the hard labor."

He shrugged. "That was standard procedure at Farthing. Feels like old times. Sorry about your committees or whatever."

She affected a similar shrug. "I'll have my parents call and pitch a fit. I'll get reinstated."

Scarlett wondered if he was lying as much as she was. There was no way she was going to tell her parents about this. Though it might not be a terrible idea for her to impersonate her mother and call Dr. Brown. Usually white people didn't question who was really on the phone if she faked even a mild Indian accent. She'd get it taken care of—after tests were done.

Scarlett could only handle one crisis at a time.

"So, what about Rosa?" he asked. "Going to be awkward around the breakfast table."

"It was already awkward. And this doesn't let her off the hook, either."

"No," he agreed. "If anything, it makes me almost want to buy the idea that she's here as a spy. Dr. Brown is on the board. That she's so mad means we might be closer than we thought."

"Why, Mustard!" she exclaimed. "Are you *sleuthing*?"

He shrugged.

"Are you going to go call Finn now?" she asked him.

"Yeah. Probably." He hesitated. "Can I ask you what happened between you two? Before, it was like you were fighting, but then you stuck your neck out for him just now."

Yeah, and got decapitated. "Don't tell him that part."

Mustard regarded her carefully. "Are you into him? *Non*platonic power couple?"

She snorted. Why was it so impossible to believe that a girl could want something other than a romantic attachment? Let the other idiots on campus—like Orchid—get moony over some boy. Scarlett had bigger goals in mind.

"You sound just like him. Trust me, Finn likes grand romantic gestures far more than I do." Case in point: almost freezing to death running after Peacock in the storm last term.

"Oh."

Mustard had perfected that laconic Texan thing where he could seemingly be talking about the weather no matter what was under discussion. But Scarlett heard it anyway. That little extra—*something*—in his voice. The kind that had never once been in Scarlett's but was always in Orchid's when she was talking about the stupid townie.

Interesting.

And Finn had told Mustard about the project. Mustard . . . and Peacock . . . and *not* her.

The seed of an idea planted itself in her mind. She should ignore it. It was *definitely* shenanigans as Dr. Brown had defined them.

But old habits died hard.

She pressed. "Anyway, it's not like that with us. If I helped him, it's because I think his invention could be valuable."

"Yeah," said Mustard quickly. "I think it might be, too." He was quiet for a second. "Besides, with you two—he's kind of still hung up on Peacock, isn't he?"

Bin. Go.

A thrill coursed through her. She still had it. Between Orchid and Finn, Scarlett had worried she'd lost her touch. But she could still ferret out secrets. Maybe not everyone's. But this one, from this guy—this one she had nailed.

All at once, it all made sense. The secrecy, the note, everything.

Mustard wasn't a murderer. He was in the closet.

She almost felt sorry for him. Of all the boys in all the school that he could have picked, it was Phineas Plum? Airheaded, egotistical, selfish, scheming, knows-exactly-how-cute-he-is Finn?

Not to mention, the boy was straight. He'd dated Peacock. He'd hit on Scarlett. He'd once rated every one of her house-mates on a ten-point scale. With decimal points.

And yet, that was the thing with crushes. They never made rational sense. Look at Orchid and her bizarre jones for Vaughn Green.

Scarlett gave Mustard her most wide-eyed, innocent look. "I really don't know if he's hung up on anyone at the moment. You'd have to ask him." She could not resist adding, "Though I guess guys don't do that kind of thing. You know . . . talk about who likes whom."

Or do they, Mustard?

"Not in my experience," Mustard said smoothly. Very smoothly. The kind of smoothly that came from a lifetime of practice.

Scarlett was utterly delighted. She was so delighted, she forgot for a second that life as she knew it at Blackbrook was most likely over.

Sadly, the elated feeling did not last long after Mustard left Tudor House. It wasn't like she could rush to her coconspirators and dish. For once, she didn't even *have* coconspirators.

In the end, she decided to make herself some tea and try one more practice test. The sky might be falling, but the SATs were still on Saturday.

Which was another reason why Mr. Winkle's bozo tutor idea wouldn't have helped her. It was too late for that. And too late, apparently, to apply for an untimed test, too. She'd have to power through.

Despite Dr. Brown's admonishment, Scarlett could not imagine she was confined to her room entirely. After all, she needed to eat. She headed back down the hall toward the kitchen.

And found Vaughn standing by the sink. He must have just arrived at the house, as he was still wearing his dirty, worn, red overcoat. His brown wool mittens had the tops pulled back, revealing fraying fingerless gloves underneath, and his black ski cap was hanging haphazardly out of his coat pocket.

The locals here had a uniform Scarlett never quite understood. All their coats looked to be a million years old, and their wearers were utterly oblivious to mud stains or salt marks.

"Oh," he said blankly. "Hey."

As if this night could get any weirder. "How did you get by Brown?"

He narrowed his eyes. "Huh?"

"The rules are, no one gets into this house without an invitation." She made a show of looking around. "Where's Orchid?"

A slow smile spread across his features. They were not unpleasant features. Spiffed up a bit, Vaughn could be cute. Maybe Orchid saw past the trashy clothes. Then again, some people wrote love letters to murderers in prison. There really was no accounting for taste.

"Why, Scarlett, you're the last person I expected to forget that I *work* here."

She rolled her eyes. Right. Custodial. That was something she'd never had to worry about when Mrs. White was still the Tudor House proctor. Then, Mrs. White had mopped their floors, and Scarlett had never had to deal with the likes of Vaughn Green. Of course, thoughts of Mrs. White and a mop brought to mind bloodstains in the corners of the hall. Scarlett shuddered.

"Well, empty the trash or whatever and move along. I'm making tea."

"I'm not blocking your access to the kettle, am I?"

No, but she still found his presence unnerving. Scarlett had never been able to get a proper read on Vaughn. Half the time, he was this shy little music nerd. The other half, he was a total snake. He'd made a game of torpedoing her projects when she'd led the Campus Beautification Committee. During the storm, he'd made a game of getting everyone in Tudor House to suspect everyone else of murder. She wasn't one hundred percent sure he didn't know that Mrs. White was the culprit all along.

Not that she'd been the greatest judge of character lately. Orchid's revelation about her true identity had come as a shock. Finn's betrayal, too. Mustard—well, she might have guessed that Mr. Buttoned-up Colonel had a few secrets up his sleeve.

What was Vaughn's?

"Whatever," she stated coolly and brushed past him on her way to the stove. As she lit the flame under the burner, he didn't move. She did not love having her back to him. If there was a spider in the room, she wanted to keep her eye on it. She set the kettle on and turned back to him. "Today sucked, by the way, no thanks to you and that little trick last night."

"Trick?"

"You know, hiding in the pantry."

He looked at the nailed-shut pantry as if he'd never seen it before. "Oh. Right."

She shook her head. He was too weird. "Brown's on the war-path. She stripped me of all my student leadership positions."

Of course he smiled! What a jerk.

"I'm not surprised you're thrilled. Honestly, I have no idea what Orchid sees in you."

Vaughn shrugged. "Me neither." At least he admitted it. She wondered if he knew the truth about her. But, no, Orchid had sworn no one knew, not even the administration.

Or maybe that was another lie. Finn had found it easy enough to lie to her. Dr. Brown didn't even want her help. She'd poured so much of herself into this school for the last few years, and it was all going down the drain.

"But it's kind of fun, yeah?" he went on.

"You'd better not hurt her," Scarlett said. "She's my friend."

"You don't have friends," he shot back. "You have assets."

The kettle whistled. Thank goodness. Scarlett took the kettle off the stove and grabbed her mug. It wasn't true. She had friends. She and Finn were just in an off period. She and Orchid were getting very close. And she'd made great strides with Mustard tonight. She liked everyone in the Murder Crew.

Except this jerk.

Her fingers fumbled with the mug, and she splashed hot water onto the counter as she poured. "Maybe I'll transfer," she said carelessly. "Make your whole year, wouldn't it? I bet you'd like nothing better than to get rid of me."

His voice was even as he replied. "I assure you, there are at least four or five things I want more."

For her part, Scarlett couldn't think of anything she wanted more than *not* to know what else was on his list. She took a deep breath, set her features in as calm and carefree an expression as she could manage, and turned back to him.

"So, no Murder Crew camaraderie?" she asked, stirring honey into her tea.

"With you?" he shot back. "I thought I was supposed to empty the trash and scram."

"Fine." She sipped her tea. "You never liked me, and I never liked you. What a shame Orchid doesn't have better taste."

"I feel precisely the same way," he replied. "And maybe you should thank your lucky stars your fortunes are no longer tied to this school. It's going down in flames."

"That's your expert opinion?"

"No. That's my promise." His tone was as cold as the night outside.

Scarlett's fingers tightened around her mug as she swallowed. "I thought you loved this school more than life itself."

He seemed to consider this. "Me? No. Never." Then what was the point of their battle over the old boathouse? "Not love, anyway. More like obsession."

Scarlett made a face. Seriously, what did Orchid see in this guy? But if she wasn't going to let Mustard best her in a battle of words, there was no way she'd let Vaughn get one over on her. "I guess it's good to get out while the getting is good, then. Rocky Point people who get themselves too involved in Blackbrook affairs don't tend to make out very well. Mrs. White was obsessed, too."

She expected him to flinch, but he did nothing. His face was a mask of stone.

"And Rusty," Vaughn said, eyeing her carefully. "Who do you think killed him?"

She spluttered over her next sip, the hot liquid rushing in and scalding her tongue. She fought to keep her cool. "He wasn't murdered. Dr. Brown said the coroner confirmed that he died of natural causes."

"Did she?" Vaughn's tone was appreciative. "Well, that's convenient."

That wasn't what he'd said about the matter yesterday. He was crazy erratic. You never knew with Vaughn. Did he love Blackbrook or hate it? Was he friends with Rusty, or did he want to hypothesize that his old boss had been violently murdered?

"Why do you think he was murdered?" she couldn't help but ask. Had Finn been showing around the photo?

"Of course he was." Vaughn leaned in. "Murder Crew, Murder House . . . this whole place is drowning in murder. Just wait. It'll all come out eventually."

Scarlett shivered. She had heard enough. "You know what? I think I was right before. Empty the trash and get out."

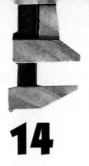

14

Orchid

Orchid was sitting at her desk, studying the ring in her hand and trying to figure out if she'd gone mad, when Scarlett burst into her room.

"You have to break up with that guy."

She looked up in shock, her fingers closing reflexively around the ring. "What? Vaughn? We're not together."

"Good!"

No, not good. Or maybe good. Orchid couldn't decide. She shook her head. "Don't you knock?" Scarlett might think that she could do whatever she wanted because she knew Orchid's real identity, but it was time to enforce a few boundaries.

But Scarlett brushed her off. "Whatever. I knew you weren't up here making out with your boyfriend, as he was downstairs being a total creep."

Orchid shot out of her chair. "Vaughn is downstairs?"

Scarlett stopped her. "Slow down, Juliet. I kicked him out. And we're seriously going to have to have a talk about your taste in men. You should have heard what he was saying."

"What was he saying?"

"Oh, that Rusty was murdered, and that murder was essentially part of this house's DNA now."

Orchid sighed. "I think he's really upset about Rusty's death. Between that and what he's going through with Mrs. White—"

"Really?" Scarlett's voice dripped with disdain. "Come on, Orchid. Don't be that idiot girl who spends her life making excuses for a creep's bad behavior."

"I'm not," Orchid insisted. "As it happens, I thought Vaughn was being a creep to me earlier, too, and I called him out on it." She pulled her phone out of her pocket to show Scarlett her recent texts.

Scarlett frowned at the screen. "He didn't write you back after that."

Orchid pocketed the phone again and shrugged. "Well, I told him not to." And he'd been in the house and didn't come looking for her, either. At least he respected her that much.

But was that just granting him more excuses? Oh, good boy Vaughn, giving her space after acting like a jerk? All is forgiven?

Her therapist said her crush on Vaughn was healthy, but maybe it was just welcoming her back into old, unhealthy patterns.

"Honestly, I've been through a lot," Orchid began hesitantly. She looked at the ring in her palm. This morning, it hadn't been there. A lot of things hadn't been there. But when she came back after class, the items were all back. It was . . . weird.

She'd told Scarlett so much. Maybe it was time to tell her this as well. Maybe it was time to tell her everything.

"I've been through a lot, too." Scarlett flopped dramatically onto Orchid's bed and threw her arm over her face. "This day has been the worst."

"Why, because you lost your pen?"

"What?" Scarlett peeked out for a second, her brow furrowed.

"You were really upset about it this morning." That part, Orchid remembered perfectly. She, too, had been upset about some missing objects. But maybe it was all just a symptom of her panic attack. Or a lack of caffeine. Or something. Because they were right where she'd left them when she got home from the cliffs.

"No! I don't even care about some dumb pen! Dr. Brown just stripped me of all my leadership positions on campus."

"What!" Now Orchid joined her on the bed. She stripped Scarlett's arm off her face to look her in the eye. "Are you kidding? What for?"

Scarlett was nothing without her titles. Long before Orchid had developed even a grudging respect for her housemate, she knew that.

"Ugh, it doesn't even matter. More of that nonsense from last night. She thought I was skulking around the halls with Mustard. But we weren't doing *anything*."

With Mustard? But why, though? "You had to be doing . . . something, no?"

"She's a control freak!" Scarlett exclaimed. "She thinks she runs everything."

Orchid bit her lip. "Doesn't she, though?"

"I mean my very ability to walk around this house," Scarlett said, seething. "Headmaster Boddy never cared about that stuff."

"Headmaster Boddy is dead," said Orchid. She folded her hands in her lap. "Rusty is dead. The woman who used to make the rules for this house is in jail. Everyone is a little on edge."

"Oh, we're back to 'give Vaughn the benefit of the doubt.'" Scarlett sat up. "Well, I'll also have you know he said he had no idea what you saw in him but that he found you 'fun.'" She made air quotes with her fingers.

Orchid blinked. "Am I not fun?"

Scarlett groaned. "It was the way he said it. Like you were a game or something."

That brought her up short. That's pretty much how he'd acted on the cliff, too. Just because a guy *said* he wasn't into games didn't mean it wasn't true.

There was a knock on the door.

"Yes?" Orchid called.

Peacock poked her head in. "Has anyone seen Finn or Mustard? I thought I told them to wait for me in the hall."

Scarlett rolled her eyes. "Girl, we're way beyond that now. Come on in."

Orchid shot Scarlett a look. "Yes. Go ahead and come into *my* bedroom, Beth."

Beth entered and perched on the edge of Orchid's desk. "I don't think I've ever been in here before."

No. No one had. Before this whole Murder Crew thing, Orchid hadn't really had any of what most girls called *friends.* She'd been too concerned about keeping her secret. But she'd walked around all day today without her glasses on, and no one had mentioned to her that she looked like a missing movie star.

Maybe no one cared anymore. She weighed the ring in her palm, then slipped it onto her finger. At least now she knew for sure where it was. Her glasses were back on her face, too, and Scarlett was currently using Bobo to pillow her head on the bed. Maybe she'd imagined it all.

The discovery of Rusty Nayler's body had triggered a panic attack. The panic attack had made her not think clearly and not be able to find her belongings. Nothing had ever been missing from her room. It was just a minor mental health incident.

She could probably still get in touch with her therapist, out west. Or maybe call Mr. Winkle back, after all.

"It's nice," Peacock went on. She touched the gilt mirror frame. "Anyway, I invited Mustard and Finn back here. I was hoping I could get them to try my anti-stress smoothies. I think we all need one after yesterday."

Orchid's mouth was still gritty from the last one. "I'll pass."

"I'll try it." Scarlett was still horizontal on the bed. "I'll try anything after the day I've had."

"What happened?" Peacock asked.

"Oh, nothing. Just your BFFs Finn and Mustard ruined my life today."

"What?" Peacock's eyes went wide. "Did Finn cut you out of a class you wanted to take? That's a thing he does, you know."

"No, he accused me of murdering the janitor."

"What!" both Peacock and Orchid exclaimed at once.

"It doesn't matter. It's nothing. He didn't mean it. Or maybe he meant it—I don't know. But he's about to be educated—oh my God!" She sat straight up on the bed, nearly smacking Orchid in the face, and clapped a hand over her mouth. "I totally forgot."

"Forgot what?"

"Nothing," she mumbled through her covered lips, but her eyes danced with delight.

Orchid rubbed her temples. What a drama queen.

"Okay, I do have a story, but I'm not going to tell you." She looked at Orchid. "I can keep secrets."

Now it was Orchid's turn to roll her eyes. "Always the mark of a real friend."

Scarlett's face lit up. "Thank you!" she said with genuine joy.

That wasn't precisely how Orchid had meant it, but whatever. Scarlett was truly having a rough day.

"You know what?" she said to Peacock. "Maybe we should all have those smoothies."

"Excellent!" Peacock clapped her hands. "I think they'll do wonders to detoxify us from all our stressors."

"If only we could detoxify ourselves from the boys," Scarlett added.

Orchid bit her lip, thinking of the last text message she'd sent Vaughn.

Yeah. If only.

The following afternoon, Orchid stood outside the door of the school counselor's office, utterly baffled. She checked the time on her phone: 5:12. She checked the note in her schedule: *Winkle, 5 p.m.* She checked the door again: locked.

Weird.

She walked down the hall, where the school secretary, Ms. O'Connor, had made a sort of ad hoc command center in the ruins of the administrative offices. There was much less damage here, though the air still smelled moldy. Orchid could not blame Dr. Brown for setting up shop in Tudor House instead.

But what had become of the insistent Mr. Winkle? He'd been on her to make an appointment with him all week, and after what had happened yesterday with her panic attack and freaking out about her belongings, she and her therapist in California had agreed that it couldn't hurt to loop him in to the conversation. And now he was AWOL?

"Excuse me?" she said to Ms. O'Connor. "I'm supposed to have a meeting with Mr. Winkle this afternoon . . .?"

"I'm sorry, I haven't seen him," the secretary confessed. "But he could have gone out the other entrance. It's a little chaotic here, as I'm sure you know."

Orchid sighed. "May I borrow a piece of paper? I'll leave him a note."

But as soon as she had it written, Orchid thought better of the matter. After all, she didn't exactly want to leave her name posted on the school counselor's door.

Instead, she opened up her email on her phone and

replied to their last exchange—you know, the one confirming that they indeed had an appointment at five.

From: *orchid.mckee@BlackbrookAcademy.edu*
To: *perry.winkle@BlackbrookAcademy.edu*
Subj: *Re: Evaluation*

> *Hi, Mr. Winkle!*
> *I stopped by the office as we discussed, but I must have missed you. Are you free any time tomorrow?*
> *Thanks,*
> *Orchid*

There. Now, at least, she could say she had tried.

And then, against her better judgement, she clicked over to her text chain with Vaughn.

Nothing.

A day later and still nothing. She hadn't reached out to Vaughn, and he had not texted her back. He'd also been absent from history class, and though she'd kept an eye on every recycling bin and restroom on campus, she hadn't see him working, either.

He might be avoiding her.

Which was what she'd asked him for, so she shouldn't be mad at him for giving it to her.

Only, she was.

Orchid went to the dining hall, picked up a very depressing-looking chicken salad, and brought it back to her room for an even more depressing dinner. Funny, she'd always liked being alone before. Before the storm. Before all of it.

She sat in her room, turning the rose gold ring on her finger. All day long, she'd waited for someone to ask her about the jewelry. Not even Scarlett had remarked upon it. Of course, Scarlett was driven to distraction lately. The one-two punch of testing and being stripped of all her leadership positions on campus committees had left her in need of far more than Peacock's anti-stress smoothies. Orchid had spoken to Rosa—Scarlett's punishment was a result of trying to break into Rosa's room yesterday.

Orchid felt a certain responsibility toward her friend. She knew what it was like to be overcome with anxiety, to latch on to things you thought you could control—like the mysterious new girl—because you were beyond terrified about those that you couldn't—like the SATs. If nothing else, she needed to get Scarlett to leave Rosa alone.

But she didn't think Scarlett would listen to her. She talked as if the two of them were best friends, but Orchid had seen the way Scarlett operated for far too long. Orchid and her secret represented another trophy, another way Scarlett could control what was going on at the school. So far, Orchid had been able to make that work to her advantage, but she also needed to stay on Scarlett's good side.

They weren't real friends. She hadn't had those in years.

For years, Orchid had hesitated to wear the ring, fearing that an orchid ring might be too on the nose. Or maybe people just figured that of course a girl with her name would have jewelry to match. When she'd chosen the name Orchid during her escape from Hollywood, it was in honor of the Steelman twins and the film they'd never gotten the opportunity to release.

It was in honor of the only friends she'd ever had.

Ever since the storm, she'd thought she had more. Not this nonsense about the Murder Crew, but in her long chat texts with Vaughn she'd begun to believe that the ice she'd allowed to encase her heart ever since she first left California was finally beginning to melt.

Well, she'd been wrong. That was all. It wasn't the first time that she'd trusted the wrong guy. Orchid could only hope it would be the last.

Her phone pinged, and—heaven help her—she perked up. But it was only an email.

From: *perry.winkle@BlackbrookAcademy.edu*
To: *orchid.mckee@BlackbrookAcademy.edu*
Subj: *Re: Evaluation*

> *Orchid,*
> *I cannot waste my time sitting around waiting for late students. Our meeting was for five p.m. I don't know how they do things in Hollywood, but in the real world, it pays to be prompt.*
> *Perry Winkle*
> *Guidance Counselor*

Orchid rolled her eyes. Well, Blackbrook wasn't the real world. It wasn't her fault she'd been late. The stupid class bell wasn't working again, and their teacher hadn't let them out until seven minutes past. She'd run over as quickly as she could!

What a jerk. And this was who the board had decided would be good for kids in crisis? Figures. She looked over the note again, and her blood ran cold.

I don't know how they do things in Hollywood . . .

Her enrollment form did not say Hollywood. Her fake parents supposedly lived in San Marino. Of course, to some people, anyone from California might as well be from Hollywood. It was a state of mind, not a town.

But still . . . there was no way Mr. Winkle knew Orchid's real identity, was there? Scarlett wouldn't spill the beans. Not to someone like him.

But it was weird, for him to act so pushy and then ghost for her being a few minutes late. If anything, that was the way egotistical producers and managers behaved in *Hollywood.* Her ex-manager Keith used to act *precisely* like that.

Orchid decided not to answer the email. She'd made the right call the first time about seeking the help of Perry Winkle.

After a bit, she collected herself and headed downstairs to the kitchen for a snack. But as she neared the ballroom door, she heard a familiar, if muffled, sound emanating from behind it.

She froze and listened harder. Yep, definitely.

Orchid closed her eyes. Scarlett would say she was a total idiot. And maybe she was. Probably she was. But she opened the door to the ballroom anyway and walked in.

Though the ballroom of Tudor House did occasionally host school dances, it was primarily used as a music or theater rehearsal space. In Blackbrook's glory days—before the storm and the murder—the choir, the band, and the improv group would meet here for practice during the week, and Orchid had grown used to slightly off-key and repetitive music drifting up through the radiator pipes most evenings. There'd been no band or choir practice since the new term had begun, though, and Orchid was pretty sure that the entire improv troupe had transferred to another school.

But the instruments were still there—a drum set, a couple of guitars, and, of course, the grand piano. A large oriental rug covered the parquet floor, and there was an old-fashioned fainting couch up against the far wall, near the fireplace.

On that couch sat Vaughn Green, cradling his guitar.

He looked up at her, and his expression nearly broke her heart. "Sorry," he said quickly. "This is where I could practice, and—"

"Yeah." She nodded.

"I wasn't going to bother you—"

"You aren't." She took a few more steps into the center of the room. "Am I bothering you?"

He gave a slight nod. "But no more than any other time." He put the guitar aside and stood. "Orchid, I'm so sorry about yesterday. I don't—I don't know what else to say. I can't explain myself. You're probably right not to want to have anything to do with me anymore."

"Is that why you weren't in history class today?" she asked. "You were avoiding me?"

He flinched. "That . . . sounds right."

"You can't keep skipping, Vaughn. Your scholarship depends—"

"Thanks, I know," he said, his tone short.

She should leave. They'd said what they had to say. Or, at least, he had. She could walk out now, and this would all be over. They could go back to not even noticing each other.

She crossed to the couch instead and touched the neck of the guitar, where his fingers had been. "I liked that song you were playing. I remember you sent me a recording of it."

It was called "Another Me," if Orchid remembered correctly.

His tone was wary as he replied. "Thanks. It's my favorite of the ones I've written."

"How many have you written?"

"Ten."

She whistled in appreciation. "That's basically your debut album right there."

He snorted. "Sure. I'm totally making an album."

She shot him a glance. "Seriously, are you?"

Vaughn sat down and picked up the guitar. She wasn't sure what to do, so she sat down next to him. A respectable distance away, of course, but on the same couch.

Who did she think she was kidding?

"All kids from hick towns have big dreams." He started strumming again.

"That sounds like the beginning of a movie."

"My mother was a musician," he said. "She used to tour all the time when—when I was little. She and my dad both. They'd leave us on Rocky Point and go all over New England."

"Us?"

He bent his head over his guitar. The chords changed. "My grandmother and me."

"The one who was Mrs. White's friend."

"Yeah."

"From here? When Tudor was a girls' school?"

"Yeah."

Orchid thought of how hard it had been on Vaughn this last month. First Mrs. White, then Rusty. All the stress of thinking the school might not reopen, or that his scholarship was in jeopardy. She'd come back to Blackbrook partially because Vaughn was there, but she'd had options. She had escape routes.

Vaughn had none of that. He'd just had her, on the other side of a text chain.

They'd been dancing around each other for so long. And what was she really mad about, anyway? That he *hadn't* kissed her when he'd had the chance?

"When did they die? You told me once, but—"

"When I was eight," he replied. "They were out on tour. Bus accident. It's kind of a blur, really. Rocky Point will do that to you. You know how it is. The winters are just this long white dream, and when we came out on the other side, in spring, my folks were gone."

Orchid swallowed. Yeah, he could write lyrics. Sad ones, but people liked sad songs. "I'm so sorry."

"That's why I think—maybe I shouldn't go into music. I have this idea in my head that it's unhealthy." And yet, he played on. The music seemed to weave a spell around both of them, as thick and dreamlike as any Rocky Point blizzard.

"The entertainment industry *is* very unhealthy," Orchid agreed. "Trust me, I'm from California." Trust her. She knew better than anyone. "I—I had this friend back home. She was a child actress. Made a lot of money, but she was totally miserable. Her mom and her manager treated her like some prize-winning racehorse. Just worked her as hard as they could. She hated the films she was in. She hated how creepy her fans were. Especially the grown-ups. Especially the men."

Vaughn nodded but did not look up from his instrument. She looked over at his close-cropped hair, at the way his hairline tapered down into that little V at the nape of his neck. He had a very nice neck.

Was that a strange thing to think about a guy? *That Vaughn Green, what a beautiful neck.* Oh, well. Men had been thinking much weirder things about her since she was a child.

She wondered what Vaughn would do if she reached out and touched his neck. She wondered when he'd last been hugged. Or when she had.

Maybe that was why she wanted to touch him so badly. She was just . . . overdue.

Maybe. But probably not.

"And she had this manager—he was crazy, a lunatic. He actually threatened to kill her in public once."

Vaughn's fingers slipped on the strings. "He'd kill her in public?"

"No, he threatened, in public," she clarified. They'd been on set. She was tired and hungry, and she wanted a break. This was where a manager should have protected her from a demanding director. This was where a parent should have. But both her mother and Keith thought of her as a wind-up doll. They played with her until they were done.

"That sounds terrible," said Vaughn.

"It was. There are lots of kids like that. On-screen they're cute and smiling and have these perfect families, but in reality, they're little prisoners. They don't get a say in anything. In how they appear. In who can come near them—" She broke off. "My friend got out, though. Other people weren't so lucky."

Like the Steelman twins. Keith had destroyed them. They'd been a few years older than Orchid, and as they were offered more adult roles, Keith had pushed for more adult presentations. Strict diets, harsh, sexy styling, pills to make sure they "stayed on track."

Vaughn's fingers stilled, and the music stopped. Silence reigned in the ballroom. Finally, he raised his head and looked her in the eye. "I'm so sorry that happened to you."

Her heart skipped a beat. "What?"

He took deep breath. "Orchid . . . I have to tell you. I know who you are. Who you—who you used to be, before you came to Blackbrook."

Her eyes burned at the way he said it. *Who you used to be.* "How long?" she whispered.

"Over break. One of your movies was on TV, and I—I just knew." His voice was so soft. "I'm sorry. I should have told you, but it seemed that you didn't want anyone to know. I didn't know how to tell you. I'm sorry."

He'd known? "All this time, you knew?"

"I don't care," he insisted. "You're Orchid McKee to me. I wish I hadn't found out, honestly." He shook his head. "It was just—I saw you, and I knew. I believe when you really care about someone, it's easy to see the truth of who they are."

"Yes," she breathed, and then she leaned over and kissed him.

15

Green

Not that Vaughn would admit it, least of all to the pretty girl currently pressing her lips to his, but he'd never been kissed before. Other kids at Blackbrook might view boarding school as one long experiment in hookups, but that was a dangerous game to play when you were Vaughn and Oliver.

But he didn't want to think about Oliver right now. Not when he was finally—*finally*—kissing Orchid.

Because he was. Kissing her, too. The stupid guitar was trapped between them, but he'd never cared less about a musical instrument in his life. His hand trembled as he reached up and touched her shoulder.

Her lips parted. Vaughn nearly died on the spot. He pulled her in. The guitar strummed its protest. Neither of them cared.

She had her hand on his neck, the side of her thumb notched under his jaw, four fingertips pressing into the nape of his neck as if saying, *closer, more.*

He shoved the guitar to the floor, and it clattered against the wood.

She broke away, panting. "Oops."

He couldn't catch his breath, either. "'Oops' the guitar, or 'oops' kissing me?" If it was the kissing, he'd go throw himself off the side of the ravine.

"'Oops' the guitar." She laughed. "I wanted to kiss you."

Thank God. "I wanted to kiss you, too." He still wanted to kiss her. He really, really liked the look of this fainting couch they were on. He thought they both might just fit.

"Me . . . Orchid," she said. "I don't think anyone's ever wanted to kiss me-as-Orchid before."

"You're only Orchid to me."

"Boy, do you know exactly what to say."

But it was true. He'd done a double take when he'd seen her on-screen. The red hair and the glittery clothes. It was her, but not really. He'd heard of the heiress movies, of course, but they'd been more popular with little girls. Still, it was Orchid.

Or Emily. Didn't matter. People took stage names. Why not the other way around? The girl he'd gotten to know in the storm, over text—that was Orchid.

I believe when you really care about someone, it's easy to see the truth of who they are.

"Orch—" But she was kissing him again, so he quickly shut up.

For not really having any idea what he was doing, he felt like he must be doing okay, since she wanted to go again. He had one hand in her hair and another at her waist, and she was tugging at his shoulders as if she wanted him to lean in—no, to *lower her down* toward the cushions, as if it was his birthday and Christmas morning and all his ships coming in at once, and apparently she had the same idea as Vaughn about how well they'd fit on this couch, and she was very soft and her hair smelled very good and—

"Wait," she said against his mouth, and he pulled away. It was hard, but he did it. "I was just thinking, Dr. Brown is on the warpath. She's been handing out insane punishments for, you know, sneaking around this house, doing things that are not schoolwork."

Vaughn had learned more in the last ninety seconds than he had in his last two terms at Blackbrook.

"Unnnh," he said, and he pressed his nose against her neck, breathing deeply.

"Vaughn." She playfully shoved him, and he sat up. She, too, scooched back into a sitting position.

He stared at her, unable to think of whole words. Orchid's mouth was wet and swollen, and he had done that.

"That was—um—" She smoothed her hair. "That was—" *Amazing. A long time coming. Something she wanted to do again, Dr. Brown be damned.* "Really nice."

Oh, no, he'd sucked at it. *Nice?* He could already hear Oliver laughing.

Those thoughts must have shown on his face, because her eyes widened. "No! More than nice! I—I'm glad we made up."

"Is that what we're doing? Making up?" No, he was supposed to tell her she was better off without him. He was supposed to protect her from Oliver—protect himself from the specter of her doing exactly this with Oliver.

"Making out, making up . . ." Orchid chuckled. "I don't know. You do, though. You knew exactly what to say. It's not a puppy dog, act, Vaughn. It's who you are."

The words fell on him like cold water. "What?"

"The other day on the cliff. You said I was falling for your puppy dog act."

Ugh, of course Oliver would say that.

"But I don't think it's an act. You put up this front where you act all tough or whatever, but that's not who you are. This"—she pointed at the space between them, at the guitar, forgotten on the floor—"*this* is who you are."

I believe when you really care about someone, it's easy to see the truth of who they are.

Vaughn had watched an Emily Pryce movie and seen Orchid McKee. Orchid had been with Oliver and decided it wasn't who Vaughn really was.

Maybe she knew his secret, too.

He swallowed heavily. His heart was already racing. He had two choices here. He could kiss her again and just stop thinking about it, or he could open his stupid, stupid mouth.

And Orchid must be right about him. It wasn't an act. He was just a puppy dog. A very stupid, clumsy puppy dog.

"Orchid, there's something I haven't told you. I haven't told anyone—"

She leaned in and took his hands between her own, and, somehow, it was even nicer than all the kissing. He stared down at their hands in a kind of wonder, at her skin against his, at the little pinkish-gold ring she wore with the orchid on it, as if she might forget her name.

"I'm listening," she said, and it was like hitting perfect chord after perfect chord. The way a song just snicks into place when it's right.

All he had to do was tell the truth.

"When I got my scholarship, it was like a miracle. Gemma— my grandmother—was dead. I didn't see any way out of this town. And then, Blackbrook—"

"I know," she said. "I know all this."

"You do?" After all this time, after all these years of not saying it—of not saying it to anyone—it would be amazing if she just *knew*.

They weren't Emily Pryce or Oliver Green. Just Orchid and Vaughn.

"You belong here, Vaughn," she said. "At Blackbrook. No matter what people like Scarlett say. You're not going to die on Rocky Point like Rusty or your grandmother. You're destined for great things." She was nodding at him.

She was so, so wrong.

"No, that's not what I'm saying," he whispered. "I've been lying to everyone. Since I got here. When you think I'm being weird, or playing games, or putting on an act—it's not that. It's that I'm not always *me*—"

There was an enormous thump from beyond the door. They both froze.

"What was—"

Orchid was already on her feet and marching toward the ballroom door. "I know exactly what it was!" she said angrily. "Scarlett. Listening at doorways is her fun new trick. I bet she's been spying on us the entire time. You'd think, after yesterday, she would have learned her lesson—"

She threw the door open.

It was not Scarlett.

It was Rosa, collapsed on the floor.

"Rosa!" Orchid screamed and knelt at her side.

Vaughn sprinted toward them. Orchid rolled the girl over. Her face was a reddish purple.

"She's not breathing!" Orchid said. "She's not breathing, Vaughn."

She wasn't conscious at all. Her hands were near her throat.

"Is she choking? A heart attack?"

Orchid's eyes widened. "Oh my God, what if it's anaphylactic shock? She said the other day she was allergic to nuts."

"Call 911!" Vaughn shouted. "I'll go check her room for an EpiPen."

"She's in the billiards room!" Orchid called.

Vaughn raced to the billiards room, but the door was locked. He backed up a couple of steps, then threw himself against the thick wood.

Slam! Pain radiated through his shoulder and down his arm, but the door did not budge.

The door to the library opened, and Dr. Brown came out. "What's this? Are you breaking into another student's room? What is wrong with you people?"

"Rosa is having an attack of some sort. We thought it might be anaphylactic shock. I'm trying to see if she has an EpiPen in her room—"

"Where is she?" Dr. Brown looked frantic.

"Outside the ballroom." He pointed. "Orchid called 911—"

Dr. Brown disappeared into her room for a moment, then reappeared with a ring of keys. She brushed Vaughn aside, opened the door to the billiards room, and cast about for anything that looked like Rosa's medication.

Vaughn just stared at the room in confusion. Maps of the campus and diagrams of every building—including this one— were hung up all over the walls. A single suitcase lay open on the floor. The desk was covered not with schoolbooks but with cameras, binoculars, and even—he noticed with some shock—a revolver.

Rosa was . . . not a student. He'd seen some funny things in people's rooms while emptying the trash cans—things Oliver said they could probably use to blackmail students, things that made him very curious about the way rich kids lived—but nothing like this.

"What the—"

"Out of the way, Mr. Green," Dr. Brown said, and pushed past him. "Go look in the kitchen for a first aid kit. I am *not* having another person die in this house."

Vaughn obeyed. He saw some of the other girls in the house coming down the stairs and out of the lounge.

"Does anyone have an EpiPen?" he gasped.

"I do!" said Violet Vandergraf. "Not that I've ever even *seen* a bee up here in the Arctic Circle. But, whatever, my mom insisted that—"

"Go get it!" he shouted at her. She turned and hurried back up the stairs.

"What's going on?" Scarlett asked.

"Rosa's having some kind of episode—she's outside the ballroom. She's not breathing."

They all hurried back to where he'd left Orchid. When they got there, they found Dr. Brown bent over Rosa, doing CPR.

"The school nurse is on her way with an epinephrine shot," Dr. Brown said.

"The paramedics are coming, too," said Orchid. "They said it'll be about fifteen minutes from the mainland."

"Twenty-five," Vaughn said, choking on the words. "It's twenty-five at least." It had been twenty-five when he'd called for Gemma. Twenty-five minutes of waiting and knowing it didn't matter anymore. That she was dead anyway. Twenty-five minutes until someone came and confirmed it for him. "Maybe thirty."

Orchid put her hand over her mouth. "This is all my fault."

Vaughn didn't stop to think about the fact that all the other girls of Tudor House were standing around. He just reached for Orchid and drew her into his arms. "No, don't say that. Whatever she ate—it was an accident."

She buried her face in his chest. "No, Vaughn," she mumbled miserably. "Don't you get it? I'm the one who brought her here!"

16

Peacock

From: *elizabeth.picach@BlackbrookAcademy.edu*
To: *ash@phoenixmanagement.org*
Subj: *Anti-stress smoothie*

> *ASH, THERE WERE NO NUTS IN THAT ANTI-STRESS SMOOTHIE MIX, WERE THERE?*
> *I gave it to our new housemate Rosa yesterday, and just now, she went into anaphylactic shock and we had to call an ambulance. They said she's in a coma and might not make it!*
> *OMG, is this all my fault?*
> *Call me!*

From: *ash@phoenixmanagement.org*
To: *elizabeth.picach@BlackbrookAcademy.edu*
Subj: *Re: Anti-stress smoothie*

> *Dear Beth,*
> *I'm so sorry to hear about your friend! No, there are no nuts in the smoothie mix. I try not to use any allergens, and I always*

make sure not to contaminate any of my mixtures because I do have so many clients with a variety of dietary intolerances. But of course, people can be allergic to any food, not only food from major allergy food groups.

It's terrible to hear that your friend is doing poorly, but I urge you not to blame yourself. You said you gave her the mix yesterday. That's a pretty long time for a reaction to occur. I don't think you had anything to do with this.

Re-center yourself. The last thing I want is for an anti-stress treatment to have the opposite effect on you than I intended. Decouple yourself from the concern that you had anything to do with this, or any control over the outcome. YOU take care of YOU.

You have your own concerns to worry about. Your own tests this weekend. Your own tournament next month. Are you getting enough sleep? I know how much you've been fretting about these tests. If necessary, maybe get some melatonin on board. I can overnight you whatever you need. You must get a good night's sleep before your exams.

While I feel deeply for this Rosa person, she can't be my main concern now. There's only one girl I care about at Blackbrook.

I am honored to share with you the illumination within,

Ash

17

Scarlett

Half an hour later, it was all over. Well, not Rosa's life—that part they said they might be able to save, which was a huge relief to everyone in Tudor House, including Scarlett. She wasn't exactly Rosa's biggest fan, but that didn't mean she wanted the poor girl to die.

This was the second time this week they'd had to have paramedics at Tudor House, at Blackbrook. And this time, it wasn't a staff member. This time, it was a student.

This did not bode well for Dr. Brown's campaign to make the campus seem safe for the students. Nor did it help lower the stress levels of those who were still willing to remain there. A lot of the other girls living in the house were already on their phones to their parents or even their parents' lawyers. Scarlett expected a call from her mother any minute now, once word got out in New York City.

The only question was whether her mother would insist she pack up *before* the standardized tests or after.

Scarlett was so upset about the whole thing that it took until the paramedics had packed up Rosa and left for her to notice that Orchid and Vaughn were standing awfully close to each other. In fact, they were even . . . holding hands!

What?

No. Scarlett felt that she'd been perfectly clear about this. Even if Vaughn Green wasn't a total weirdo, Orchid could do way better. She didn't even need to date someone in a boy band—there were better choices right here at school! Tanner Curry, for example—total hunk. Although maybe he was dating Amber Frye. Clay Hopwell from the crew team— although, maybe he'd transferred to Groton? Scarlett couldn't remember. That was how much she was slipping!

Or Orchid could even stick closer to home. Everyone in the Murder Crew had crushes on the wrong people. Scarlett could arrange things much better for them. She spent a few relaxing moments on a self-care fantasy in which her friends actually took her advice as to whom they should be dating. Wouldn't it be splendid if Orchid was . . . maybe in love with Peacock? Beth wasn't a football player or a rower, but movie star and tennis phenom had serious potential as a power couple.

Vaughn now had his arm around Orchid's shoulders. Scarlett wondered if he smelled like custodial services. Maybe Orchid didn't have a well-developed sense of smell. Ironic for a girl named after a flower. Though Orchid wasn't really named that, was she? Did orchids even have a scent?

Ugh. These were the things she was going to be up tonight wondering about, rather than reviewing her binomial formulas.

"I should go to the hospital to be with her," Orchid was

saying, presumably to Vaughn, though Scarlett was totally close enough to hear. "I feel responsible."

"Why?" Scarlett couldn't help but blurt. "Because you tripped over her body? Because Dr. Brown was the one who had to perform CPR?"

Orchid shook her head, exasperated. "I don't have time to get into this with you, Scarlett."

Scarlett rolled her eyes. *Well, make the time.* Things were certainly a lot better around here when people took her opinion into account. When Scarlett had run the school, there were one hundred percent fewer murders.

"I can take you to the mainland," said Vaughn.

"You have a car?"

"No." He ducked his head into the neck of his parka. "But I know where Rusty kept his spare keys, and I don't think he's going to be needing his car for a bit."

Orchid's face lit up. "Oh, thank you. That would be amazing."

"Um, no, it wouldn't!" Scarlett said. She could not stand idly by and listen to this. "You're going to go steal a dead man's car to take Orchid on an unauthorized trip to the mainland to go visit some girl that neither of you actually know? After the week Dr. Brown has had and the punishments she's been handing out? Are you even listening to yourself?"

Orchid and Vaughn exchanged glances.

"Let's, um," Orchid began, "go discuss this somewhere private."

And before Scarlett could protest again, Orchid had herded Vaughn and her into the study. Seemed the custodial staff still hadn't finished their work on the fireplace. Plywood and tools littered the floor in front of the hearth. Scarlett very nearly mentioned something to Vaughn about the mess. But she was a bigger person that that. Instead, she merely flopped onto the couch and folded her arms over her chest. Vaughn did not stray from Orchid's side. Figured.

"So," Orchid began, folding her hands in front of her and addressing Scarlett as if she was giving an oral report. "Rosa was . . . not a student."

"What?" Scarlett asked, though Vaughn gave a nod, as if he'd just had his own suspicions confirmed.

"She was a bodyguard. I hired her to protect me after last term."

What? Well, at least that explained Rosa's utter disinterest in getting to know anyone, in talking about her last school— even the maps she'd caught a glimpse of in the girl's room.

It did not, however, explain why Orchid had never told her. Especially after Scarlett had nearly been suspended over her suspicions of the new girl.

"My stalker may not have killed Headmaster Boddy, but he was still out there and causing mischief. It seemed safest to—"

"Orchid!" Scarlett said, casting warning looks at the townie. "Maybe we should talk about this somewhere, you know, *more* private?"

Orchid sighed. "Vaughn knows, Scar."

It couldn't have hurt worse if Orchid had hauled off and slapped Scarlett across the face. "You told *Vaughn?*"

Vaughn, too, appeared taken aback. "You told *Scarlett?*"

Scarlett was giving him a dirty look when Orchid stepped between them. "Quit it, both of you. Yes, I told Scarlett. She's my best friend here. And no," she said, turning to Scarlett, "as a matter of fact, I didn't tell Vaughn. He figured it out all by himself."

"Creeper," Scarlett mumbled. And then what Orchid had said sank in.

Her best friend? *Really?*

Scarlett was now sitting on the edge of her seat. "I thought you got all that worked out back in California."

Orchid perched on the sofa beside her. "I mean, I checked it out with the lawyers. The restraining order is still in place. He denied having anything to do with my financial hiccup last term, or with the letter I got."

"Couldn't they check the letter for fingerprints or something?" Scarlett asked.

Orchid rolled her eyes. "You watch too much TV. It was sent through the mail. And just in this house, you touched it, I touched it, Mrs. White touched it when she sorted the mail . . . There are no usable fingerprints. His argument to my lawyers was that it was probably just a crazed fan, and the thing with my tuition was probably just my own irresponsibility."

Scarlett pursed her lips. Questionable taste in boyfriends aside, Orchid was anything but irresponsible.

Vaughn put out his hand. "I'm going to need you to back

all the way up for a minute. Orchid, you hired a *bodyguard*? Because you have a *stalker*?"

"Catch up, lover boy," Scarlett snapped at him. She looked at her friend. "I want to talk about how you moved a body-guard into Tudor and didn't tell anyone, including me."

"I want to talk about why you think you need a bodyguard," Vaughn said.

"That's why she was in the billiards room by herself," Orchid explained. "We thought her having a roommate might make the fact she wasn't a student too obvious."

"*We?* So Dr. Brown knew?" Scarlett was furious. She'd been punished despite the fact that she had been right—Rosa Navarro was very suspicious, indeed. And Orchid had never even told her! "I can't believe I went to you for comfort after Dr. Brown caught us trying to sneak into her room!"

"Can someone tell me about this stalker?" Vaughn cried.

Scarlett glared at the both of them. "It's her old agent."

"Manager," said Orchid.

"Whatever."

"The guy you told me about, who forced you to do jobs you didn't want and didn't protect you from your actual crazed fans?" Vaughn asked. "The one who threatened to kill you?"

Orchid nodded. "Keith Grayson. And it's worse than that."

Vaughn's eyes couldn't get any wider, but Scarlett had already heard this story.

"I had these two friends—Jen and Kate."

"The Steelman twins?" At Scarlett's skeptical glance, he shrugged. "What? Even Rocky Point got reruns of *All Ours.*"

"Yes, the Steelmans," Orchid said. "Or Steelmen? Anyway, they were clients of Keith's, too. Only five years older than me. And it was, like, the *second* they turned eighteen, he had them on this whole other career path. It was . . . it wasn't okay. I was just a kid, but I still understood what was going on. I even tried to talk about it to Jen once, but, you know, Keith had her convinced. He was going to make her a star. She just had to dress as he told her and eat like he told her and get the plastic surgery he told her to get and take the pills he told her to take. He had complete control over them, just like he did of me. I saw it coming for me, like a runaway train, and—" Her voice broke.

Scarlett saw Vaughn take a step closer and reach out and grab Orchid's hand. To comfort her.

"I had a bodyguard I trusted, but that's about it. He was the one who kind of pointed out to me that the stuff Keith was letting fans do to me was screwed up. But then he was killed in a car accident with the paparazzi—" She looked at Vaughn. "I told you about that, remember? During the storm?"

"You said it was your uncle," Vaughn said.

"Yeah. Well, anyway, maybe that's why I was so quick to hire Rosa. A bodyguard made me feel safe. After he died, there was no buffer between me and Keith. And I was doing this movie with the Steelmans—*Three Orchids*, it was called."

Orchid looked down at her hand, and Scarlett followed her gaze to see a tiny orchid ring there.

Well, that explained the name, at least.

"I don't know that one," said Vaughn.

"It was never released. Jen and Kate died less than a week after firing Keith."

Vaughn took a breath. "How?"

Orchid bit her lip and didn't respond.

Scarlett finished for her. "Their car was found at the bottom of the cliff that their house sat on in the Hollywood Hills. They were both inside."

Orchid's whole face crumpled, and she reached for Vaughn's hand.

"An accident?" he asked.

"No one knows," said Scarlett. "There were investigations, but nothing was ever conclusively proved. Some people said it was a carjacking, some that it was a murder-suicide plot or some drugged-out party gone horribly wrong. Guess you don't get tabloids at Rocky Point."

Vaughn was not taking the bait. "If it was around the time my grandmother died, I wasn't keeping up on celebrity news, no."

"Anyway," Orchid broke in, "I testified against him in one of the investigations. I don't know if Keith killed the Steelmans, but I do know he abused them. I do know they were scared of him. I was scared when I fired him. He wound up settling a civil suit with the Steelmans' family, and the movie got shelved, and—" She covered her face with her hands. "That's when he threatened me. That's when I knew I had to get a restraining order and get out of Hollywood. For good."

Vaughn was practically on top of them. "But it's been years. Why would he come after you now?"

"I don't know—maybe it took him this long to find me? All I know is, after I got that letter, I couldn't take any chances. A bodyguard protected me before." Her voice was rising, frantic. "But now I've done it again. A bodyguard dying, for me!"

"Hey," Vaughn said, and now he was kneeling at her side. "Rosa's not dead. She's going to be okay. I'll go get Rusty's car. Screw what Dr. Brown says."

Scarlett bit her lip, feeling guilty. "Dr. Brown won't even know," she promised Orchid. Vaughn gave her a questioning look over his shoulder. "I'll cover for you. Both of you."

Orchid lifted her head. "Thank you, Scarlett."

Scarlett felt a lump in her throat. "And don't feel guilty about this. Rosa wasn't even injured in the line of duty or whatever. She accidentally ate a nut. This is not your fault. It could have happened to her anywhere."

The door opened, and all three of them looked up to find Peacock standing in the doorway. "I'm so glad I found you guys!" she announced, letting herself in and squeezing onto the couch. "I'm so worried about Rosa!"

"Us, too," said Orchid. She scooted over a bit to give Peacock more room.

"I think this whole thing might be my fault," Peacock said.

"*Your* fault?" asked Orchid, sniffling.

"I gave her a smoothie yesterday. One of the new mixes my life coach Ash sent me. What if it had nuts in it?"

"Did you ask him if it did?" Vaughn asked.

"Yes, and he said no!" Peacock exclaimed.

"Then I think you're pretty safe," said Scarlett. "Besides,

you said you gave it to her yesterday. A nut allergy would appear quicker than that."

"That's what Ash said, too," Peacock whined. "But look what happened last year! All I did was *yell* at Boddy, and everyone blamed me when he got murdered!"

Oh. *Oh.* She wasn't worried about Rosa. She was worried about what people would think of her *regarding* Rosa. That, Scarlett was sorry to say, she felt better equipped to handle.

She looked at Orchid and Vaughn. "Go do your thing. I'll handle Beth."

"What?" Peacock asked.

"Best you don't know," Scarlett said quickly, and Orchid and Vaughn made themselves scarce. She'd deal with the rest of it later. Like how Orchid had totally let her believe that Rosa was just some innocent fellow student, even though she completely didn't act like one.

She turned to face Peacock. "Look, Beth," she said, "no one thinks you murdered Boddy. No one thinks you murdered Rusty. No one thinks you poisoned Rosa. No one thinks any of those things. Get those thoughts out of your head."

"But during the storm—"

"During the storm we all said a lot of crap," she stated firmly. "We were alone and scared, and it was, like, a natural disaster. This is just a string of unlucky accidents." Probably because this fool school was falling to pieces without her leadership skills, but whatever. An argument for another time. "And I, for one, am extraordinarily sorry if I ever gave you the idea that I thought you were capable of murder."

Peacock hunched her shoulders. "Actually, you didn't," she said softly. "You were one of the only ones."

See? At least someone appreciated her judgment. "Murder Crew forever," she said in solidarity.

"Kind of the opposite of that, though, right?"

"Yeah," Scarlett conceded. "Totally the opposite of murder."

Peacock, thank goodness, looked relieved.

"So, tell me more about this life coach. It sounds like you really like him."

"I do!" Peacock nodded. "I just feel like he's there to help me get my life on track. Blackbrook is a mess, and the tests this weekend are going to be a total bloodbath, but if I just listen to his advice, I know I'll make it through."

Scarlett had to say, the idea of people paying her to give them life advice sounded like an absolute dream job. Maybe *that* was the future for her. "Does it require a master's degree or something?"

"Not that I know of." Peacock shrugged. "He's just . . . really insightful and intuitive."

Bingo. At least the way things were going with her test prep.

"He came really well-recommended. My parents said the tennis pro at their club raved about him."

Scarlett wondered how you got started in that line of work. And how much she could charge. Scarlett was absolutely positive she'd be able to provide accurate information on Ayurveda. She wanted to sit down with Peacock, or maybe this Ash fellow, and go over it all. She wanted that so much more than another drill on quadratic equations.

Her phone buzzed. She imagined that the campus grape-vine was going wild about Rosa's attack.

She checked her phone.

No, not gossip. Finn.

Finn

> Well? I'm still waiting for an explanation.

"Oh. My. God." She shook her head in disgust. With all the excitement, she'd almost forgotten Finn's little intrigue.

"What?" Peacock asked.

"It's your stupid ex-boyfriend," she explained, showing her the text. "He's trying to pin Rusty's death on me."

"On you?" Peacock exclaimed. "Like he did with me and Boddy during the storm!"

Ooh, good point. This was turning into a bit of a pattern with Finn, wasn't it? At least, every time he was trying to deflect attention from his precious, secret little project.

She was so done with his crap.

She texted back.

> Boy, are you barking up the wrong tree. Go ask Mustard what he knows. I think you'll be VERY surprised.

There. At least he wouldn't be *her* problem anymore.

18

Plum

Finn stared at the text message as if he could decode it as easily as a chemical equation. Go ask Mustard? What was that supposed to mean?

He'd spent the last two days concocting and discarding plans to retrieve his work, with little success. He'd even gone so far as to sneak over to Tudor House and try to figure out if there was a way he could break into the conservatory. Since it was closed off, if he could somehow get in through one of the windows, it was likely no one would notice. Right?

Wrong. Dr. Brown, it seemed, had thought of everything. Large boards covered the inside of all the lower windows of the conservatory. If there was a way in, it wasn't through a window.

Finn was running out of ideas.

There were rumors that there were other ways to access the underground passages, stories of Blackbrook students from the distant past who'd found underground tunnels all over the campus, built for rumrunners taking their wares across Rocky Point from Canada. Tall tales and legends of parties past, of times that Blackbrook boys and Tudor girls found all kinds of interesting uses for those tunnels.

But no one Finn talked to seemed to have the slightest idea how to get inside one now. Granted, he'd only talked to three people. It's not like he wanted word to get around school that he wanted inside the tunnels. Three other people, at least, knew about his project now—Peacock, Mustard, and Scarlett—not to mention whoever had leaked it to Boddy last term. He didn't need anyone putting the details together and breaking into the passages without him.

Go ask Mustard.

He wasn't about to take Scarlett's advice at face value. Not after her private meeting with Mustard, who, by the way, had *not* called him after. Which Finn had specifically asked him to do. Which meant that in said private conversation, Scarlett had undoubtedly recruited Mustard to her side, probably by filling the new kid's head with stories of how—whatever, how sneaky or untrustworthy or backstabbing Finn could be.

Which was really unfair, because *if* he was, it was only because he'd learned all his best tricks from Scarlett.

And now she wanted him to go talk to Mustard about it? Finn wished he knew her angle.

And he really, really wished he knew if she and Mustard had teamed up to steal his invention.

On the walk home from the temporary chemistry lab, Finn noted that the paths seemed more crowded than he was used to since the school had reopened, as if everyone on campus was out and about. Two girls walking abreast approached him, clutching big bags and pillows in their arms.

"What's going on?" he asked. Had another dorm been flooded? This school had truly seen better days.

"I'm not spending another night in the Murder House," said the first girl, Violet. "It's cursed. Someone is dying in there every other day now."

"She's not dead," corrected Amber.

"Uh, yeah, because I gave her my EpiPen," Violet said, and hefted her pillow in her arms.

"Who's dead now?" Finn asked. "Or—what happened? Exactly?"

Amber hugged her pillow to her chest. "The new girl, Rosa Navarro. She had some kind of attack. They had to get an ambulance. They said they don't know if she's going to make it." She shook her head. "I don't know if I believe in curses, but I'm staying with my boyfriend tonight. If Dr. Brown doesn't like it, she can expel me. My father already said he can get me into Horace Mann if this place goes under."

Finn knew nothing about Rosa except that she liked his being in Tudor House as little as Mrs. White once had. "What about everyone else? Did you guys see—"

"The rest of the Murder Crew?" Amber drawled. "Of course. Last I saw, Peacock and Scarlett were in Scarlett's room—which, by the way, is so much bigger than the one they gave us, Vi."

"I know! I think that's because she lived there before, though. She must have dibs or something."

"And Orchid and Vaughn Green were going somewhere in some old junker of a car."

Violet leaned in. "Do you think they're a thing?"

"I do!" Amber replied. "I haven't decided what I think about it, though. Do you think he's hot?"

"He could be hot," Violet agreed charitably. "He's got that kind of grungy thing going. Have you heard him sing?"

"I have. Okay, so he's hot. Is *she* hot?"

"If she'd brush her hair. She's kind of grungy, too. Or emo."

"Definitely emo. What do you think, Finn?"

"They're both attractive," Finn said without thinking.

The girls gave him a look.

"Okay, whatever," Amber said. "So, have we got the Murder Crew covered?" Her eyes widened. "Well, not Mustard. Come with me back to Tanner's room. Mustard's going to flip, I bet. From what Tanner said, he got into this whole thing with Rosa the other day."

"What? Really?" Violet pounced on this.

"Not like that," Amber said. "Or maybe it is like that? I don't know. They had a fight at Tudor or something. Mustard got into mad trouble."

"Like a fight-fight?" Violet asked. "Why is Mustard always getting beaten up by girls?"

"Do you think that's true, what they say?" Amber asked. "That Peacock punched him out during the storm?"

They looked at Finn, who was still trying to figure out what Mustard and Rosa could have gotten into a fight about.

"Yes," he confirmed. "But I don't know if it was really the

punch. It was mostly that he fell and cracked his head on the floor."

"Ew," said Amber. "Anyway, he was put on cleaning duty."

"Wow . . ." Violet fell into step beside her friend. "He's super hot, isn't he?"

"Super hot," Amber agreed. "I should totally set you two up."

Neither of them asked Finn's thoughts on Mustard.

He trailed behind the girls all the way back to the boys' dorm, relieved to have an excuse to go ask Mustard anything. He probably should have done it before, when Mustard hadn't called him after his conversation with Scarlett.

But he hadn't. He knew Mustard was in Tanner's room. He knew where Tanner's room was. But if Mustard wasn't going to call him, then he probably had his reasons.

The girls burst into Tanner and Mustard's room. "Did you hear? Did you hear about Rosa?"

"I mean, I got your sixty texts," Tanner said from where he was sitting at his desk. Mustard, too, was in his desk chair. He looked up, and his eyes met Finn's.

Tanner nodded at Violet. "Is she getting the couch?"

"Our bed's a little crowded," Amber shot back with a smirk.

Finn leaned against the doorjamb.

"What up, Finn?" Tanner asked.

"More dead bodies, apparently."

"I said she's not dead!" Amber pointed out.

"Hey," said Mustard, to Finn alone.

"Hey," Finn replied.

"Are you sure Dr. Brown is cool with this?" Tanner asked his girlfriend. "Have you heard of the punishments she's been handing down? She stripped Scarlett Mistry of all her leaderships. She gave Mustard here hard labor. My folks will kill me if I so much as get detention." He affected a snotty voice. "It does not *reflect well* on the Curry tradition at Blackbrook."

"If we're not sleeping here, then I'm pitching a tent in the dining hall," Amber insisted. "But I'm not spending another night in the Murder House."

"Can I talk to you?" Finn asked Mustard. He cocked his head toward the hall.

"Yeah," said Mustard. He grabbed his coat and a backpack sitting by the side of the desk, and the two of them left the others to bicker about sleeping arrangements. They walked side by side down the hall, then, as if by unspoken agreement, took the stairs and exited into the night.

Mustard was very big, Finn thought. He'd thought it the first time he'd seen the new kid picking up Karlee and Kayla and carrying them across the flooded campus during the storm. He thought it now, when they would have been walking shoulder to shoulder, except for Mustard's shoulder being a few inches above his and notably broad, especially under the layers of his down jacket.

"Is that whole thing cool with you?" Finn asked. "The girls sleeping at your place?"

Mustard shrugged. "At Farthing, we were in bunks, twelve to a cabin. This isn't so bad."

Finn's eyes widened. He thought it was bad ever since the

storm, when the damage to the dorms meant he was assigned his new roommate, Jin. Jin and Finn—someone in administration must have gotten a good laugh out of that. Jin, however, kept mainly to himself and slept on a schedule that made Finn wonder if he was keeping to Beijing time.

"So, this Rosa thing . . ." Finn began.

"Yeah. I heard it was a nut allergy . . ."

"Do you think it's a coincidence?"

Mustard looked over at him. "I'm seriously done investigating anything on this campus. It's only ever gotten me into trouble."

Finn nodded. "Yeah . . . so what happened, there?"

Mustard stopped. "You didn't get my email?"

"Your email?"

"Yeah. I emailed you yesterday. I didn't have your number—"

Finn shook his head. "I didn't get an email."

Mustard's expression changed right away. He looked—relieved. "Oh. I thought you were just ignoring me. Finn Plum at Blackbrook, right?"

"Phineas," Finn replied. "With a *P-h.* My email is Phineas Plum at Blackbrook."

"What kind of name is that?"

"What kind of name is Mustard?"

Mustard stopped on the path, looked away, and scrubbed a hand through his dark hair. "Actually, my name is Samuel. Samuel Maestor."

"Yeah, I figured your parents didn't name you Mustard—"

"With an *S-M.*"

Finn's mouth snapped shut.

"Like on that note you found. The one you showed to Scarlett?"

Oh. *Oh.*

He looked around the campus. It had cleared out some from earlier, but there were still a couple of kids wandering here and there.

They couldn't go back to Finn's room. Jin would be there, probably asleep. And there was still a party in Mustard and Tanner's.

But he did know somewhere private. As long as he could still get in.

"Come on." He grabbed Mustard by the sleeve of his parka and pulled him off the path. He probably could have let go of the tether at any point. But he didn't. Not until they were standing under the shadow of the old chemistry building. Like so many others, the building had been flooded in the storm and was not currently in use. Electrical problems, they said.

But Finn knew a way in.

He leaped for the fire escape ladder, and it screeched down until the bottom rested in the dirt.

"Subtle," said Mustard under his breath.

Eh, no one was looking. "Trust me."

Mustard snorted. "Right."

Finn started to climb.

Mustard waited until Finn had reached the platform on the second story to follow him up the ladder, which he did so quickly that Finn was left speechless and also completely embarrassed by what he was sure was his own comparatively awkward climb.

"Where are we going?" Mustard asked.

"Room 203," Finn said as he jimmied open the window. Ah, room 203, his old friend. His old partner in crime. If he'd only trusted room 203 during the storm, he wouldn't be in this mess at all. He should have left his work there. It would have been safe. Untouched.

One of many mistakes he'd made.

Mustard climbed in behind him, then stood looking around the cold, musty-smelling chemistry lab. It was all shadows and amber glow from the sodium streetlamp just beyond the window. Most of the supplies had been stripped out—all the glass flasks and beakers and burettes. The scales and hotplates, the ring stands and clamps, the class computers, and the jars of solutions and powders.

It was mostly countertops and stools now. Mustard put his backpack down on the former and sat on the latter, facing Finn.

Now that they were here, in the dark, Finn had completely forgotten what they were going to talk about. He could not get a good look at Mustard's face in the shadows. He did not know where to put his hands.

"That note," Mustard said at last. "The one you found on Rusty's body . . ."

"Yeah."

"It was for me."

"*For* you?" Finn asked skeptically.

"Yeah. I found it in my school mailbox."

Well, that would explain why it had his initials on it instead of his nickname. Finn shook his head. "Your mailbox? Then how did it get onto Rusty's body?" Oh no. *Oh, no.* Had he brought a killer up to an abandoned chemistry lab?

"It was a shakedown," Mustard said now. He stood and reached for the backpack.

Finn tensed. This was the part where he was going to be murdered.

But when Mustard turned back around, he wasn't holding a weapon. He was holding . . . Finn peered through the darkness.

"Is that . . . is that my digital scale?"

"Yeah," said Mustard. "At least I hope so. Otherwise, I paid a lot of money for nothing."

Finn leaped forward and grabbed it out of Mustard's hands. "I thought I'd never see it again." Somehow, he resisted hugging the scale. He gave Mustard a suspicious glance. "But . . . how did you get it?" And where was the rest of his stuff?

"I'm trying to tell you," said Mustard. "I'm—I'm doing it badly. I thought Rusty and I had a deal, you know? I'd heard the rumors about those passages in the woods. I thought it might be a back way in to the ones under Tudor. I offered him a little cash, and he took it. Brought the scale but said he couldn't get it all. He wanted me to go out there and look for myself. I figured he was trying to get more money out of me—"

"Oh my God," whispered Finn. "And you *killed* him?"

Mustard gave him an incredulous look. "You moron. I got you your files."

He slid the backpack over. There, inside, was a black box that looked just like Finn's computer, as well as his binders and folders. The ones he'd left in the passage under the conservatory. The ones with his entire future inside them. He put the scale down on the counter and touched the edge of the backpack with reverent fingers.

Then he breathed out for what felt like the first time in weeks. It was there. It was safe. His dye. His beautiful black dye. Mustard had gone and found it.

For him.

Mustard was standing there, close, watching him. Finn's eyes must have adjusted to the darkness, because he could see Mustard just fine now. His deep brown eyes, even the little bumps on his jaw from razor burn. Razor burn! Finn had never had to shave a day in his life.

He shook his head in disbelief. "So you didn't kill him?"

"What is with you people?" Mustard whispered harshly. "You're really fond of getting me alone in a room and then accusing me of murder. Why would you bring me up here if you thought I was a murderer?"

Finn turned to face him fully. He didn't back up. "Because I don't think you want to murder me."

Mustard was quiet for a moment. "What do you think I want to do?"

What was happening? *What was happening?*

He swallowed. "I think you want to kiss me."

There were three utterly awful seconds in which Finn was positive that he'd guessed wrong. Possibly fatally wrong.

Then Mustard nodded. "Yeah, okay."

And then he did kiss him. Hard.

Finn had been kissed plenty before, but not like this. Not this full-body onslaught thing, with his head between Mustard's hands, and his back biting up against the countertop, and their bodies pressed together from thigh to sternum. Maybe Mustard was a murderer after all, because Finn thought he might die. He'd forgotten how to breathe. He still didn't know where to put his hands, and they somehow ended up just . . . clutching the lapels of Mustard's parka, as if they both might be swept away.

And then, just as quickly as it had started, Mustard pulled his mouth away and rested his forehead against Finn's, panting.

"Okay," he gasped. "Okay."

Finn's hands slipped down to his sides. He was breathing hard, too, but he was scared to move. He was scared to speak.

So, instead, he tilted his face up, just a bit, and pressed one more soft kiss to the corner of Mustard's mouth.

The other boy jumped back as if he'd been bitten by a snake.

Finn's hands shot up defensively.

Mustard wiped at his mouth with the back of his hand, staring at Finn with haunted eyes.

Finn's hands lowered, and he straightened. His heart pounded in his chest. "Have you ever done that before?"

"Yeah," Mustard said roughly. "Once."

19

Mustard

The sky did not fall. Lightning did not strike him down where he stood. Mustard could detect no scent of fire or brimstone.

But he'd said it.

Plum was standing there as if there was absolutely nothing wrong. Mustard didn't know whether to run away or grab him again.

"Have you?" he choked out.

"No," said Plum, pretty simply, and Mustard wished that lightning would hurry up and smite him. "I mean . . . I've kissed people before. But not—" He gestured to Mustard.

Oh no. No no no no no. "Right," he managed. "So."

"So." Plum took a step forward, and Mustard stumbled back.

It had been that little kiss at the end that did him in. That soft press of Plum's lips to the corner of his mouth. He'd never done that before. Never. That time—that other time—it had been hard and harsh, too. Like if it wasn't overwhelming, they'd be in enough control of themselves to stop. Like they had waited too long already and they had no time to waste.

Less time than they'd even thought. Less time than they'd hoped for.

But no one would ever catch Plum and Mustard here, in this abandoned building, on this empty campus. He bet people hooked up in these flooded-out buildings all the time.

Just like they did in the secret passages.

"It's okay," Plum said.

It was not okay. It was never okay. But it felt good to hear Plum say it. Straight freaking Finn Plum.

Maybe straight. Who was Mustard to say?

A straight boy would not do that soft little corner kiss thing. Mustard would never do that soft little corner kiss thing.

Well, he'd *want* to.

He clenched his fists and breathed.

Plum stuck his hands in his pockets. There was a smile on his pretty face. "Just so we're clear, you did not kill Rusty?"

Mustard glared at him. "What is wrong with you?"

Plum let out a short bark of incredulous laughter. "Many, many things. Ask anyone."

He had. He'd asked both of Plum's ex-girlfriends, and they'd both said he was a selfish, self-centered, backstabbing prick.

It had not helped Mustard as much as he'd hoped.

He didn't know what to do, so he zipped up his jacket. "All right, well, you have your stuff. I'm going to go." He headed to the window.

"Sam," came Plum's voice. "Wait."

He paused at the sill. "Mustard," he grumbled.

"I'm not calling you Mustard, you fool. I kissed you."

He turned around and looked at the other boy. "You kissed someone named Peacock, too. Maybe that's your thing."

"But I call her Beth."

Her.

What the hell was he doing? This was a mistake. This had always been a mistake. It had been a particularly bad mistake last time, when he'd been even more careless and had gotten caught. It might be a monumental mistake this time, because it was with Plum, and Plum was not a person to be trusted. Everyone said so.

But then there was that little corner kiss that Mustard figured he'd remember until the day he died.

Plum was still studying him in the dim light. His glasses were fogged up from cold, or maybe from heat—Mustard didn't know. Plum was the chemist here.

"When was the once?" Plum asked.

"What?"

"You said you did it before once. When?"

Mustard gave a little shake of his head. "No way."

Plum blinked. "Why won't you tell me?"

"Because you collect secrets and use them as currency."

Plum laughed again. "You're the one who knows my secrets, Sam."

Mustard. *Mustard.* He'd earned it. He wanted it used.

"You know about the dye." He gestured to the backpack. "You went out of your way to get it for me."

Oh. Realization washed over him. That's what this was. Some kind of twisted thank-you. "Well, consider it even, then."

"No. I mean—" Plum threw his hands in the air. "That wasn't what I meant. I don't want this to be currency."

"It was stupid. It was a mistake." He opened the latch.

"I'm obsessed with how hot you are."

Mustard turned around again. "What did you say?"

Plum was walking toward him. "I used to think about it . . . a lot. And I thought it was because I was jealous. You could pick up Beth like she was a sack of potatoes. I could never do that. So I figured, you know, I was just thinking about it all the time because I wished I was as attractive as you."

Mustard frowned. "Is that a compliment?"

"But now I think I was just . . . attracted to you."

Mustard fought the urge to clap his hand over Plum's mouth to get him to shut up. Or whatever else it took. "Got it. Glad we had this chat."

Plum's hand was on his lapel again, his fist tugging him forward. The first time Plum had grabbed him and pulled him off the path, Mustard had lost his breath. He wasn't sure he'd caught it again.

"Stop."

"Come on." He tugged harder.

Mustard put both hands on Plum's chest and shoved. The other boy stumbled back on his heels.

"This isn't a game," he growled. "You don't have a clue."

"Probably not," he said with a shrug and a smirk. "Scarlett thinks I'm a total idiot about anything that doesn't come in a test tube." He hugged himself. "I didn't know I liked doing what we just did until I did it."

Exactly. Mustard felt hot red rage building behind his eyes. He was—this way—and he was not okay. And Plum—wasn't gay?—and he was totally fine with kissing another boy. That wasn't fair. That wasn't *right*.

Just like his father said.

"Do you want to know what happened to Rusty?" he asked in a low, dangerous voice.

In the light from the streetlamp beyond the window, Plum's face went pale. "What?"

"You think I'm a murderer . . ."

"No, I don't—wait—" Now he looked scared. Good. Good. This was terrifying. "You're not, are you?"

Mustard swallowed thickly. "I told you. It was a shakedown. Rusty said he couldn't find all your stuff, and he'd need me to come with him. I thought he was after more money. So I went. He took me way out into the woods—"

Finn was shaking his head furiously.

"—to this tunnel thing. He let me in. It was really dark. I was . . . I got a bad feeling."

"You got a bad feeling," Finn repeated. "What kind?"

"The kind of bad feeling you get when you're alone in the dark with a strange old man," Mustard snapped.

"Oh," said Plum, his voice flat. "That."

"So I thought, I can navigate these tunnels, I can get there on my own, I can get your work and get out, and I won't have to pay him."

Finn had drawn closer again. "What . . . what happened to Rusty?"

What happened to Rusty? What happened to Rusty?

He'd been up nights wondering. Worrying. Too petrified to consider the truth.

"We weren't alone," Mustard forced himself to say. "In the tunnels. He must have brought some people from town. I didn't know what they were going to do to me." He clenched his jaw. All kinds of bad things happened to people like him.

"Mustard," Plum breathed. "You saw them?"

He nodded miserably. "I spotted a guy in a mask. And I heard them, shouting at one other. They were going to get me. So I hid."

He hadn't been looking for Plum's invention at that moment, just for a way to get behind a wall, away from whoever was searching for him, whoever was screaming and banging around the tunnels, promising severe retribution.

"Hid?"

"Yeah. I'm really good at hiding."

The corner of Plum's mouth turned up. "Apparently."

"Shut up."

"But you didn't kill Rusty?" Plum pressed.

"No." Mustard shook his head miserably. "Eventually, I got into the passages under Tudor House. I found the rest of your work, and I broke out through the lounge entrance. I had to sneak out. I didn't go back."

"So you don't know what happened?"

"Of course I know!" Mustard hissed. "Rusty and whoever else was in the tunnel were a couple of small-town punks looking to start something. When I wasn't available, they must have turned on him."

Finn frowned.

It was the frown that did Mustard in. Of course he couldn't convince someone else. He hadn't believed it himself, not really.

Mustard dug into his eyes with the heels of his hands. He felt sick. "Or," he said slowly, painfully, from behind his palms. The words were as thick as mud. "Or we interrupted a drug deal or something, and I wasn't there to protect Rusty."

Not very *Leave No Man Behind* of him. He was a failure all around.

After a minute, he felt Plum's fingers on his wrists, gently tugging Mustard's hands away from his eyes. Plum's pretty face lay just beyond. He wasn't smiling anymore, but his expression was gentler than Mustard had any right to.

"It's not your fault," Plum said.

That was not remotely true. "If I hadn't suspected him of—I don't know, being a creep . . ." He didn't finish. If he hadn't been so certain that creeps looked for people like him . . .

Wasn't that what his dad always said? Everything would go wrong if he stayed on this path. Farthing was just the start. He would not have the career he wanted, no matter what the government's current policies were. The military wasn't policies, his father always said. It was people. And people did not find it okay.

Even if Finn Plum did.

"Or maybe they would have gotten you, too," Plum said.

Mustard hung his head. Plum was still holding him by the wrists, and it was . . . surprisingly comforting. He took deep, gulping breaths, and then he felt it.

Plum's forehead against his. Not pressing hard, like Mustard had a few minutes earlier. Another soft, gentle touch. *Reassuring.* He was just *there.*

The other boy, at Farthing, hadn't been reassuring. His father certainly hadn't been. Mustard's marching orders had been clear. He was supposed to come to Blackbrook and keep his nose clean, not get involved in two separate murders and make out with a cute guy in an abandoned building.

But Plum just kept being there.

Undeniable. Inevitable. Like lots of things were, he supposed.

He'd thought he could do this thing—that he could get Plum's stuff for him, and it would be enough. That it didn't mean anything, that it certainly didn't mean he wanted more out of Plum. But, of course, it all went wrong. It always did.

"I have to tell someone."

"Let's not rush into anything," Plum replied softly.

Mustard lifted his head. "Rusty was murdered. You were right about that. Not about Scarlett or me, but . . . it wasn't natural causes or whatever stupid story Dr. Brown is peddling. I have to tell someone."

Plum shook his head. His hands slipped down onto Mustard's hands, and he squeezed. "You're already in trouble with Dr. Brown. You really want her to know that you were sneaking around in the tunnels? Think this over."

"I am thinking it over."

"You'll get expelled. *Again.*"

He flinched. And he'd deserve it. Again. "There's a murderer somewhere under this campus. Or maybe even *on* this campus."

"Stop trying to be Captain America," Plum insisted. "Remember what happened last time you tried to stop someone you thought was a murderer."

Yeah, because Plum had led him to think it. "I didn't mean figure it out myself. I meant, like, call the cops."

"How do you plan to do any of that without revealing why you were down there to start with?"

All at once, Mustard understood. He shook free of Plum's hands and moved away. "I see. You're still about protecting your precious dye."

Plum's mouth narrowed into a line. "Yes, of course I am. But I'd also like to protect you. You stuck your neck out for me. We're a team. And—whatever this was—"

"Oh, God, stop talking," he begged.

"Make me." There was challenge behind those glasses, inside that smirk.

Mustard gave a hollow laugh. "You really are a jerk, aren't you?" He pushed away from the sill, away from the light. "I'm not going to be talked out of doing the right thing." Or—or kissed out of it, or anything else. "Keeping your invention secret was one thing. Covering up a murder is another."

"I don't want you to cover it up . . . exactly," Plum said. "Look, I already got in trouble for being down there and finding the body. I can't get in any more trouble. I'll take the lead here. Share my concerns about what I saw that night. And I have the pictures. He was bleeding—we know that now. We can figure out a reasonable way to tell this story . . ." His face brightened. "We'll ask Scarlett! Scarlett is great at figuring out angles. When we used to scheme together, she was the idea person. I just handled the tech . . ."

"We're *not* telling Scarlett," Mustard stated firmly. "Are you nuts? You want to tell her—what? *This?*" He gestured between them. "What happened with Rusty?"

"I want us to get help figuring this out."

"There's no us."

Plum smiled crookedly. "Oh, there's an us. We have *secrets* now, man. *Lots* of them."

Mustard groaned. He was done for.

"Don't worry. We'll figure out how to fix it. I'll keep you safe."

"Really? The guy who lost his million-dollar dye in an underground tunnel? In a flood? You're going to keep *me* safe?"

Plum clucked his tongue. "*Million*-dollar? Don't lowball me like that. Ten figures, easy."

Mustard's eyes widened, and he looked over at the backpack full of Plum's work. Seriously? And he'd left it *underground?* "You're a bigger idiot than I thought."

"So, what do you want to do?" Plum said, exasperated. "I know you—you aren't going to cover it up. But you can't confess the whole story, either. Let me help you."

Every part of him wanted to say yes. But it was too danger-ous, for too many reasons.

"All I need to do is say I saw a head wound on Rusty," Plum argued. "That I'm worried there was foul play. After what hap-pened with Headmaster Boddy, I'm sure that's enough. Maybe the police even have a list of shady characters on Rocky Point. If it was a drug deal, like you think, it could be open and shut."

Mustard thought this over. That was a good point. After all, whether from Blackbrook or Rocky Point, there weren't a lot of people who could have been in those tunnels that night.

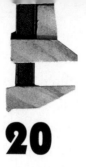

20

Green

Rosa's condition was deteriorating. Vaughn did not want to knock the fine doctors at the regional medical center on the mainland, but they just didn't have the advanced equipment that a large, cutting-edge hospital would have. Brain-cooling pads or hyperbaric chambers or whatever.

Orchid was beside herself. "We should have had her airlifted to Portland," she sobbed.

Vaughn didn't know what to do except hold her. Which he didn't mind at all.

They'd passed the whole night that way, side by side in hard plastic medical-center chairs. Vaughn slept, on and off, his face buried in Orchid's hair, the scent of floral shampoo and dry-cleaned wool sweater at once exactly what he'd hoped she'd smell like and like nothing he could have ever imagined. The fluorescent lights hummed off-key in the discolored ceiling tiles above them. The linoleum beneath their booted feet was scuffed and pitted. The intercom was scratchy and distorted.

But the music in his head made up for all of that.

He was halfway through a new song. A love song. He'd never successfully written a love song before, for all the obvious reasons. For all he knew, this one would stink, too, but right now, with Orchid's hand in his, it felt really, really good.

Last night, she had kissed him, and the shell around his world had cracked in two. The secrets he held, the ones that were the very fabric of his life—they didn't matter anymore. She had secrets, too, but she was moving on. She'd escaped from her nightmare. He could escape from his.

Oliver had been sending messages all night, but Vaughn hadn't responded. He didn't want to let his brother into this moment, this stolen evening that no grungy hospital or harsh lighting could diminish.

He was not exactly *grateful* for Rosa's accident. That would be cruel. But he was grateful for this time.

Orchid had been getting messages, too. He felt her phone buzzing in her pocket as she dozed on his chest. Her brow furrowed in her sleep every time the phone went off.

Which was a lot.

"Orchid," he whispered finally. "Your phone."

She mumbled something and handed it to him.

"No, I meant—"

"Three, three, one, one," she said, then snuggled her face into his sweater.

Vaughn blinked. Was that her lock code? She was giving him her lock code? Vaughn wasn't positive, but that seemed like a very boyfriend/girlfriend kind of thing to do. He entered the code on the screen, and, sure enough, her phone opened to him.

Thirteen messages from Scarlett. From that morning. He opened the messaging app.

Scarlett

Are you coming back?

Scarlett

I really hope you're still at the hospital and not, like, in Vaughn's bed.

Scarlett

What's going on with Rosa?

Scarlett

OMG, Orchid, answer me.

Scarlett

!!!!

Scarlett

Well, now I just think Vaughn murdered you and dumped the body.

Scarlett

Call me as soon as you can.

Scarlett

Brown is on the warpath. She wants to know where you are too.

Scarlett

She says anyone caught skipping school is going to get suspended. Did you get permission from her to go off campus?

Scarlett

SUSPENDED, Orchid. Are you listening to me? SUSPENDED.

Scarlett

I hope you took your phone. Maybe it's just locked in your room right now and I'm texting into a void.

Scarlett

Or maybe Vaughn did murder you and dump the body. Vaughn, if you're reading this right now over the dead body of Orchid McKee, know that I will hunt you down. I will not rest until her death has been avenged.

Scarlett

> ORCHID. CALL ME. Don't forget our
> tests are TOMORROW!!!!!!

Vaughn would have laughed if he wasn't afraid of disturbing the girl sleeping on him. If he were Oliver, he'd probably text back some creepy response about how he had, in fact, killed Orchid and was now using her phone for selfies.

But Vaughn was the good twin.

Which reminded him: it might be time to check his own messages. He shifted in his seat carefully, so as not to disturb Orchid, and pulled out his phone. His messages were not as amusing to read as Scarlett's had been. Oliver was pissed mostly that Vaughn hadn't met him last night, as promised, for their little quest. But he'd saved a good amount of rancor for the fact that apparently Vaughn had had access to a car and had never told Oliver.

That's because you're a terrible driver, Vaughn texted back. The last thing Rusty would want was his car at the bottom of the Rocky Point ravine.

Oliver was not appeased, nor was he going to let it go.

Vaughn sighed. He supposed he should wake Orchid. Unlike himself, she had no one to fill in for her at class.

Maybe in a few minutes. Gently, he brushed Orchid's hair out of her face. This girl had *kissed* him last night. She'd kissed him a lot.

Not for a while, though. Whatever Scarlett had texted, it

wasn't like Vaughn had driven Orchid out here for another make-out session. It hadn't seemed right to do anything other than hold her hand and let her rest her head on him while she slept. She was too upset—guilt over Rosa's condition, guilt over the death of her earlier bodyguard, and, of course, whatever baseline fear for her safety had led her to hire a bodyguard to begin with.

This girl was the kind of person who hired bodyguards. The kind of person who *could*. Vaughn wasn't sure he could really wrap his brain around that.

Scarlett kept texting, in ever more outrageous combinations of capital letters, exclamation points, and freaked-out emojis. If anyone needed one of Peacock's anti-stress smoothies, it was her.

"Hey." He nudged Orchid gently. When her eyes opened, he handed over her phone. "Scarlett seems to think we need to get back to Blackbrook."

Orchid scrolled through the texts with a single lazy finger. "Scarlett thinks you're a psychopath."

He chuckled. "Yeah, she's got some pretty colorful descriptions on there of how I supposedly murdered you."

She sat up and stretched. "Yeah. Although, also, she really does thinks you're a psychopath." She squeezed his shoulder. "Try to be nice to her, huh? I'm going to go check with the doctors."

He was nice to Scarlett. Mostly. She was never nice to him, though. She was never really nice to anyone. Vaughn didn't know when Orchid had started caring so much about Scarlett, enough to let Scarlett in on her most closely held secret.

Oliver buzzed him again. Vaughn was sending his angry reply when Orchid returned, her face pale.

"They say there's no reason to be here. She's not waking up anytime soon." She shook her head. "I got a message from my lawyers. They contacted the agency I hired Rosa from, and got in touch with her family. I arranged to have them flown out here . . . just in case."

Of course that made sense, but still. Vaughn's mind boggled. Orchid was arranging for other people's plane flights. He'd never even been on a plane.

He'd stolen—er, *borrowed*—a car stained with grease and mud and motor oil and driven her to this hospital and let her sleep on his scratchy, moth-eaten old sweater. He'd pretended she was Orchid, but she was a movie star.

"We need to get back," she said now.

"Yeah, Scarlett was pretty clear about that."

"We can't do anything to endanger your scholarship."

Vaughn shook his head and looked away. "Don't worry about me. Dr. Brown will never know. Worry about yourself."

"I can explain myself to Dr. Brown. She knew who Rosa was, remember?"

Oh, yeah. "Wait, how did you explain needing a bodyguard at the school?"

"They think I'm some trust-fund baby. All I had to do was say that after last term, my parents' agreeing to let me come back here was contingent on me having private protection."

Made sense. "You must be a very smooth liar."

She gave him a weak smile. "Yeah, well. Acting." She grabbed her coat off the chair. "Ready to go?"

On the ride back, Orchid seemed lost in thought. She toyed with the zipper on her coat, while Vaughn fought to get Rusty's ancient heater working hard enough to keep their breath from freezing in their throats. As they approached Blackbrook, Orchid fidgeted in her seat.

"I don't know if I can be here without knowing Rosa has my back. Her presence made me feel safe. Not just because of Keith, but because of all of it. The deaths, the storm. I thought I was doing better—finally moving past it all—but maybe I was just kidding myself. I felt okay because I'd *bought* protection." She gave him a guilty glance. "And it wasn't like I was really even doing that okay. I had a whole panic attack the other morning when I thought some of my stuff from the old days had gone missing from my room."

"Orchid—" he began.

She laughed mirthlessly. "Let me just sit here and get slapped upside the head with my privilege for a second. I'm not afraid it'll kill me. Unlike whatever else is happening out here."

He wished he could deny the danger. But what had Rocky Point ever given him except trouble and tragedy? "I have your back. And seven million texts say Scarlett does, too."

"True." She bit her lip and seemed to consider him, like one might a horse. "How are you with a gun?"

He gave her what he hoped was his most intimidating look.

"I'm actually an excellent shot. Remember: rural Maine, born and bred."

"Have you killed a moose?"

Killed one? Hardly. That was like asking if you'd killed an elephant. "Hitting a moose is like hitting the broad side of a barn. It's getting the chipmunks that makes you a badass."

"You are not allowed to use the words *chipmunk* and *badass* in the same sentence." But she considered what he'd said. "Fine, you're hired. But what will I do at night?"

Vaughn swallowed. Did she want him to volunteer for that duty as well? "I—" His mind went blank. Smooth, Vaughn, real smooth.

"I suppose I'll have to rely on Scarlett," Orchid said quickly.

"Good idea," he said, recovering. He grinned at her. "We both know she's way scarier than me, gun or no."

And then she really smiled. It was enough to keep him warm all the way back to Blackbrook.

He pulled up outside of Tudor House, which was silent and dark. He wondered if anyone at all was inside now.

"I'm going to go take a shower and then hurry to class," she said as they got out of the car.

"Me too," he said, then added quickly, "at home."

She giggled. "Right. So . . . see you in history class?"

Oh no, history class! He wondered if he could convince Oliver to switch with him.

She did this little twist thing with her body, as if she wasn't sure if she was walking off or not. It was really cute. She was really cute.

He was in so much trouble.

"So, until later?" She was clearly asking him a question. What was the question?

She twisted more, the bottom half of her body listing toward Tudor, the top half toward him.

"Vaughn?" she prompted.

Oh. *Oh.* She wanted him to kiss her goodbye. Right there on the lawn. In the sunlight. In front of everyone. This was definitely a boyfriend/girlfriend thing.

Vaughn could take a hint. He caught her by the hand and pulled her in. She was smiling—maybe a little too broadly as their mouths met, her teeth scraping his lip. He grimaced. Not smooth. Not smooth at all.

But Orchid only laughed and put her hand against his jaw, her fingers in his hair. "Here."

Yes, it was much better this time, with their mouths lined up just right and her hand softly stroking the side of his face. Vaughn wondered, idly, if actresses had kissing lessons, and that's why Orchid was so good at this, though he didn't know if Emily Pryce had ever been in a kissing movie.

"Bye," she whispered, still standing close. And then she blew her bangs out of her eyes and headed up the steps to the porch, and Vaughn floated back to the car, where he was so warm on the drive across the ravine to Rocky Point, he considered cracking open a window.

21

Peacock

From: *elizabeth.picach@BlackbrookAcademy.edu*
To: *ash@phoenixmanagement.org*
Subj: *Testing*

> *Hey, Ash,*
>
> *I feel like I screwed everything up. It's the day before the most important test of my life, and I couldn't sleep. I'm not saying your methods don't work—of course I'm not saying that—but I keep hearing about how other kids are getting special dispensation to take untimed tests due to stress or whatever, and it's, like, okay, smoothies and inner peace are great and all, but are we on the right track here?*
>
> *Can you call me?*
>
> *I am honored to share with you the illumination within,*
>
> *Beth*

22

Green

By the time he got back to his house, all Vaughn wanted was a shower and a nap. Fortunately, he could count on a few more hours before Oliver returned from classes and got on his case about his insane quest.

Alas, it was not to be. Instead, he found Oliver waiting for him, packed up and ready to go.

"You're supposed to be in class," Vaughn said, though he was too tired to put much anger behind his words. Of course Oliver was skipping. Of course.

"What, and ruin your alibi with your *girlfriend?*"

"Stop it. Dr. Brown said if we step out of line again, we're out."

"Like I care what she thinks? Brother, when we're done with them, they'll be begging us for scraps."

He didn't want anyone begging for scraps. He didn't want to destroy the school. He especially didn't want to remain conscious this afternoon and crawl around underground, but when had his wishes ever mattered to Oliver?

Vaughn was herded unceremoniously back into Rusty's car, and out they drove to the woods.

"I don't know why you think this is going to be any better," Vaughn said with a yawn as Oliver thrust a flashlight into his hands and shoved him toward the mouth of the tunnel.

"They did it in one of these tunnels, and we're going to search until we find out which one it was."

Vaughn brushed aside leaves and vines until he found the metal grate covering the tunnel entrance. The lock was broken and lay on the ground, and the hinges showed bright, fresh scratches, as if they'd been recently forced.

He hesitated.

"What are you waiting for?" Oliver asked. "Is it locked? I can get the crowbar out of the trunk."

"It's open," Vaughn said softly. He thought about Rusty's body, lying forgotten in the secret passage under Tudor House. He thought about Dr. Brown telling everyone that he'd died of exposure. Rusty, a Maine native. He thought about the time, during the storm, when the two of them had volunteered to take a rowboat across the flooded ravine, and it had capsized, and Vaughn had stood on his side of the rushing rapids, praying that Rusty made it out of the water alive. He remembered being so relieved when he saw the old man, soaked and freezing but waving heartily from the far side of the cliff.

What had Rusty been doing in here the night he died? Had Rusty, too, been involved in this lunatic quest for revenge? Was there more that Oliver and Mrs. White weren't telling him?

Vaughn swallowed past a lump in his throat. He didn't want to do this. He didn't want to go look for evidence that his dead grandmother had had her work stolen from her by some dead Blackbrook kid. He didn't want any more death.

"Fine." Oliver pushed past him into the tunnel. Wordlessly, Vaughn stumbled behind him.

Biting cold and the damp of the earth greeted him. Ice lined the walls, and mud crunched beneath their feet. Mrs. White had once told him that all these tunnels connected somewhere. And yet for all of Oliver's exploration of them since the storm, he hadn't been able to locate the evidence she'd told him that she and Gemma had kept hidden all these years.

But maybe Mrs. White had been lying to Oliver, sort of the way she'd lied to everyone in Tudor House about not being a murderer.

Oliver stopped a few feet ahead of him, swinging his flashlight in wide arcs. "This doesn't make sense."

Vaughn sighed. He was so tired. Tired and hungry, which only made the cold penetrate more. His feet were numb, and his fingers ached inside their mittens. "What doesn't?"

"I was here already. Just last week. This doesn't connect to the passages. It just goes to some hobo hideout."

Best news Vaughn had heard all day. "Oh, great. Well, then, this is a dud, too. Can we go?"

"No!" Oliver spun to face him, and Vaughn almost jumped back at his brother's expression. He'd seen him in many moods: angry, jealous, suspicious, triumphant. But this one was new. This one was confused. And . . . scared.

Vaughn only recognized the expression because he knew what it looked like on his own face. But he'd never seen Oliver scared in his life.

"Rusty told you about this place?" Oliver insisted.

"Yeah. He said this was the only way he knew of to get into the secret passages from outside of Tudor House."

"But Linda pointed me to some other entrance!" Oliver shouted at him. "And neither of them went where they were supposed to."

Vaughn held up his hands. "I don't know what to tell you. Maybe she didn't remember."

"She lived in that house half a century—"

"If Gemma wanted her old work found, maybe she shouldn't have put it underground," Vaughn snapped. "Think it through, Oliver! If there was really anything for *anyone* to find, maybe Linda would have come down here and gotten it sometime in the last half century." Vaughn gestured around the muddy, frozen, rubbish-clogged tunnel. "Look at this place! Do you really think this is a lab where a bunch of student scientists invented a special glue?"

What scientists in their right minds would put a lab underground, on an island? That was something out of a James Bond movie, not real life.

"You never believed it, Vaughn. You never believed it because you never believed anyone in Rocky Point could make something of themselves—except you." Oliver clenched his jaw, then spun around and shot off into the darkness.

Vaughn, dejected, followed. His flashlight sputtered, and he switched to the light on his phone.

Oliver was bobbing and weaving down the tunnel, ducking into alcoves and whipping around turns. Vaughn had to jog to keep up with him. As he got closer, he heard his brother murmuring under his breath.

"What's going on?" he asked.

But Oliver didn't answer. He just kept running. Vaughn wondered how many hours his brother had spent in the tunnels of this island, like some kind of snake, searching endlessly for a treasure that did not exist.

And how long he'd make Vaughn look.

"Stop!" he shouted.

Oliver turned.

"What are you doing?" he asked. "Why don't we just go home? Stop looking for some get-rich-quick answer. Don't try to challenge the patent. Study for our tests, study for our classes, go to college, and just get *out*. We're doing well at school—Dr. Brown even said so. Why don't we stop letting this place—*haunt* us like this—and just get out?"

"Easy for you to say, with your rich Blackbrook girlfriend," his brother scoffed.

"Can we leave her out of this?"

"How do you expect that to work, by the way?" Oliver asked. "You won't want me to pretend to be you with her, and she won't want me ignoring her. So how do you think we'll pull it off?"

"I—I don't know." He was too tired to figure it out right now. But they would figure it out. They always made it work . . . somehow.

"I do," Oliver said, his voice low and dangerous. "You'll cut me out."

Vaughn stood there, dumbfounded.

"You'll cut me out of Blackbrook the second it's no longer convenient for you to share it with me."

It had never been convenient. It had never once been convenient to sneak around and hide and make excuses for all the blank spaces in his memory. "I wouldn't do that."

"You already want to do my history project for me so you can hang out with her."

Vaughn had no response.

Oliver kept going. "This is how it'll start. A history project. Then a class. When we accept our two college scholarships, how are we going to choose who goes where? Will you get first pick? And what if we only get one scholarship? Will you be the one to take it?"

"We'll figure it out when—"

"Yeah," Oliver sniffed. "This is me figuring it out. You work your angle, Vaughn, and I'll work mine. Good twin/bad twin. Isn't that how we always do it?"

Vaughn was breathing hard. "Stop."

"No." And then Oliver turned and walked off into the darkness.

Vaughn had no choice but to follow. After a few more yards, the corridor turned and widened somewhat, into a tiny nook.

"See?" Oliver said, shining the flashlight around. "Some hobo hideout."

It certainly looked that way. A mattress on the floor. Blankets and boxes. Old newspapers taped to the walls. A conglomeration of rusted chairs and tables, plastic bags, and what looked like the bent spokes of a bicycle wheel. Broken bottles and glass.

"I think that's what someone would say if they saw your little collection in the boathouse," Vaughn replied. For years, Oliver had been nicking what he could from classrooms or lazy students. Rich Blackbrook kids shrugged off the occasional missing phone or pair of earrings. When the storm hit, he'd graduated into larger items. Mrs. White had lied about a looter murdering Headmaster Boddy—but not about there being a looter.

The main problem, as Vaughn saw it, was that Oliver was better at stealing than fencing. For all that his thievery put their position at the school in danger, they were still living off ramen noodles.

Vaughn peered more closely at the walls. The newspapers stuck there were probably for insulation. Some were old, stained with moisture and faded with time. Others appeared brand-new, reporting details of Boddy's murder, including photos of the old headmaster and even of Mrs. White. He hadn't seen these articles; it's not like they subscribed to the paper, and no journalists had come looking for Vaughn, thank goodness. A few students' parents were quoted, including the Silvermans and the Goulds, saying they would not be sending their children back to the school, and the Picachs and Currys, saying they would. Peacock's parents sounded like their daughter's own personal PR team, discussing her skill at tennis and how proud she was to play for the school. Tanner's dad, John Curry III, a school board member, said that attendance at Blackbrook was a Curry family tradition and that the event—however tragic—should not define the school's long and glorious history. The Blackbrook staff seemed to have precious little to say; they were buttoned up tight about the murder, even though their public relations staff were likely spinning just as hard as they could.

Vaughn shook his head. Maybe Oliver was right. Blackbrook was going down in flames, no matter what they chose to do. Maybe it wouldn't even last until they had a chance to graduate, especially with all these new scandals to contend with.

He stepped back, and the toe of his boot caught on a box under one of the sagging old card tables. The ancient cardboard tore like tissue paper, and the contents spilled out.

"Oops." Vaughn knelt on the damp earthen floor. Papers, yellowed and crumbling at the corners, had fallen out, along with stacks of envelopes, the rubber bands holding them together long since disintegrated. Silverfish swarmed from in between the pages.

"Come on," Oliver whined. "This isn't what we're look-ing for."

Vaughn shoved the papers back into the hole in the box, but an even bigger avalanche of envelopes toppled out. "Besides," he said, "the hobo might come back soon."

His brother snorted. "Unlikely. I scared him off pretty good the other night."

"You did?"

"I told you," he said harshly. "I've already been in this tunnel. There's nothing here."

Vaughn scowled. Just like his brother to harass a home-less man. Well, the least he could do was not leave the alcove a total mess. He was stacking the envelopes neatly when the handwriting on one of them made him stop dead in his tracks.

It was his own name.

"Oliver . . ." he whispered.

"There's got to be another entrance," his brother was saying.

Vaughn flipped to another envelope. "Oliver—"

"Maybe a trapdoor? Or a hidden passage?"

"Oliver!" Vaughn cried. He waved the letter at his brother. "Look!"

His brother shone the flashlight on the paper. His brow furrowed. "Gemma?"

Oliver tried to snatch the papers out of his hands, but Vaughn whirled around and hunched over them, balancing his flashlight in the crook of his arm as he swiped dust and creepy-crawlies from the pages.

Olivia Vaughn
Tudor House
Rocky Point, Maine

September 12, 1970
My dearest Olivia,
I will not allow us to be derailed by such puny obstacles as your parents have deployed, no more than by any other complication. I have secured enrollment at a nearby school—Blackbrook Academy. It isn't Phillips Exeter, but I never much cared for Latin, anyway. We will find a way to continue our work.
Soon, my love,
Dick

"What the hell?" Oliver said from over his shoulder. "A letter to Gemma?"

Vaughn fought to keep his hands from shaking. There *had* been something to find down here. "I think—I think it's from Dick Fain."

"What do the rest of them say?"

Vaughn opened another one.

November 3, 1970
Dear Olivia,
They told me at the house that you aren't feeling well. I hope they aren't getting to you. I know the kind of line they like to peddle

at Tudor. I'll be in the usual place, working all weekend. I haven't figured out the latest wrinkle. I need you to help me.

All my love,

Dick

January 20, 1971

Dear Olivia,

I know you're upset, but believe me: this is the best outcome for everyone. We talked about this. Neither of us wants to give up our future. Remember NASA? Remember all our plans? The town is beautiful. It'll be very happy here.

Please see reason. We're so close to everything we've worked for.

Love,

Dick

February 9, 1971

Dear Olivia,

Your friend Linda came to see me today and told me of your plans. You know what I am going to say. Linda agrees with me that it's nonsense. Do not throw your life away. The formula works. I can't do this without you. Please don't force me to make this choice.

Love,

Dick

September 20, 1971

Dear Olivia,

Thank you for the picture of Angela. You are right—she looks like a most agreeable baby. I'm sure she is quite the delight.

I am afraid I have no plans to return to Rocky Point, this fall or ever again. I have made my choice, just as you have yours. I have a meeting next week with Northeast Chem. A fellow here, John Curry, helped me set it up. Don't worry—I will always make sure both of you are taken care of. But you know where I stand on this issue. I never wanted this, for either of us.

  With deepest regrets,
  Dick

Vaughn could not believe what he was reading. Gemma's story had been true: she had invented the glue with Dick Fain. And then there'd been the story she'd never told any of them:

Dick Fain was his grandfather.

23

Peacock

From: *elizabeth.picach@BlackbrookAcademy.edu*
To: *ash@phoenixmanagement.org*
Subj: *Re: Testing*

> *Hey, Ash,*
>
> *I do feel better now. Thank you so much for calling me and talking me through it. I'll take the melatonin at bedtime, just like you suggested. Thanks for thinking ahead and sending it along. You really do think of everything.*
>
> *I wish I had thought about the untimed thing a month ago. I talked to my parents, and they said that they might be able to swing it before the makeup test—but I'll need to see a real doctor. Not you, and certainly not this sad excuse for a school counselor.*
>
> *I don't know. Do you think it's cheating? Is it still cheating if everyone does it? It's like the scoring thing all over again. Everyone does the same thing, and then I get blamed for it. It doesn't seem fair, does it?*
>
> *I am honored to share with you the illumination within,*
> *Beth*

24

Orchid

O rchid checked the bathroom for the third time, but there was no ring to be found. She was very close to unscrewing the drains. She'd already turned her room upside down and sent a group text to all the residents of Tudor House, most of whom were quite reasonably avoiding the premises ever since the night before.

All she knew was that she'd worn the ring to the hospital, and why would she have taken it off there? No, what was most likely was that she'd taken it off before she went for her shower that morning. But then, where was it?

Maybe she *had* lost it in the hospital. She'd thought it had fit all right, but cold weather could make your fingers shrink. Or something?

Or maybe she was going nuts.

Her phone dinged.

Amber

No idea, sorry! I haven't even been back to the house since everything went down. How IS Rosa, btw?

Thanks anyway. She's still critical.

Amber

OMG! I can't believe this is happening again!

Neither could Orchid. All of it was happening all over again. She put down her phone and checked her jewelry box. Again. She paced around the bedroom, caught herself wringing her hands, then heard another ding from her phone.

Amber

You have an orchid ring? That's so cute. Should I get a violet one?

Violet

Ooh, maybe we could get Rosa a rose one. Like as a get-well present?

Amber

Do you think she will? Get well, I mean.

Orchid cringed and swiped away from the group text. She opened up her thread to Vaughn, who, despite his promise, did not show at history class.

He hadn't answered her text about it, either. It stared up at her, mockingly.

> Um . . . did you fall asleep? Where are you?

Maybe she had asked too much of him, last night and this morning. They had kissed, like, *once*, and here she was, burdening him with her entire life story and obliging him to stay up all night with her in uncomfortable hospital chairs and asking him to drive her around Maine in a semi-stolen car.

Okay, they'd kissed twice. And it had been *awesome*.

But she shouldn't be letting anyone in like this. Her confession to Scarlett during the storm had been a necessary one, and apparently her confession to Vaughn had been entirely unnecessary—but, either way, it shouldn't have happened. The more people who knew her secret, the more danger she was in of losing the new life she'd built for herself. What if Dr. Brown tried to call Orchid's "parents" regarding the accident? What if Mr. Winkle knew more than he was letting on about her Hollywood past? If Vaughn had guessed, maybe the counselor had, too? Maybe everyone knew, maybe that's how Keith had found her, maybe he was on his way now . . .

Orchid realized she was wringing her hands again.

The ring wasn't in her room—that much was certain. And

if she stayed there fretting about it, she was going to have another panic attack. Instead, she headed downstairs, into the brightly lit and intensely empty public area of Tudor House.

"Hello?" she called. "Anyone here?"

"In here!" Scarlett's voice floated out of the study. Orchid followed it inside to find the other girl bent over a stack of math formula flash cards. Her usually sleek hair was in a messy topknot shot through with three number two pencils. Her oversized Blackbrook hoodie sported coffee stains. Her eyes were shadowed and red-rimmed.

All right. So they were all balls of stress.

"Are you ready?" Scarlett asked her. "I'm not ready. Here, quiz me on volume formulas." She shoved the flash cards in Orchid's direction.

Orchid stared at the formulas, feeling more removed than ever. She flopped down on the sofa. The study was still in disarray from whoever had come to close up the entrance to the secret passage. There were two-by-fours and an open box of tools piled near the fireplace. She wasn't surprised. The custodial staff had been overworked before Rusty's death, and she'd had Vaughn on the mainland this morning, instead of at his job.

"I'm shocked that Dr. Brown isn't canceling the test, with everything that's going on."

"Did she say she was going to do that?" Scarlett pounced. "She didn't say that, did she?"

"No . . . I just . . . I can't even think about this right now. I'm going to have to rely on the makeup test . . ."

"If you just take the makeup test, that's the only chance you'll have. You won't be able to improve your score—" Scarlett fumbled with her cards.

"I spent all last night in the hospital—"

"No one made you do that," Scarlett said. "You're Rosa's employer, not her sister."

"I feel responsible—"

"If you want to feel responsible," Scarlett snapped, "how about you feel responsible for all the *actual* students that you've put in this really stressful situation so that you can sail around campus with your private bodyguard? If you didn't totally overreact and hire Rosa, she never would have been here to collapse and throw this entire house into another crisis."

Orchid was taken aback. "This isn't my fault!"

"I beg to differ. If you'd told us what you were doing, maybe Mustard and I would not have gotten into trouble. I need to absolutely ace this test tomorrow, since you and your secrets wrecked the extracurriculars on my college applications. How about an apology for that?"

Orchid wasn't sure what to say. "Look, I know you're stressed. We're all stressed. I'm not sure I even feel safe around campus without Rosa here. Did you see my text about my ring?"

Scarlett rolled her eyes. "Yes, you lost your ring again. Misplaced it for the second time in two days. Does that mean your stupid stalker has found you? I don't know. Last time you lost your ring, Rosa was sleeping downstairs, so maybe she sucked as a bodyguard from the start."

"That's not fair!"

"No!" Scarlett shouted, her eyes aflame. "You know what's not fair, Orchid? That I have been standing by you, and working with you, and keeping your stupid little secret, and you didn't even trust me enough to let me know that Rosa was working for you. The other day, when I asked you about her, you could have just told me, and I never would have gotten in trouble. We're supposed to be *friends*, Orchid, but you have hurt me worse than anyone else has."

Orchid's heart was pounding. "We're friends, Scarlett? Really? Or am I just another asset on your list? You're special because you've collected a movie star who owes you every little detail about herself? What she's doing and who she's doing it with? You even think you can tell me who to *date*—"

"Oh, get over yourself!" Scarlett yelled. "You obviously don't want my advice about Vaughn, so whatever. And, yes, I *have* been your friend. Maybe you're the one who doesn't know what friendship is. Because I kept your stupid secret, and I covered for you with Dr. Brown when you stayed out all night, and I have never once tried to take advantage of you over your real identity."

Give her a break! It was the subtext of every single one of their conversations. She should date a football player or a pop star, indeed!

"Quite honestly," Scarlett added, "I would do a way better job with your fame than you ever did."

"What the hell is that supposed to mean?" Orchid said, her tone withering.

Scarlett waved her hand dismissively. "See? You never even cared to ask what was up with me. And I'm the bad friend here? And, while we're on the topic, let's talk about your precious boyfriend. Who oh-so-innocently recognized you. Yeah, right! He's an aspiring musician, Orchid. You think he wouldn't love to hitch his wagon to an actual star?"

Orchid glared at her. "That is not remotely what is happening here."

"Sure, it's not." Scarlett shrugged. "Because you know everything. You have a stalker so dangerous that you have to install a personal bodyguard in this house, but as soon as she's not here to protect you anymore, the worst said stalker can come up with is to sneak into your room and steal your ring? Which I guess he already did once? Except you got it back, so maybe it was just under the rug or something." She threw her hands up in the air. "Has it ever occurred to you that this is all in your head?"

"You saw the letter!" Orchid insisted. "Is that all in my head?"

"No. But it's easy to write a letter."

"It was way more than just a letter!" she cried. "He threatened to get his revenge on me when I gave a statement about him after my friends were found dead. Dead, Scarlett!"

"I swear, that would have impressed me more before I stumbled across two dead bodies myself."

Orchid was not amused. "You have no idea what Keith Grayson is capable of. All his clients left him. He couldn't get work in the industry any longer. He brought it all upon himself, but he totally blamed me. And three years later, I'm getting creepy letters from him! And you think this is all in my head? What about that trick he pulled with my tuition last term?"

Scarlett crossed her arms over her chest. "What did your lawyers discover when you told them about that?"

Oh, that's where this was going? "Nothing."

"And what did your private bodyguard find out, while she was still on the job?"

"Nothing," Orchid began, "but that's not the—"

"Well, then," said Scarlett. "So maybe all these people are happy to keep taking your money and reassuring you that you're safe. And if that's what you need to feel safe, maybe it is a good use of your money, or your time, or your fame. How much *did* you spend, by the way?"

"That's none of your business."

Scarlett pursed her lips. "I can tell you this for free, Orchid: there's no one coming after you. You are safe. The only people who got hurt in this house because of your past are Rosa . . ."

Orchid reeled back as if slapped.

". . . and me."

Orchid narrowed her eyes. "Yeah, you're a real friend. You don't care about me or about what I'm going through. You just care that you got in trouble."

"*Of course* I care that I got in trouble." Scarlett nodded, her eyes wide. "But you don't care at all what you did to me. You never did."

That wasn't true! If Scarlett had just . . . minded her own business, none of this would have ever happened! Orchid had been protecting herself.

"You know, I have a reputation on this campus for stabbing people in the back," Scarlett said, "but I think you've definitely won the title this time."

She gathered up her work and shoved past Orchid on the way out.

Peacock's large frame filled the doorway. "What are you two fighting about? I could hear you all the way upstairs!"

Oh, great. Add another member of the Murder Crew who now knew her secret. And Peacock was probably the worst choice of all for keeping her mouth shut.

Scarlett shot Orchid her most disgusted glance, as if she'd read her mind. "Nothing. We're having an enormous fight about absolutely nothing at all, except how important some people *think* they are, even though no one really cares."

"You don't know what you're talking about," Orchid hissed.

"Don't I?" Scarlett shrugged. "Ask yourself what would bother you more, Orchid. That you're right, and you actually have this problem, or that I'm right, and you have no reason to keep hiding except for the one in your head."

And then she left. Orchid clenched her teeth. She finally understood how it was that Peacock had thrown a candlestick at the headmaster last term. If there'd been a candlestick around, she might have bopped Scarlett with it.

Instead, she had a handful of flash cards.

She'd known that trying to make friends was a bad idea. Everything had been so much easier when she kept her nose in a book and never spoke to anyone.

And Vaughn still hadn't texted her back!

"I care," Peacock blurted, and Orchid looked at her.

"About what?"

She looked at Orchid. "About . . . about all of it. I care that we're all fighting again. That's what happened during the storm, remember?"

"Yeah, I remember," Orchid said. She slapped the cards down on the table. Under no circumstances would she be returning them to Scarlett tonight. Either Scarlett had the formulas memorized by now or she should let it go.

"Do you think it's just stress about the test?" Peacock asked. "Or about Rosa?"

"Or whatever other disaster is befalling Blackbrook today?" Orchid finished. She ran her hands through her hair and massaged her temples, as if that would make anything better. "I don't know how we're supposed to take standardized tests in the morning. And do well on them? Dr. Brown is kidding herself."

"That's what I think, too!" Peacock said. "I was just talking about this with my life coach. He keeps saying that if I'm really that nervous, I should look on this as a practice test, but Scarlett says colleges are going to average out the scores of all the tests we take, so if we really blow this one, then it's not like they'll care it was only for practice." She shook her head. "I have more chances for a comeback in a tennis match."

Orchid sighed. "What else does your life coach say?" Maybe what she really needed tonight was a taste of good, old-fashioned, California weirdo wisdom.

"Well, he also said maybe I could get an anxiety diagnosis so I can do an untimed test next time. Do you think that's cheating?"

"Only if you don't have anxiety," Orchid answered honestly.

Peacock seemed to consider this. "Don't we all have anxiety, especially after what we've been through?"

Orchid had to agree. Speaking of which . . . "What, exactly, did you hear of Scarlett and my conversation?"

"Aside from a lot of screaming about how you haven't been there for her?" She shrugged. "I don't know. To be honest, it sounded like she was already upset and just looking for a target. I used to get like that all the time. I would take it out on my opponents or even my teammates. I mean—you saw me with Mustard. With . . . with Headmaster Boddy." She hung her head. "I have been working so hard on all of that. But I'm not sure it's making me a better person. I feel as scared as I ever did before."

Orchid thought about that. She, too, had been fighting to be a better person. She'd told herself over and over that Orchid McKee was much better than Emily Pryce. She was stronger, bolder, smarter. She was a student and a scientist.

But she'd been hiding, too. She'd been panicking about who knew her secret and what they were going to the do with the information. She'd been papering over her problems with money. She'd been telling herself that even this little romance she was cooking up with Vaughn was too much for her to handle.

Maybe Peacock was right, and this was just stress talking.

"We're scared because this place is scary," she said. "We're scared because there's no one here telling us that it's going to be okay."

"Ash tells me it's going to be okay," Peacock replied. "He said take some melatonin, drink some water, and get a good night's sleep, and I'll feel better by tomorrow."

"That sounds nice. You should keep him around." Maybe she should try getting a life coach. Having a manager had been a disaster. Having a bodyguard hadn't worked out so well, either, both times she'd tried it. "What's melatonin, anyway?"

"Some sleeping aid," Peacock said. "Ash said it's totally natural, so I can take as much as I want."

Orchid made a face. "I mean, arsenic is totally natural, too. Poisonous mushrooms are totally natural. Natural isn't always a good thing."

"You sound like Finn."

"Don't tell me that!" Orchid exclaimed.

"Do you want some or not?" Peacock shook the bottle at her.

Orchid thought about it. Despite everything that was going on, she had still managed to sleep last night. In a hard hospital chair, too.

But she'd had Vaughn with her. Vaughn, who smelled of Maine ice and old wool, who had dropped everything to drive her out to the hospital, who had stayed with her all night and then kissed her the next morning, when she hadn't showered or changed or brushed her hair and probably looked like the farthest thing possible from a movie star.

Vaughn, who hadn't responded to her all afternoon.

"Well, give me a couple, and I'll think about it." She held out her hand, and Peacock shook two pills into it.

"I am honored to share with you the illumination within," said Peacock, clasping her hands and bowing in front of Orchid.

Orchid looked at the pills. "Except in this case, I guess it's more *lights out?*"

Peacock laughed. "Yeah, I guess it is."

Then they parted ways.

But back in the hall, Orchid thought better of it. After all, this was how things had begun with the Steelman twins. Pills to help them sleep, help them wake up, make sure they didn't gain weight or feel pain or do anything other than exactly what Keith wanted, when he wanted them to do it. So many pills, it had been easy to write off what happened to those girls as a party drug–fueled accident. Or a suicide pact.

But Orchid knew better.

Jen and Kate had been planning to run away. They were going to start new lives, away from all the prying eyes and the demands Keith made on them. They were going to start over, as normal girls, with normal lives, like the orchids in the film the three of them had made.

They'd never gotten the chance.

So Orchid had taken it. She'd lived the normal life the Steelmans had wanted. Or at least, she planned to.

And maybe that meant ditching the bodyguards. It definitely meant not taking any pills not specifically prescribed to her by a doctor. She dropped them into the wastebasket and headed up the stairs.

Maybe Scarlett was right. Maybe Keith had dropped his plans for revenge. Maybe the letter was from someone else who had tracked her down. Maybe it was even from someone who had, despite her precautions, recognized her here at Blackbrook.

Like Vaughn had.

Orchid thought about what Scarlett had said, that Vaughn's interest in her was because he, too, was an aspiring performer and might think she had some kind of influence in the entertainment industry. She thought about all the clips of him sitting in his room and performing songs he'd sent her over the last month.

She thought about how sheepishly he'd confessed to her last night that he'd known all along who she really was.

You're Orchid McKee to me.

That's what he'd said. But was it true?

As if she'd summoned him with her thoughts, her phone buzzed in her pocket.

Vaughn

> Sorry. I fell asleep. Everything okay?

Nothing was okay. She and Scarlett were screaming at each other. Rosa was in a coma. Her ring was missing. People were dying.

> Not really. Everyone in this house is flipping out over the tests tomorrow.

Vaughn

> Oh, so totally normal, then?

She smiled in spite of herself.

Vaughn

> Any word on Rosa?

> No change. Do you think you can come by tonight?

There was no answer. Orchid bit her lip and started typing.

> I know it's silly. We have the test and everything. And you should get your rest. You really need to ace it. It's just, I don't know, it's been a weird couple of days and—

A new text buzzed through.

Vaughn

> I have a couple of things I have to do
> tonight, but I can come by after. If
> you don't think Dr. Brown will freak.

Orchid deleted her half-typed message. Vaughn was coming. That was all that mattered.

> I don't think she's even around
> tonight. But thank you for making the
> time! I missed you in history.

Did that last part sound needy? Oh, well, too late now. She went up the stairs and back into her room. Screw Scarlett. Vaughn wasn't after anything. He just liked her, same way she liked him.

Right?

She closed the door behind her and sat down on her bed. Maybe she should have taken those melatonin pills. Although that might mean she'd be out before Vaughn arrived.

She reached to put her cell phone on its charging pad next to the bed and froze.

Her orchid ring was sitting right there on the bedside table, plain as day.

25

Plum

Finn had given up entirely on the concept of sleep. He knew every other junior on campus was either going to bed early or squeezing in one more practice run. But he couldn't bring himself to care one tiny bit about a standardized test. What did it matter? He had his dye. If he wanted to go to college, he could go. If he didn't, well, maybe he'd start a lab of his own.

His skin seemed to buzz. Most of his classes today had been an utter blur. He'd spent all of chemistry, for instance, staring longingly out the window at the actual chemistry building, where his precious dye was even now safely hidden behind a ceiling panel. Where he and Mustard had placed it. After kissing.

Because that was the other thing that had happened.

There was a part of Finn that wondered if he should be freaking out right about now. Mustard certainly had been last night, even though the other boy had claimed he'd made out with a guy before. But Finn felt—well, not fine, but certainly not freaked. Like everything else, he put it in a data file along with whatever other point of reference he could suddenly recall—a love of a certain series of superhero movies, or the way he used to get tongue-tied around his older brother's swim-team buddies—and he came to the only rational conclusion: he did like girls, but . . . also . . . guys?

He wondered what amazing discovery he might make next.

Finn had spent the day alternately excited and terrified to see Mustard again. Sam? He really, really wanted to be called Mustard, apparently, and Finn supposed he should respect that, even if it was completely ridiculous. They hadn't seen each other, though, which was probably a good thing, as he hadn't the slightest idea what he was supposed to do. How he was supposed to behave.

What it all meant.

There was a time that he could have brought any or all of this up with Scarlett, but Scarlett had ignored his existence in all their shared classes today. He'd even eaten lunch with Beth—or what passed for lunch, because he'd had the dining hall's vegetable soup and grilled cheese sandwich, and she'd had three so-called "brain-boosting" cocktails that looked and smelled like something that might grow in the secret passages under Tudor House.

Finn wasn't entirely sure about this life coach of hers. But given how stressed she seemed to be over her tests, he didn't want to rock the boat until afterward.

He also couldn't talk to her about Mustard. The nice thing about this whole life-coach business was that it seemed to solidify whatever truce they'd come to during the storm. They were friends now, he and Beth, and though he was certain that friends should not let friends drink mushroom smoothies, he still wasn't entirely clear on when friends should talk to friends about who they were making out with. Especially if said friends used to make out with each other.

But he had to talk to *someone.*

He looked across the dark room at Jin, who was lying on his bed, watching a movie on his laptop with his headphones on. Jin was a very considerate roommate.

"Hey," he called, and waved.

Jin looked up.

"Don't you have your test tomorrow?"

Jin shook his head, and his eyes never left the screen. "Nah, man. My parents made me take it over break in Singapore. In case this place didn't open again." He grinned. "So glad to have that over with. You?"

"Yeah," Finn said. "But I don't know. I can't really get myself excited about it." The one practice test he'd taken, back before the storm, he'd aced math and done well enough on verbal not to be embarrassed.

"Well, you're already a shoo-in for . . . wherever—MIT, Caltech, Stanford—where do you want to go, anyway?"

"Yeah, any of those would be fine." Finn shrugged. "Hey, do you have a girlfriend?"

Jin's brow furrowed. "Why are you asking?"

"I don't—no reason." Finn spun his chair back around. *Good talk, roomie.*

"I'm kind of talking to someone online," Jin said then. "I don't know if that counts."

Finn looked down at his hands. "I never know what counts."

"Is this about you having lunch with Peacock?" Jin asked. "I saw you today, in the dining hall. You two getting back together?"

"Ah," Finn said. "No, that's all over."

"She's hot . . ."

Finn stood up. "You know what? I'm going to go for a walk."

"Attaboy," said Jin, and snapped his headphones back into place. "Go get her."

Hardly. Finn put on his winter gear and headed into the hall. But instead of leaving the building, he just went upstairs, as if his feet were making all his decisions.

Maybe not his feet. But certainly not his head.

And then there he was, outside Tanner and Mustard's door. He bit his lip, took a deep breath, and knocked.

A few moments later, Tanner answered the door, his expression more serious than Finn had ever seen it.

"Who died?" Finn asked. Tanner did not smile. Finn felt cold. After all, this was Blackbrook. "Oh my God, who died?"

"What do you want, Finn?" Tanner asked tonelessly.

"Is, um, Mustard here?"

"No." There was a sound in the room behind him. Tanner's girlfriend, probably. Maybe he'd interrupted a breakup.

"I'm going to go," said the voice. It was one Finn recognized. "Thanks for listening."

"Yeah," said Tanner. "I'll talk to you later."

The door opened wide, and Vaughn Green emerged.

"Hey." Finn nodded to Vaughn. "Were you looking for Mustard?"

"No," Vaughn replied simply. He pushed by and headed down the hall.

With nothing better to do, Finn followed. "Hey, wait up!"

Vaughn cast a glance over his shoulder. "What do you want, Finn?"

Why did people keep asking him that? He didn't know.

"I—um—I can't sleep."

"Yeah, well, join the club."

"The Murder Crew?"

"Whatever." Vaughn headed down the stairs toward the exit.

Finn followed. Out on the lawn, Vaughn seemed to shrink into his coat, some natural Maine posture to protect against the elements that Finn had never properly figured out. He wrapped his scarf around his face one more time and jogged to catch up.

Vaughn was walking toward a junky car parked on the street.

"I didn't know you had a car," Finn tried.

"It's Rusty's."

Finn tripped over his feet. Right. Rusty. Rusty Nayler, whose corpse had fallen on Finn's head a few nights ago. Rusty, who had been murdered.

Finn had promised Mustard he'd try to help.

"Can I talk to you about—about Rusty?"

Now Vaughn turned around. He, too, looked like death warmed over. Finn supposed the old man's death had hit Vaughn pretty hard. They had worked together on the custodial staff. He had Rusty's old car.

Finn would have to be careful. "I'm really sorry about all that, by the way."

"At least you found him," Vaughn said. "Who knows how long he might have been left to rot in there otherwise? It's not like anyone at the school cared that he was even gone. I worked with him, and it took—it took even me too long to notice." He looked out over the campus, which was choked with caution tape and darkened, abandoned buildings. "You think there's any hope for this place? Or is it just going to fall to pieces, anyway?"

"I don't know," Finn said. "Maybe it would be better if it did?" It would certainly be better for him. If there were no Blackbrook, there would be no claims on his work.

"Maybe." Vaughn sighed. "What were you going to ask me about Rusty?"

"Well, it's not really a question. It's just—remember how Dr. Brown said he died of natural causes?"

Vaughn narrowed his eyes. "Yes?"

"I—" Why was this so hard? "I—I don't know if it was. I think maybe he was murdered."

Vaughn snorted. "Why, because this is Blackbrook?"

"No, because he had a head wound. I saw it."

Vaughn was silent.

"I'm not sure what to do. Tell Dr. Brown, or the police? I don't know how to go about saying anything. Do you know his family?"

"He doesn't really have any family on Rocky Point," Vaughn said. "Are you sure it wasn't—I don't know—something that happened after he died?"

"Yes," Finn blurted. "Because that's not all I know."

Vaughn came closer. "What else?"

"A couple of days ago in the tunnels under the school, there was some kind of fight—I don't know if it was students or townies or what. But Rusty was down there that night."

Vaughn's eyes were wide. "What! How do you know about any of this?"

Finn shook his head. "It doesn't matter."

"It does!" The other boy looked frantic. "I—I didn't say anything to you, did I?"

"What are you talking about?" This was why Finn needed Scarlett. He needed a way to tell this story without implicating himself or Mustard. This was not Finn's specialty. Scarlett would be able to find a reasonable lie, a believable excuse.

Vaughn grabbed him by the arm. "What do you know?"

Finn tried to yank his arm back. "Nothing! Rusty went down there to get something. For—"

"Yeah." Vaughn let him go. "For a payout. I know how Rusty operates—operated." He cursed under his breath. "You said it was a fight with townies? Townies, you're sure?"

"I don't know. Maybe. I can get into the details at the police station. That's what we should do, right?"

"No!" Vaughn cried. "I mean—let's figure out what's going on, first."

Now, that, Finn was surprised to hear. He figured Vaughn, of all people, would want to see justice done. Besides, Rusty was dead. It wasn't like the man could get in trouble for taking bribes now. "But—"

"Why is Dr. Brown insisting it was natural causes?" Vaughn went on. "And—I mean, does it have anything to do with whoever was bribing Rusty—and—" He stumbled backward. "Maybe they didn't even realize it was Rusty . . ."

"The townies who jumped him?" Finn asked. He should say not.

Vaughn looked like he was about to be sick. Finn felt worse than ever. All he'd wanted to do was get a little input, a little help. But who knew what can of worms he'd just opened?

"I gotta go," Vaughn mumbled.

"To see Orchid?"

"Um . . ." Vaughn shook his head. "Yeah." And then he hurried away to his car.

"But Tudor is right over there!" Finn pointed, but Vaughn got into the car and drove off.

Finn watched the red taillights vanish into the distance and thought there was a better than even chance that Mustard had once been in that car. With Rusty.

Well, this was just perfect. He hoped he hadn't made things worse. All he was trying to do was protect Mustard.

And his dye. Of course.

But also Mustard. Because Finn was pretty sure that if he'd somehow inadvertently managed to implicate him in Rusty's murder, there wasn't a chance in hell that Mustard would ever kiss him again.

26

Mustard

The group of Blackbrook students who had gathered to take their tests on this still, foggy morning looked more like they were lining up for a firing squad. Mustard could have sworn he'd seen more enthusiastic expressions on the faces of Farthing plebes about to go on a four-day survivalist hike.

He didn't understand it, personally. From everything he was given to understand, their parents were paying their extraordinarily high tuitions to Blackbrook so as to ensure that, even if they were idiots, they'd be duly selected for acceptable Ivy League or Ivy League–adjacent colleges. They could simply put their names on the test and walk away, just as easily as their parents could put their names on the buildings they donated to the schools they wanted their children to attend.

Money talked in this world. Mustard had picked up on that right away. He'd even tried to make it talk for him, for all the good it had done.

He'd been surprised to see Tanner so stressed out, last night as well as this morning. His roommate never seemed upset about anything, but Mustard had heard him tossing and turning all night long, and when Mustard came back from the shower this morning, he'd caught the tail end of a fight he was having with someone on the phone. Mustard wasn't sure what the argument was about. Maybe he'd been hoping for a last-minute reprieve. Mustard knew a bunch of his classmates had made alternate arrangements, due to the stress and anxiety of just being at Blackbrook.

Mustard had taken a practice test. His score was adequate. It would be enough for him to get into West Point, if West Point would have him with an expulsion on his record.

And if not . . . well, the army didn't even require standardized test scores to enlist.

All of that, of course, assumed that he didn't get kicked out of another school.

Their proctor showed up eventually and unlocked the door to let them all into the testing room. It was one of the nicer rooms at Blackbrook—one of the nicer ones remaining, anyway—with wood paneling, spacious desks, and giant windows to let in daylight. Not that there was much daylight to be had today. The fog was thick and slate gray, and the air felt heavy, as if half of the sea itself had blown in over the island.

He watched the students shuffle in, some with travel mugs full of coffee, others with fistfuls of number two pencils. He tried not to think too hard about who was there and who wasn't. Of the Murder Crew, he saw only Scarlett and Peacock, and both girls looked ready to vibrate out of their socks with nerves. Orchid and Green were MIA.

So was Plum.

Mustard wondered if Plum, too, had gotten out of the tests. Or if he should call him. Just in case.

"Okay," said their proctor, "let's get settled in here. I want to get started on time. Everyone, take your seats."

Mustard found a seat somewhere in the middle. Scarlett, he saw, was sitting in the front row, and Peacock was sitting beside her. Tanner was with Amber, who had brought enough pencils for the entire class.

The hairs rose on the back of Mustard's neck just as the door opened.

"You're late," said the proctor. Every eye in the room turned toward the newcomer.

Plum.

"Sorry," said Plum. He scanned the room, and his gaze snapped to Mustard, as if a magnet connected them. Uh-oh. Plum skirted around the rows of desks and slid into a seat beside him right before Violet Vandergraf could do so.

This wasn't good. Mustard looked down at his desk, where he'd apparently pressed the tips of both of his number two pencils too hard into the surface and broken them.

That wasn't good, either.

"Hey," said Plum under his breath.

"Hey," Mustard replied. Could he borrow more pencils from Amber? Was there a pencil sharpener up front?

"I have to talk to you."

People were passing back thick envelopes with the test materials sealed inside.

"Not a great time."

"I think I might have made a tiny mistake yesterday."

"Oh yeah?"

"No talking!" the proctor called out from the front of the room.

"Sorry, ma'am," said Mustard. "I broke my pencil."

Amber's head popped up. "Here, have a few of mine." She started passing them back.

The proctor crossed her arms. "Okay, now, is everyone adequately supplied?"

There were nods all around the classroom.

"Mustard," Plum hissed under his breath. "I think I might have let Vaughn know too much about . . . things."

Mustard's head whipped up. "What things?"

Plum held up his hands. "What you told me. About . . . Rusty . . .?"

Better. Not much better, but better. "You told him?" He gritted his teeth. "You were supposed to *help*, not—"

"I thought I *was* helping. Vaughn was close to that guy. And I figured maybe he'd know his family in Rocky Point, but—he got really upset."

"What are you telling me?"

Finn shrugged. "I don't know. Maybe nothing. I figured maybe I could talk to him this morning before the test, but I was waiting out by the bridge to Rocky Point, and he didn't come in. So then I thought maybe I'd missed him, but he isn't here, either."

"Ahem." They both looked up to see the proctor standing between them. "I thought I was very clear about the 'no talking' instruction. What's next, you guys fill in the bubbles with ink?"

"Sorry, ma'am," said Plum.

Mustard frowned, toying with the edge of his test packet. Green wasn't here at the test, and neither was his girlfriend, Orchid. Wherever they were, they were probably together.

"Hey, Scarlett," Mustard called. "You didn't happen to see Orchid this morning, did you?"

Scarlett turned in her seat, rolled her eyes, and said, "Like I care what she's doing."

That surprised Mustard. She usually cared what everyone was doing.

The proctor frowned. "There are students missing? Dr. Brown assured me no one would be late."

"There are several students missing," volunteered Violet.

The proctor went back up to the front desk and shuffled through her papers for what Mustard assumed was a list of the kids taking the test.

"No one talked to Orchid?" Mustard addressed the room. All the girls from Tudor House exchanged guilty glances.

This was why barracks were better than all these private rooms. No one was ever late to anything if everyone slept in the same room.

"I hope she didn't oversleep!" cried Peacock. "I was just— so involved this morning, I didn't even think to knock on everyone's doors . . ."

"She's fine, trust me," said Scarlett. "She's not going to have any problem getting into the college of her dreams. People like her never do."

"What's that supposed to mean?" asked Amber.

"No. Talking!" announced the proctor, her eyes wide with disbelief. "Now, excuse me for a minute while I call Dr. Brown. Do not unseal those packets. And do not talk." She exited the room.

Of course, everyone started talking at once.

Peacock thought Orchid and Vaughn must be back at the hospital on the mainland. Maybe Rosa had taken a turn for the worse overnight?

Amber and Violet opined that that was why they all should have been given untimed tests, just from the stress of living in Tudor House.

Scarlett rubbed her temples and told everyone to calm down and that if Orchid and Vaughn missed their tests, then it was their own fault.

Plum picked that moment to turn to Mustard. "Hey, so . . . here's the thing. On the off chance that the two of them are . . . I don't know, going to the cops on the mainland right now? Is there anything in the secret passage that might connect things to you? Or, um, me?"

Mustard shushed him. "This is not the place to discuss this."

Plum looked around. He was by far the chillest person in the room. "Then let's get out of here."

"Don't you care about the test?"

Plum shoved his packet away from him. "Not as much as I care about you not getting framed for murder."

For a moment, the chaos in the room seemed to fade away. Mustard caught his breath and looked at Plum—really looked. The floppy brown hair falling over his glasses, the winter-pale skin, and the slight blush that grew as Mustard kept looking— from his cheeks to his jaw and down his neck, right into the collar of his button-down shirt.

And then he realized that everyone else had grown silent, and that was probably why Plum was blushing.

"What do you mean, *murder*?" Scarlett asked. "Who got murdered?"

"Headmaster Boddy?" prompted Violet. "Duh."

Mustard looked around. Every person in the room was now staring at him and Plum. Some of them had stood up.

"Are you talking about Rusty?" Scarlett continued. "Was that a murder?"

"Yes," said Plum.

Mustard glared at him.

"I told you that the other night, Scarlett," he went on, with a meaningful glance at Mustard. "Remember? I told you I thought he had a head wound."

"Oh my God," said Violet. "That's—that's *two* murders in Tudor House. I'm never sleeping there again!"

"Why would anyone murder Rusty?" asked Amber. "The cleanup isn't going that badly."

"Maybe he found out something he shouldn't," said Scarlett. "About the school's plans for Rocky Point. Just like with Mrs. White, except they decided to shut him up first."

"But Mrs. White was the murderer," said Peacock. "She didn't *get* murdered."

"Please stop saying 'murder'!" begged Violet.

"Guys," said Tanner. "Calm down. Rusty was a townie. No one on campus knew him like the locals. If someone held a grudge against him, isn't it more likely that it was one of them?"

"Yes!" Plum pointed at Tanner. He shot Mustard a triumphant smile. "That's exactly what I think. Some feud on Rocky Point."

"Oh my God," said Amber. "Is that why Vaughn isn't here? Did he murder Rusty? Is he on the lam?"

Mustard shut his eyes. Sure, divert attention from him and refocus it on the only purely innocent kid on this campus. The one who'd done what Mustard should have from the start and gone to the police with the information he had.

Mustard's choice was clear.

Outside the room, their proctor had noticed the commotion and now came back in, her expression appalled. "What is going on in here? Everyone back in your seats. If you all don't get your behavior under control at once, I'll be forced to collect your packets, and you'll all get zeroes."

"Really?" asked Scarlett in her signature withering tone. "How are you going to score us if we haven't even put our names on them yet?"

"In your seat, young lady." The proctor pointed. Scarlett sat.

The others followed suit. Mustard, too, after a moment.

He looked at his test packet.

He thought about Green, who had raged at the idea of Dr. Brown covering up Rusty's true cause of death. He thought about how he would have felt in Green's shoes, to learn that other people in the Murder Crew might know the truth and were hiding it for selfish reasons.

He thought of the way he'd hidden in those passages and listened to shouts and screams and didn't go back to help Rusty.

And how maybe Rusty was dead because of him.

"All right," said the proctor from the front of the room. "When I give the signal, you may open your test packets. You will have sixty-five minutes for the first section."

Mustard stood up. "I need to be excused."

The proctor was unmoved. "You should have gone to the bathroom before this."

"I'm not going to the bathroom," he replied. "I'm—I'm just going."

He dropped his pencils on his desk and walked out. Gasps erupted behind him. The proctor shouted to get everyone's attention.

And then the door shut behind him. Blissful silence. Icy Maine fog. Mustard started down the hill.

"Sam!"

He kept going.

"Mustard!"

Now he stopped and took a breath. He turned around to find Plum racing after him, his coat unbuttoned, his scarf streaming behind him like a flag. Plum had abandoned the test. For him.

Or, more likely, for his stupid dye.

"What are you doing?" he asked when Plum reached him. It came out sounding very annoyed. Which was probably for the best.

"What are *you* doing?" Plum panted.

"I'm going to the cops."

"That's what I was afraid you were going to say." Plum shook his head. "Don't do that unless we have a plan."

"That is the plan," said Mustard. "I'm going to the cops, and I'm telling them what I know."

"All of it?"

"I'll leave your precious dye out of it, if that's what you're asking."

Plum was fighting to keep up. "That's actually *not* what I'm asking, but while we're on the subject, how do you intend to do that? What reason did you have to bribe Rusty to get into that tunnel if it wasn't to get the dye?"

"I was trying to sneak into the girls' dorm, of course," he said. "Everyone will believe that."

Plum was quiet. Because Mustard was right. Everyone would believe that. It was easy to believe that of someone like Mustard. What was hard to believe was the other thing.

They walked on, and with every step, Mustard's heart pounded harder. They reached the administration building and stepped into the shadow of the colonnade.

Mustard felt the touch of fleece-covered fingers on his freezing hand. "Wait."

He looked at Plum. The other boy was still out of breath,

his cheeks bright pink from the cold. His eyes were intent on Mustard when he spoke. "I know you think you have to do this, and maybe you're right. I'm certainly not the person who can tell you whether you're wrong or right—about anything, maybe." He smiled and lifted his shoulders. "But . . ."

"But what?" Mustard asked him. Their hands were still touching, but Mustard could not bring himself to move away. "You're not going to come up with a clever solution this time, Professor. This is what it is."

Plum's mouth became a narrow line. "Okay." He nodded. "Then we go together."

"What?" Mustard asked, disbelieving.

"We go together," he said again. "Murder Crew forever."

His fingers tightened around Mustard's.

The fog was thick. The campus was deserted. And the shadows beneath the colonnade were very, very deep.

27

Peacock

Beth

Hey, Ash. I know it's early out there, but I could really use a super quick pep talk before my test. REALLY nervous here. Can you call me?

Beth

I hope you get this before the test starts. Totally freaking out. A bunch of the kids who were supposed to show up did not. Do you think they got last-minute excuses to take the untimed version? It's so unfair.

Beth

I feel like at least Orchid would have told me if she'd gotten it. I saw her last night. But she's not here.

Beth

And Vaughn isn't here, either, and I don't think he would have gotten one. Right? He's a scholarship kid.

Beth

Not that I'm saying that only rich kids can get diagnosed with anxiety. Vaughn probably is under more stress than all of us. Mrs. White was supposedly his godmother. And he worked for Rusty. Okay, gotta go, they say the test is starting. Fingers crossed!

Beth

OMG, Ash, all hell just broke loose. Plum announced that Rusty was MURDERED, and then Mustard WALKED OUT of the test. The proctor Flipped. Her. Lid.

Beth

She's calling Dr. Brown now. I don't even know if this test is still happening.

Beth

It's not still happening . . . right?

28

Orchid

Orchid woke up to the type of dreary morning that was a signature at Blackbrook all winter long. A deep fog blanketed the campus, shrouding everything in a gray twilight that could as easily be seven A.M. as noon.

She rolled over and reached for her phone to check the time, but the charging station by her bedside table was empty. She felt around in the covers for it, remembering dimly that she'd fallen asleep with it clutched her fist, waiting late into the night for a text from Vaughn that had never come.

He'd stood her up. Again.

She sat up in bed and ran a hand through her wild nest of hair. She'd fallen asleep in leggings and a sweater last night, reluctant to change into pajamas in case Vaughn had at last shown up. She checked the floor for her phone. It had to be around here somewhere. Though Orchid figured it must still be pretty early, as her alarm hadn't gone off. And she knew her phone had enough juice to last until morning without being charged. If it was time to get up, her alarm would have woken her.

No phone on the floor around her bed.

The familiar sense of panic rose, hot and itchy, in her throat. No. No. No more panic attacks. No more freaking out over missing items that turned out later just to be misplaced. Her phone was around here somewhere.

She shook out her duvet, listening for the telltale thump of her phone flying free of the covers and landing on the floor.

Nothing.

Super annoying. But she didn't have the luxury of fretting about it this morning. There was a test to get to. Orchid went over to her laptop and opened it up.

The time was 8:53.

Okay—now freak out. The test was supposed to start at nine!

How had she not woken up? Why had no one come to get her? What a time to be in a fight with Scarlett! Scarlett would have woken her, surely! You know, if they were speaking to each other.

She grabbed her coat and a stocking cap for her wild hair, slipped her feet into her boots, and made for the door. Halfway to the stairs, she wondered if anyone else had slept in.

"Hello?" she called. She ran down the stairs into the hall. "Is anyone still here? The test is about to start!"

"In here!" called a voice from the study. It sounded like Scarlett.

Orchid shook her head. It would be just like the other girl to have fallen asleep on her precious flash cards last night.

"Scar?" she said, and headed toward the study. "Come on—we have to get to the testing room."

She stepped inside, and her gaze went immediately to Scarlett's favorite study spot.

But Scarlett wasn't there.

Behind her, she heard the door shut. A chill stole across her skin.

"Hi, Emily," said a voice.

Somehow, she turned, although every muscle in her body was frozen as solid as the ice outside the windows. Standing in front of the door was a man in a soft blue sweater and a pair of sweatpants. He'd put on weight since she'd seen him, a little middle-aged paunch. His hair was longer and streaked with blond. But his eyes were the same as ever, alight with interest when they landed on her, as if she were a bug he might choose to examine or squash at will, and on his face he wore a cruel, eager smile.

Somehow she spoke, although the words sounded breathy and trembling. "Hi, Keith."

He gestured to the chair by the fireplace. "Have a seat."

"No, thank you," she replied. The blood rushed in her ears. Her heart pounded so hard, she thought it might burst from her chest. "I have a test to get to."

"Yes, I know. Everyone is already there. I think you're going to miss it, though." He pointed again. "Sit."

Her entire childhood, she'd been forced to do exactly what Keith Grayson said, whenever he'd said it. Her mother hadn't helped her. No one had. And even though she'd been free for three years, that tone in his voice was one her body wanted to obey. It knew the consequences if she didn't.

Orchid sat. "I knew you were coming for me."

"Of course you did," he replied. "I told you I was."

"But the lawyers—"

"Well, I wasn't going to tell anyone else, was I?" He came a step forward but kept his body firmly between her and the door.

Orchid glanced at the window. What if she screamed?

Keith noted the direction of her focus. "The nice thing about this house, I've learned, is that it's very far away from the rest of campus."

He'd learned? How long had he been there?

"No one will bother us, and we certainly won't bother anyone, no matter how loud we might get in this conversation."

She got it. No point in screaming.

"All your housemates are at that test," he went on. "They can't miss it. It's too important. And your terrible headmaster is trying to right the ship. And your bodyguard?" He shrugged. "She wasn't very useful in the end, was she? So fragile. How could someone with such a terrible allergy get so far in this business? I guess that's why she never made it in the Marines . . ."

Orchid swallowed. "Did you poison her?"

"What an imagination you have, Emily!" he exclaimed, and clucked his tongue. "First all those lies about the pills I gave the twins, and now this?"

"You *did* give the twins pills," she said sharply.

"I suppose you got warped, growing up in the fast lane in Hollywood," he continued, as if she'd said nothing.

"You put me in that lane!"

"And you keep blaming everyone else for your own problems. Your own failures. And then you ran away. But you aren't doing any better here, are you?"

Orchid kept waiting for the panic attack to take her away. But it wasn't. She felt—not calm, but not out of control, either. She felt like a fighter. "I'm doing great here. I love my life. And I don't have to deal with any more creeps."

She saw it—the flare of rage in his eyes. The lips pulled to a tight, thin line. "Really? What about that boy you've been seeing?"

"Vaughn's not—"

"Oh, he's a creep, all right. He sneaks around the secret passages of this house even more than I do."

Orchid didn't even know where to start. "He—what are you talking about? Vaughn would never—"

"I saw him, Emily. I confronted him, down in the passages. You think I don't look out for you, but I do. I always have. You're the one who has been ungrateful."

Orchid couldn't listen. He was lying. What possible reason would Vaughn have to be sneaking around the secret passages?

And how would he get into her locked room, anyway?

Mrs. White was his godmother.

He worked custodial.

No! Orchid clenched her hands into fists. "Did you steal my phone? And my ring? And my bear? And then put them back?"

And if so, how would *Keith* have gotten the keys to her room?

Keith was silent for a second, just looking at her. Then he smiled broadly. "See? You don't even know. Was it me? Was it your boyfriend? Did it happen at all?"

"Stop it!" she shouted.

"You're a real mess. But so is every other kid at this school. Trust me, I've been keeping careful track."

Maybe she should just keep him talking. Like in the movies. You kept the bad guy talking, and eventually someone showed up to help.

Hopefully.

So Keith had been lurking in the passages. He'd been sneaking into her room while she slept. She shuddered. She didn't know what he was talking about when it came to Vaughn, though. Vaughn hadn't been in the passages—that was Finn and Scarlett.

And . . . Rusty. Orchid bit back a gasp. Vaughn had always insisted Rusty could not have died from natural causes. What if he was right? What if Keith had killed him and taken his custodial keys so as to have access to all the locked rooms of the house—

She heard the buzz of a phone. Maybe it was her friends, wondering where she was as the test began.

It buzzed again.

And again.

Keith chuckled. "Are you looking for your phone, Emily?"

"Why, do you have it?" she managed to ask without her voice shaking.

"I have *my* phone," he said. "You can't be trusted to manage your own things, it seems."

"Not if you keep stealing them!"

"I thought we decided it was your sneaky boyfriend doing that. It's definitely what they'll say later."

Her heart dropped into her stomach. *Later?* "What's your plan, Keith?"

He pulled a phone out of his pocket, glanced at it, and shook his head. "All you girls are such train wrecks. It's really sad. You have so much potential. Is it bad parenting, you think?"

"Yes," Orchid said. "And even worse management."

He gave her a dangerous look. "Watch your mouth. I spent three years rebuilding what you stole from me, the reputation you demolished. And why? That's the part I could never understand, Emily. You were leaving the business. It wasn't like I was going to make any more money from you."

She couldn't believe this. He thought it was about money?

Keith looked sincerely gutted. "Why did you need to destroy me so thoroughly?"

"I did nothing to you," Orchid said. Her eyes burned with unshed tears. "You did it all to yourself. I had to tell the truth, to make sure others weren't hurt, the way you hurt me. The way you hurt the twins."

"The twins!" Keith crowed. "I didn't hurt them! They fired me. They fired *me*. That was the start of the whole mess. All I did was make them a massive success, and they wanted to just walk away?"

Run away, more like. But they hadn't gotten far. The twisted remains of Jen Steelman's car had been found at the bottom of the canyon near their house in the Hollywood Hills. Jen and Kate had both been inside.

"Bad things happen when you leave me," Keith said. "It happened to the Steelmans, and it happened to you."

"Nothing bad has happened to me," Orchid forced out from between clenched teeth.

"I'm sorry, weren't you kidnapped and held at gunpoint by your dorm mother last month, after being stranded on a flooded campus where your headmaster was killed in front of you?"

Well, he had said he'd been keeping track. Orchid hugged herself. Of course, the story had been in the news. She'd been careful that her own name had never appeared. The only kids named were the ones who had come forward to issue statements. That would never be Orchid McKee.

"And then more murders on campus. Even your own bodyguard!"

"Rosa is not dead."

"Yet," Keith observed. "But she's going down. Just like I'm going to rise again. Like a phoenix from the ashes."

He sounded ridiculous. "You always did have terrible taste in scripts."

He glared at her. "I'm not even in show business anymore. Didn't the lawyers tell you that?"

"They also told me you were obeying the terms of the restraining order."

"Huh." Keith looked thoughtful. "You, know, I don't think there are any restraining orders against me. Not the me I am now, anyway. You're not the only one who can change your name."

That wasn't how restraining orders worked, though, was it? "What's your new name?"

"I think you already know it."

Orchid felt the panic there, fuzzy, on the edges of her brain. But she understood the feeling, as well as the adrenaline keeping her head clear. It wouldn't last forever, though. She tried to think. *Already know it?*

She didn't know anyone new. That was the whole point of her life now.

His phone buzzed again. Orchid gestured to it. "Well, whatever you're doing now, you sure seem popular. Why don't you just get back to it? Leave me be?"

He looked at the phone and sighed. "She's so needy. Do you ever remember being quite so needy?"

"Quite so needy as—" she began, but then he pointed the phone at her, and her words died in her throat.

Text messages from Beth Picach. Lots of them.

"Oh my God," Orchid whispered. "*You're* Peacock's life coach?"

"It sounds so much more uplifting than 'manager,' doesn't

it? And so much less regulated." He mocked clasping his hands together and bowing. "I am honored to share with you the illumination within."

So he *had* poisoned Rosa. What else had he managed to get Peacock to do? "You should leave her alone," Orchid said. "I've seen what she's like when she's angry."

"Well, I don't ever intend for her to be angry at me," Keith replied. "She worships me. I help her. That's what I do, Emily. That's what I'm good at. Advising stupid little girls like you. If you'd listened to me, you wouldn't be in this mess. Hiding out in this disaster of a school, dating that dangerous boy—"

"Vaughn isn't dangerous."

"We'll see," Keith said easily. Orchid felt cold. "Do you know he's been visiting the murderer in jail?"

Vaughn had been visiting Mrs. White? Her eyes widened. But, no, it must just be another of Keith's lies. "That's not—"

"Lord only knows why he killed his boss."

She shook her head vehemently. "No one will ever believe Vaughn killed Rusty. He was devastated when he heard about it!"

Keith looked amused. "What a good liar he is! The parts he plays . . . he's a better actor than you are."

"Shut up." That's what Scarlett had said—that Vaughn was playing a game with her. That he was using her for her fame.

Now Keith laughed. "Oh, Emily! You have no idea, do you?"

Keith was making it up. He always made things up.

"I wonder how he'll kill you."

Orchid couldn't think of a comeback.

"Maybe he'll drag you underground and leave you there to freeze," Keith said. "I've been in the tunnels under this school. They are very dark and very, very cold. A body could sit under there for days, and no one would notice. Like the janitor's did."

"He didn't do that," Orchid forced out. "Stop saying that."

"Everyone will be saying it soon enough," Keith said, his tone smug. "Or maybe he strangles you. Can't blame him, really. You're such an annoying little brat. He'll kill you the second you turn on him." He came closer, his hands moving toward her as if ready to strangle her himself. "And you will turn on him. Ungrateful bitch."

Orchid hugged herself tighter and pushed back into the cushions. Oh, how she wished that stupid passage was open right about now.

His phone buzzed again.

Maybe if he kept ignoring Peacock, she'd leave the test and come home. Orchid glanced out the window again. The campus appeared deserted. Were they all at that dumb test?

Keith clucked his tongue at his phone screen. "Just another desperate little girl who can't handle her own life. Like you were. She's been very useful, though. Even if she couldn't get you to take those pills last night."

Orchid shuddered. She was very quickly running out of options. No one was coming back to Tudor House, that much was certain. She needed to get out of there!

"Or maybe it's a little more subtle. Maybe people will just think you killed yourself. All these deaths. All the stress. Sleeping through your exams! You're already so fragile, Emily—maybe you woke up this morning, decided you couldn't hack it, and slit your wrists." He straightened and, for a second, stared right past her, as if imagining her gruesome death. "Well, whatever. I'll decide after."

She darted up from the chair and raced for the door.

He caught her by the throat and slammed her back into the cushions. All the breath whooshed from her lungs as he held her pinned there, as easily as a bug.

"The trick is to make the story believable. It was so easy last time."

She was about to die.

"I knew it," Orchid sobbed. "I knew you killed Jen and Kate."

"Oh, I didn't kill them," Keith said. "The fall did."

29

Scarlett

"You may begin."

Scarlett stared at the first question. Were those words even in English? She certainly didn't understand them.

This is what she did understand:

Last month, a storm had swept through this campus, obliterating everything in its path. Headmaster Boddy had lost his life. Everyone in Tudor House had lost their sense of safety. Nothing at Blackbrook would ever be the same.

Scarlett wasn't the same, for sure. Before the storm and the murders, she was confident in her place at this school. Comfortable in her position in this elite world. She and Finn had their roles locked up tight, and she had never given much thought to what that meant or what it made her.

She thought she had a best friend, but she only had a partner in crime. Or not even that, as Finn had been lying to her about his work.

Then Orchid had confided in her. And she hadn't asked Scarlett for anything except to be a friend. Someone she could tell her deepest, darkest secret and trust that Scarlett would, in fact, keep it for her. And over the month or so that followed, Orchid had been there for her, doing practice tests or chatting after classes. Peacock, too, had shared her smoothies and her silly, New Age encouragements.

And when Orchid kept secrets, it wasn't like Finn, who was doing it for his own advantage. It was because she was scared. She was scared of her past, scared enough to hire a body-guard to keep her safe, scared enough not to tell even Scarlett about it.

Question 1:

If the preceding paragraphs are taken as fact, then what possible reason would Orchid McKee have to be absent from the testing today?

A) Orchid purposefully withheld information from both Scarlett and Peacock that she had secured a make-up date while lying to the other girls about thinking it unnecessary.

B) Orchid decided not to take the test at all and instead plans a triumphant return to Hollywood, despite every single statement she has ever made to the contrary.

C) Orchid stayed up late making out with her jerk boyfriend, and the two of them even now are curled up in the back of Rusty's car some-where, and if they both sleep through the test, they totally deserve it.

D) Orchid was right to hire a bodyguard, right to freak out when said bodyguard collapsed, and even more right to freak out last night when her stuff went missing. Again.

Scarlett tapped her pencil against the sheet. Why did she suck so badly at tests? She was supposed to be smart.

She sneaked a peek at the other students. They were all bent over their tests, concentrating.

It was weird, though. Why would Orchid and Vaughn be a no-show? Why would Mustard walk out?

Why would Finn follow him?

Why would anyone murder Rusty Nayler? At Blackbrook or on Rocky Point?

She buried her head in her hands and groaned.

"Silence!" demanded the proctor.

Scarlett lifted her head. She looked down at her test. And she was suddenly one hundred percent sure of the answer.

"I don't care about any of this." She threw down the pencil and stood.

There were a few gasps. Everyone was staring at her. Peacock's jaw was practically on the table.

"I have to go," she said. She grabbed her coat and headed for the door.

"Sit down, young lady!" the proctor cried.

Scarlett did not sit down. She headed out. There was a bit of a shuffle behind her, and a few moments later, Peacock appeared at her side.

"Hey," Peacock said, a little breathless, "I'm ditching, too."

"Go back inside, Beth," Scarlett warned her. She looked back at the classroom, where most of the kids were staring at her, and the proctor was already on the phone, probably to Dr. Brown.

"No way," said Peacock. "Mustard left. Finn left. You left. Vaughn and Orchid never even showed. Murder Crew forever, right? If you guys are going to fail, I'll fail, too."

Scarlett shook her head. "I don't have the time to tell you why that makes no sense."

"Where did the boys go?" Peacock asked. "Are they looking for Vaughn and Orchid?"

"I don't know." Scarlett beelined for Tudor House. She could just . . . check on Orchid, right?

"Well, has anyone tried calling them?" Peacock whipped out her phone. "I'm not even sure I'm getting reception right now. I've been texting my life coach, but he's not answering me."

Scarlett shot her a look. "Texting him . . . from the test?"

Peacock shrugged. "Yeah. Why?"

"Maybe it's good you left before you got kicked out."

"No, silly," said Peacock. "I mean before the test started. I know she said to put away our phones." She tapped out a text. "I'm trying Orchid."

"Me too." Scarlett pulled out her phone and called. No answer. "Maybe she and Vaughn ran off together."

"Good news, then," said Peacock. She pointed over Scarlett's shoulder.

Scarlett turned to see Vaughn driving up in Rusty's car. She waved at him, and for a second, she thought he might veer the car right into them. But instead, he pulled over and rolled down the window.

"Have you seen Orchid?" Scarlett asked him.

"No. Why aren't you at the test?"

"We're looking for Orchid," she replied. "And . . . you." She couldn't believe it. She'd just thrown away her future to make sure that *Vaughn Green* was okay. What was happening?

"Why weren't you at the test?" Peacock asked him.

"I overslept. Have you seen Finn Plum?"

"Yeah," Scarlett said. "He went looking for you, too."

"Technically, I think it was Mustard looking for you," said Peacock. "And Finn just tagged along."

"Mustard," Vaughn repeated, narrowing his eyes.

"Well, Finn thinks Rusty was murdered," Scarlett explained.

"By who?"

"We don't know that part. Are you sure you haven't seen Orchid? Or talked to her?"

"No," Vaughn mumbled.

That was plenty. Scarlett hadn't given up her future for this loser. She had to check on her *actual* friend. Though she was relieved that Orchid was not, in fact, in the back seat of the car with hickeys all over her neck. What was it the test prep materials said? If you could narrow your choices down, you had a better chance of guessing the right answer.

And Scarlett really hoped that she wasn't right.

She had to get back to Tudor House. She started walking in that direction.

"Wait!" Vaughn rolled alongside her in the car. "Shouldn't Orchid be at the test?"

"We all should be at the test, dude. But this is what we're doing instead, because Blackbrook is a trash fire." Scarlett walked on.

Vaughn said something like, "No argument here," and kept pace with her.

Peacock let out a shout. Scarlett stopped, and Vaughn braked. They both looked back at Peacock.

"Is that Mustard and Finn?" she asked, pointing toward the colonnade of the administration building. "Finn!"

Scarlett peered through the mist. Sure enough, the other two boys on the Murder Crew were skulking around under the colonnade.

Beside her, Vaughn gunned the engine. "Hey!" he shouted. "I gotta talk to you!"

Finn looked over at the car heading up the hill toward them, then grabbed Mustard's arm and bolted. The two boys shot across the muddy green toward the edge of campus.

Vaughn, in the car, lurched to the right and jumped the curb in pursuit.

Scarlett and Peacock stood on the sidewalk, staring in disbelief as Rusty's old car kicked up mud and ice as it crossed the green. The boys kept running, vaulting yellow caution tape and skirting downed trees.

Peacock and Scarlett exchanged glances, then took off after them.

Well, Peacock took off. Scarlett was not dressed for a race across a mud slick. Her fleece-lined booties slipped and slid on the surface of the green, and she was soon outpaced by the tennis star. She watched in frustration as all four of them rampaged through what little of the picturesque Blackbrook campus remained. She trotted after them, avoiding the worst of the mud and the deep grooves that Rusty's car had left in the soft earth of the green.

Mustard and Finn were headed toward Tudor House, but she saw Finn go down as soon as he hit the yard—tripping, perhaps, on one of the slate flagstones lining the walk to the front door. Mustard stopped, too, turning to help him up.

Vaughn did not look like he was going to stop. The car hopped over the edge of the curb on the green and splayed, a mud-spattered beast, in the street in front of Tudor House. The door opened, and Vaughn spilled out, still shouting.

Peacock caught up to him right before he descended on the other boys. From this vantage point, it looked like she was trying to get between Vaughn and the others.

Scarlett started sprinting again. Screw her shoes.

By the time she arrived, it was a full-on shouting match.

"Just tell me what you saw!" Vaughn was screaming at Finn.

"I'll tell the police, thank you very much."

"You'll tell me, punk!" he cried. "Before you start accusing people of *murder*!"

"Hey!" screamed Peacock. She stood between them, both arms stretched wide. "Hey! No more violence, okay? No one is accusing anyone of murder."

"Speak for yourself!" He batted Peacock's hands away.

"Finn didn't see anything!" Mustard blurted out. "*I* was the one who was there that night."

"Mustard!" Finn hissed in warning.

Vaughn's arms dropped to his sides. He took a breath. "So, what did you see?"

Mustard frowned.

Scarlett raised her eyes heavenward. This was ridiculous—and then she saw him. The man in Tudor House, standing right there in the study.

"Guys—" She pointed.

They all looked.

The man turned toward the window. There was someone with him—Orchid. Orchid was in the study with a strange man!

But before Scarlett could even wave, she saw her friend dart toward the fireplace.

And before Scarlett could even scream, Orchid lifted her arm and bashed something down on the man's head.

30

Plum

All five of them forgot everything they were doing and dashed toward the door of Tudor House. They crowded inside and ran through the hall to the study.

Vaughn got there first. He opened the door to a terrible scene—Orchid was standing in the middle of the room, a bloody wrench gripped firmly in her fist. The man lay on the floor in a growing pool of blood.

"Orchid!" Scarlett screamed. "What did you do?"

Orchid held her free hand up to her throat. Her eyes were as big as dinner plates and flowing freely with tears. "He was going to kill me. He was going to—" She dropped the wrench, which clattered to the floor and into the blood.

Finn almost backed out of the room right then and there. But then he caught sight of Beth.

She was standing over the body, and her mouth was open in a silent scream.

"Beth?" he asked.

"Ash!" she gasped. She collapsed on top of him. "Oh my God, Ash!" Before he could stop her, she'd rolled the body over and put her ear over his chest. "His heart is still beating. He's alive! Someone call 911!"

The man's face did not look as if he could possibly still be alive. It was pale and still, his eyes were open, and there was blood everywhere.

Finn knelt as near as he could bear, given all the blood. "Beth . . ."

"This is my life coach!" she cried. "Help him! Do you know CPR? Get something to stop the bleeding!"

Finn grabbed a pillow off the couch. "Here. Press this against the wound." He had no idea if that would do anything.

Mustard was already on the phone, reporting the emergency.

"Wait," said Scarlett. "Your life coach? Tried to kill Orchid?"

"His name's not Ash," Orchid whispered. Her voice was gravelly, and her hands were still cradling her throat. Above her fingertips, he saw red marks, as if she had been choked. "It's Keith. Keith Grayson."

"What?" Scarlett gasped.

"He's my old manager. He's been stalking me for years."

Finn gave her an incredulous look. Why would Orchid have a manager?

Orchid seemed to crumple before his eyes, and Vaughn stepped in and caught her in his arms.

"It's okay," he said softly, his lips against her hair. "It's okay."

It was most definitely *not* okay. This guy was bleeding out on the rug. Beth was screaming for help, and Mustard was shushing her so he could talk to the authorities on the phone.

Plum turned to Beth. "It's okay," he lied to her. After all, it looked like it was helping Orchid. He covered her hands with his and pressed the sopping pillow to the poor man's head wound.

"He was going to kill me," Orchid repeated, sounding stunned. "He was going to kill me and make it look like—"

"The police are on their way," Mustard announced.

"That's not good enough," said Scarlett. "Remember how long they took to get here for Rosa? He's going to bleed to death before they get past the ravine."

For a minute, no one said anything.

"Rusty's car," Vaughn blurted. "It's on the lawn. Let's get him into that, and we can drive to the hospital. There's only one road out to the point. We'll have to see the ambulance when it comes."

"That's a great idea!" Peacock said. "I'll go with you. I'll keep pressure on the wound."

"Okay." Vaughn nodded. He looked at Finn. "Will you help me carry him to the car?"

Finn nodded wordlessly. A few minutes ago, this kid had been about to kick his ass. But you know what they said:

Murder Crew forever.

"No, Vaughn!" Orchid shook her head, her eyes wild. "Don't leave me!" She clutched at his shoulders.

Vaughn captured her wrists in his hands and pulled her away from him. "I have to. Don't you see? He's going to die if we don't get him out of here. I can't let you become a murderer. I just can't."

"Vaughn—"

But the boy had already turned away.

It was difficult to load the man into the back seat of Rusty's car, and Finn was pretty bloody by the time it was all done. Beth was in the back seat too, cradling her life coach's head in her hands and applying more pressure with a towel Scarlett had conjured up from somewhere in Tudor House.

"Let's go!" Beth begged. "Before it's too late."

Vaughn looked out his window at Orchid, his expression pained. He looked like he was about to say twenty different things before he landed on, "Wish us luck," and they drove off.

The other four watched them go.

Scarlett had her arm around Orchid.

"He was going to kill me," Orchid said again. "I swear."

"Yeah," said Scarlett. She hugged Orchid closer. "We believe you."

"I'm sorry," said Finn at last. "Who was that guy again?"

"No one," said Scarlett.

"My manager," said Orchid, her tone completely flat.

"What manager?"

"None of your business, Finn."

"It doesn't matter," said Orchid. "Everyone is going to find out now, anyway. I *killed* him."

"He's not dead yet," said Mustard. "Maybe Green will make it to the hospital in time."

Finn examined his blood-covered shirt. Not likely.

Seconds later, Dr. Brown and a few of the other teachers streamed over the hill, racing toward Tudor House.

"What is going on?" she shouted at them. "We just got a call from the police, and—" She stopped dead on the path. "You four! Of course!" she seethed. "What happened?"

Scarlett stepped in front of the others. She was the least drenched in blood. "Dr. Brown, there's been an intruder on campus. You know the stalker Orchid hired Rosa to help protect her from?"

Wait—the what? Finn stared at Scarlett in disbelief.

"He broke into Tudor House this morning."

"Last night," Orchid said softly. "At least. Probably lots of other times, too, and he—"

"He took Orchid hostage," Scarlett went on, undeterred. "That's why she wasn't at the exam this morning."

Dr. Brown looked past Scarlett to Mustard and Finn. "Is that what you two were screaming about to the proctor when you ran out?"

Sure. That sounded pretty good. "We were very concerned about Orchid's safety." Finn stared daggers at Mustard.

"Yeah," the other boy agreed. "We didn't know if he had something to do with Rusty Nayler's death."

Figures. Mustard always had to be Captain America.

"Probably," Orchid said, her voice cracking. "He said he'd been hiding out in the secret passages."

They were now drawing a crowd. Blackbrook students from the lower classes were coming up over the hill to see what all the commotion was about. With a flick of her wrist, Dr. Brown deployed the other teachers to keep the kids away from the vicinity.

"But what *happened?*" she insisted. "The police said there was a report about a man bleeding to death."

Orchid began to cry again, and Scarlett hugged her close.

Dr. Brown rolled her eyes and herded them all back into Tudor House. She took one look at the blood-drenched study, decided against it, then shut them all in the dining room.

"No secret passages in here," she said.

She left, and Scarlett rolled her eyes and pulled out her phone. "First things first," she said. "We call your lawyers."

"I don't know their number," said Orchid. "They're in my phone. He took my phone."

"Well, you know their names," she replied evenly. "And I know how to do an internet search."

"They aren't—" Orchid put her head down on the desk. "They aren't *criminal* lawyers."

"Wait," said Mustard. "You have lawyer*s?* Like, plural?"

"That is not the topic under discussion here," Scarlett snapped. She entered the information Orchid gave her and started searching. "Don't worry, Orchid. They'll take care of this. You were *stalked.* You were *threatened.* You had to hire a bodyguard who was then *poisoned,* and—"

"Rosa was a bodyguard? I *knew* she was military," he said triumphantly. He looked at Finn. "I knew it."

Way to focus on the wrong thing, Mustard. "Rosa was poisoned?" Finn asked instead. "How?"

"Probably Peacock's smoothies," said Orchid, in that same toneless way, as if words were nothing more than air being pushed through her lungs, with no feeling or meaning behind them. "She was allergic to nuts, and somehow, Keith knew . . ." She bit her lip. "If Rosa dies, too, it's all my fault."

"Shh." Scarlett patted Orchid on the hand. Her other hand held her phone up to her ear. "It's going to be all right. Hello? Yes? I need to talk to the representation for Orchid McKee—er, Emily Pryce. It's an emergency."

Finn stared at Orchid, at the rat's nest of brown hair, the blood, and the tear-streaked face. "Emily Pryce? The actress?"

"Get with the program, Plum," Scarlett snapped, then returned her attention to the phone. "Hello, yes?"

Finn looked at Orchid, who covered her face with her hands. He turned to Mustard.

Emily Pryce? he mouthed.

Mustard lifted his hands. *I don't know who that is,* he mouthed back. Then he crooked his thumb at Orchid. *Her?*

Finn supposed that had to be it. The age was certainly right. He hadn't seen an Emily Pryce movie in years, though. Not since he'd been a little kid.

He thought about Orchid when she didn't look the way she did right now. When she was just her regular level of grungy. Could she be Emily Pryce? The movie star? Hiding out at Blackbrook?

Mustard gestured for him to meet him in a corner of the room, which Finn thought wasn't exactly private, but Scarlett was busy on the phone, and Orchid was lost in her own little world.

"Are you okay?" Mustard asked.

"Um, yeah," said Finn. Ten minutes ago, he'd been kissing

Mustard in an alcove by the administration building. Then he'd almost gotten his ass kicked by Vaughn. And now . . .

Now he was a witness to a possible murder?

"I'm just confused."

"I'm not," said Mustard. "Not anymore. Orchid said that guy—Keith or Ash or whoever—was hiding out in the tunnels. That's the answer."

"It is?"

"Rusty and I must have surprised him when we came in the other night. And that's why Rusty was killed. Not townies. Keith."

Finn nodded. "Yeah. That makes perfect sense."

Mustard rubbed his hand through his hair. "He must have been a real maniac. I can't believe I escaped. And he poisoned Rosa, too?"

And then he was brought down by a petite teenage girl with a hand tool. "Orchid's lucky," Finn said. "And you're lucky."

"I know."

Finn reached for his hand, but he yanked it away and went back to the table.

Orchid was staring straight ahead. The blood on her hands was drying to a cracked brownish red, and the marks on her neck were darkening into bruises. Finn wondered if they should get her some ice.

"He was going to kill me," she said again.

"Yeah," Mustard said, nodding in understanding. "I know what that feels like."

Finn sat down next to Mustard.

"He was going to kill me and blame it on Vaughn," she added, then squeezed her eyes shut.

"What a creep," said Mustard.

Finn nodded in agreement. He thought back to that morning, how he'd waited for Vaughn out by the bridge over the ravine. The townie had hurried off the night before, so he'd never been able to explain to him why he was bringing up Rusty's death. And then this morning, when Vaughn hadn't shown up for the test, he'd worried that he was going to the police with a half-understood tip.

And then, when he'd chased after Finn, he'd looked so angry. He'd looked like he was ready to run both of them down with his car.

He'd claimed Finn was accusing someone of murder.

Very weird.

Of course, none of it mattered now.

He reached across the table and patted Orchid's blood-spattered hand, though he doubted he'd be as good at comforting her as Vaughn had been. "I'm sure they got to the hospital in time."

"I should call Vaughn," she said. She patted her pocket. "Oh, yeah. Keith stole my phone."

The door banged open, and Dr. Brown stood there, glaring at all four of them. Behind her stood the school counselor, Mr. Winkle, his arms laden with first aid kits, water bottles, and blankets.

Scarlett stepped forward. "We've already called Orchid's lawyers. And the police should be here soon. We're just waiting to hear from the others about whether or not they've intercepted—"

"Sit down, Miss Mistry," Dr. Brown stated in the kind of voice that might turn lesser people to stone.

Scarlett dropped to her seat as if her limbs had suddenly lost power.

"The police have just called," she announced. "From Rocky Point."

"Thank God!" Orchid cried. "Did they make it to the hospital in time?"

"Who was in that car? Rusty Nayler's car?"

"What do you mean?" Scarlett furrowed her brow. "It was Vaughn Green and Beth Picach and the guy. The stalker guy."

"Keith Grayson," Orchid added flatly.

Dr. Brown closed her eyes for a long moment, and when she opened them, there were tears shining in them. "Rusty Nayler's car went over the bridge. The police found it at the bottom of the Rocky Point ravine."

31

Peacock

From: *elizabeth.picach@BlackbrookAcademy.edu*
To: *phineas.plum@BlackbrookAcademy.edu*
Subj: *Re: When you get this*

> *Finn,*
>
> *Thank you so much for writing. I haven't been up to writing back, but I wanted to let you know that I'm still alive.*
>
> *I almost deleted that for sounding stupid, but it's true. I am still alive. It's hard to think about it, that I'm alive, and they aren't. There are so many things it's hard for me to think about. Like how Ash was using me. Like all the things he lied to me about. I thought I was becoming a better person, but it was all fake.*
>
> *I don't know how long I'm going to be here. My parents won't tell me anything, and they must have told the doctors not to, either. Everything is in a cast. I'm writing this with voice recognition. Basically, I've got one hand and one foot without bandages, but that leg's shot, anyway.*
>
> *I do not think I'll be playing tennis this season. Or next. Or maybe ever.*

I probably shouldn't have walked out of the test. I probably shouldn't have gotten into the car.

I have a whole list of things I should not have done.

I cry a lot, and then I think of Vaughn, and I feel bad for being so upset.

The police asked me what happened. So did Scarlett. I wish I remembered. Or maybe I don't. Who wants to remember driving off a cliff?

My parents have really limited visitors, due to all the press, but I'm sure they'd be okay with you or any of the other Murder Crew.

We really need a better name.

Beth

From: *phineas.plum@BlackbrookAcademy.edu*
To: *elizabeth.picach@BlackbrookAcademy.edu*
Subj: *Re: When you get this*

Dear Beth,

I don't think what you and Ash were doing was fake. (Okay, that alkaline water thing was fake, but not the rest of it.) Unfortunately, I know a lot about using people, and I've come to the conclusion that it's all on the person doing the using, not the other way around. What I'm saying is, he may have been using you, but you weren't using him. All that stuff you learned about being a bigger person was real. The Beth I knew before could never have written me this letter.

Things here are about like you'd expect. Scarlett's not letting anyone talk to Orchid, which Mustard keeps trying to convince me is the right choice. He says hi, by the way. If we can, he and I will come visit you this weekend.

I'm so sorry you're going through this. I wish there was something I could do. I don't know if it's too late for me to switch to engineering. I'd invent you bionic limbs. You'd be back on the court in no time.

Love,

Finn

From: *elizabeth.picach@BlackbrookAcademy.edu*
To: *phineas.plum@BlackbrookAcademy.edu*
Subj: *Re: When you get this*

They're broken, not amputated. Jeez, get over yourself.
Beth

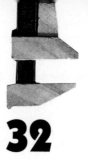

32

Orchid

Orchid looked at the form in front of her. Bile rose in her throat. "I don't know what to put."

Her lawyer, Bianca Landis, gave her a sympathetic smile. They were all like that. Gentle. Reasonable. At least to her. To the prosecutors in the DA's office, it was another situation entirely.

"Just say what happened. Like we talked about."

What happened. Sure.

I, Orchid McKee, a.k.a. Emily Pryce, was being held hostage by Ash Kingman, a.k.a. Keith Grayson, in Tudor House. He had stalked me for years. I had a restraining order out against him. After receiving threatening letters that I believed to be from him, I hired a bodyguard to protect me at Blackbrook. A day after she was found unconscious due to what we believed to be an unrelated allergic response, he broke into my room, stole my phone so the alarm wouldn't wake me up, then took me captive when he knew I would be alone. He threatened to kill me and make it look like my boyfriend had done it. Then, when I tried to run, he said he'd make it look like a suicide.

But I stopped him. When he was distracted by my friends fighting outside the window, I grabbed the nearest weapon I could, and I hit him with it.

I, Orchid McKee, killed Keith Grayson. In the study. With a wrench.

She pushed the sheet toward Bianca, who looked it over, then pushed it back with a sigh. "Let's try it again, with about eighty percent less drama."

Orchid sighed. She picked up the pen.

Scarlett slapped her hand down on the page. "How about you just write what you want, and Orchid will sign it?"

Bianca wore that special kind of frown that only appeared when Scarlett spoke to her, the one that came with three new wrinkles in her forehead. "Orchid has made it quite clear—"

"I'm not signing anything where I don't take responsibility for what I did," she said for the fifteenth time.

Bianca sighed. "Orchid. Listen to me. The DA has already said that they will not be pursuing charges against you for assault, due to the obviously critical position you were in. It would be great if you just . . . didn't use words like 'killed' in your statement."

"Especially because you didn't kill anyone!" Scarlett went on. "We don't know if Keith would have died."

Orchid looked down at her hands. She felt like she'd killed a lot of people.

Rusty.

Rosa.

Keith.

Vaughn.

None of them would be dead if not for her.

"Maybe . . . struck?" Scarlett suggested? "You *struck* him with the wrench? So you could escape?"

Sure. Fine. Whatever. Let them revise her confession to their hearts' content. Orchid shook her head and made the changes required, then signed it.

Bianca looked relieved. "That should wrap this all up. Please don't talk to the press."

"We know," said Scarlett.

Bianca glared at her. "Is she paying you for this?"

Scarlett lifted her chin. "I'm considering it an unpaid internship."

As soon as they were alone, she whispered, "I mean, we're really just friends, right?"

"Friends," Orchid agreed, nodding. She gave a halfhearted fist pump. "Murder Crew forever."

Scarlett cringed. "We really need a better name." She bustled them out into a waiting town car, and, soon enough, they were on the road back to Blackbrook.

The school hadn't even shut down, which had made everyone realize that the former delay in opening had nothing whatsoever to do with the murder on campus and everything to do with simple storm damage.

And damage was what concerned the staff there now. Damage to the carpeting in the Tudor House study. Damage to the railing of the bridge over the ravine.

Damage to the reputation of the school.

More deaths on campus. The death of a student. The attack on another. The grievous injuries of a third. And, of course, the average test score had plummeted.

Like a car to the bottom of a ravine.

Orchid squeezed her hands together in her lap and stared out the window. Eighty percent less drama might be a tall order.

They passed through the village of Rocky Point, and she felt it like a vise around her heart. One of these houses was Vaughn's. It was there that he'd learned to walk and read and play the guitar and . . .

She reached for the phone in her pocket. They'd found it among Keith's things in the secret passage. At least it, too, hadn't been destroyed on the rocks in the ravine.

Scarlett saw the phone in her hand. She cleared her throat.

"You don't want me to play it." It wasn't a question.

"You can play it."

"You never liked him."

Scarlett shook her head and looked out the window. "No. But I didn't want him to die."

Orchid pulled up the video.

Vaughn had sent it to her while they'd been separated over winter break. They'd texted each other endlessly, back and forth between Maine and California. Stupid stuff, jokes, and snippets of Vaughn's music.

Those were the things she'd clung to in the past week. Vaughn's voice, his fingers moving expertly across the strings. As if he were still alive.

"He said he had ten songs," Orchid said now. "I only have a couple of them. I wonder if he gave them to anyone else."

Scarlett shrugged. "Maybe the music teacher. I don't know if he was really close to anyone else on campus. Before the storm, I don't think he had any friends. He was always so busy working or studying. I used to be jealous of him, because he took so many more classes than I did, and his grades were still as good as mine. It felt like magic, or like he had a Time-Turner or something. But I guess he was just good. You know, that's why he got a scholarship. And I used to give him such a hard time."

"I know."

"I'm sorry I called him a creep."

"I know." Orchid looked out the window. Keith had said it, too. He'd said all kinds of things about Vaughn. That he sneaked around in the secret passages. That he visited with Mrs. White.

But they were lies. You couldn't trust a murderer.

They were coming up on the ravine bridge. Scarlett straightened in her seat, and her hand tightened on the door handle.

It was silly, really. Their driver was a professional, and the railing had been fixed already. The car rumbled across the bridge and up the slope toward campus.

"Stop," Orchid blurted.

The car slowed.

"Orchid . . ." Scarlett warned.

"I have to," she said. "I'm sorry."

"You don't have to," Scarlett replied. "We're supposed to have that session with the crisis counselor."

"I don't need any more sessions." Especially not with Perry Winkle. He was still a jerk.

"Mustard and Finn are coming to this one."

"I'll be there," Orchid said. She knew how much Mr. Winkle cared about punctuality. "I just have to do this first."

The driver cleared her throat.

Scarlett scowled. "I'm not coming with you," her friend said. "This is morbid."

"I'll go alone. You don't have to worry about me."

"I'm not worried about you," Scarlett said. "Come on. You took down your childhood boogeyman single-handedly. I'm worried about everything else. Bad things happen when we're not a team, remember?"

Orchid squeezed her hand. "We are a team. Not the Murder Crew. We're the Survivors."

And then she got out of the car. After a long moment, it continued to climb the hill without her.

She hugged her arms around herself and zipped her parka up all the way. The day was cold and grim, with black clouds blowing in off the sea and the feel of rain in the air. As if pulled by an invisible thread, Orchid made her way to the edge of the cliff.

I can't let you become a murderer.

Those had been Vaughn's almost-final words to her. And she didn't know if they were even true. No matter what she and her lawyers had decided to put down on that paper, she felt like a murderer. She didn't know if this was how Mrs. White had felt during the storm, her hands bloody, her panic rising as she hid bodies and kidnapped kids and drugged Mustard. Every action had set off a chain reaction of disaster. She'd run away from Keith three years ago, and now, four people were dead.

She sidled to the very edge of the cliff. They'd cleaned up everything, though she could still glimpse shimmering bits of metal or glass shattered on the rocks below. Just last week, she'd been standing on this cliff with Vaughn. They never did get to have their stormy cliff kiss, like characters in some romantic movie.

Vaughn had never gotten quite a lot of things.

She looked at the video, paused on her phone. Just like his parents, he was dead before his music could ever really make a mark. It wasn't fair. And it was all her fault.

She sat on the rock and pressed play. The sound was weak and tinny under the whistling wind, but she could still make out the undeniable Vaughn-ness of it all.

It is the truth beneath my skin
It is the game I'll never win
My only secret shameful sin . . .
I want to be
Another me.

When the song was over, Orchid wiped the tears from her eyes and put the phone back in her pocket. She looked around, but no one was out there on that blustery day. She had no idea what people were saying on campus or in the press. Scarlett and her team had kept her pretty well protected. Orchid had given up any pretense of resistance to Scarlett managing her affairs, or to maintaining secrecy about her true identity. As long as the paparazzi left her alone, she couldn't bring herself to care.

And she had to hand it to Scarlett—for all the other girl had not approved of Orchid's relationship with Vaughn while it was happening, she had never once made a comment about them only being together for a day or two or intimated that Orchid was making a big deal out of nothing.

Orchid knew, rationally, that she and Vaughn weren't some great, world-ending love affair. But he'd been a person, and he'd been alone in the world, and he'd had hopes and dreams, and now he was dead. He had no family. Who was going to remember Vaughn Green if she didn't?

The sky opened, and freezing rain began to pummel the cliffside. Orchid yanked her furry hood around her face and started up the hill toward the school. The rain fell harder.

Shivering, she redirected course toward the old boathouse. Scarlett would not be pleased by the delay, but Orchid was pretty sure she wouldn't be thrilled by a case of pneumonia, either, so Orchid would simply wait out the storm among the old crew shells and sailing skiffs.

She stepped onto the porch of the rickety old structure. The boards creaked beneath her feet. The door was sticky— she thought. She slammed her shoulder against it, and she heard something metallic pop as it gave way.

Oops. Had it been locked? The dangling latch hook on the doorjamb would indicate that, indeed, someone had attempted to keep the door closed from the inside.

Which was odd.

The interior was the usual mishmash of boats and buoys, mostly covered with tarps. Grimy windows did little to illuminate the dark, shadowy space.

Orchid immediately felt the hairs on her neck rise. It was creepy. Perhaps she should have braved the weather and a sprint back up the hill to Blackbrook. After all, this cliff was haunted now.

But places weren't haunted; people were haunted. Funny, it had been Peacock who had told her that, last week. Orchid wondered, now, if it was Keith who'd told Peacock that. How ironic.

She'd laugh if it weren't so unbelievably ghoulish.

There had to be a lantern or a flashlight around here somewhere. Orchid crossed over to a table covered in boxes, old paperwork, and equipment, as the wood creaked and groaned around her. It was a motley assortment, and she wasn't entirely sure who on the crew team had thought it was a good idea to leave all these electronics lying around the old shed—she counted at least six laptop computers and probably a similar number of tablets, cell phones, and even what looked like a telescope. But there was a chair, and Orchid thankfully sank into it.

The boats swayed on their hangings, knocking gently together. The storm raged outside.

Orchid turned on the flashlight on her phone. There, among all the electronics, was a stack of old envelopes tied together with string. Her eyes fell on the address on the top of the stack, and she did a double take.

Olivia Vaughn
Tudor House
Rocky Point, Maine

Acknowledgments

Some books are gifts. This one came at the perfect time. I'd like to thank all six of my main characters for behaving in such shocking and amusing ways without me having to fight them too much about it. (And you too, Oliver. I know you always feel left out.)

But even with their cooperation, I couldn't have produced this book without my people. My awesome agent, Kate, who emailed exclamation points; my patient and enthusiastic editor, Russ, who said I could kill as many people as I wanted; the whole team at Abrams; the generous folks at Hasbro; my wonderful parents; my fantastic kiddos, who love playing Guess Who! Clue with me; and of course, my actual partners in crime: writer friends Marianne and Kyla and Leah and Jon and Mindy and especially Lenore, who came up with the name Perry Winkle and will not rest until everyone knows it.

DIANA PETERFREUND is the author of fifteen books for adults, teens, and children, including the Secret Society Girl series, the Killer Unicorn series, *For Darkness Shows the Stars*, and *Omega City*. She has received starred reviews from *Booklist, School Library Journal*, and *VOYA*, and her books have been named in Amazon's Best Books of the Year. She lives outside of Washington, DC, with her family.

After the death of one of their own, the Murder Crew comes face to face with the long-buried secret at the heart of Blackbrook—all as prom looms around the corner. Turn the page for a sneak peek at the deadly conclusion to the sping-tingling trilogy!

1

Orchid

Vaughn Green was singing again.

Orchid McKee looked up from the textbook she had been trying, and failing, to read for the last fifteen minutes. The Tudor House dining room was empty except for her. She cocked her head to the side, wondering if she'd imagined it.

But no, that was him. And it wasn't a song she recognized, either.

Weird. She'd thought each of his songs was etched permanently in her memory. By now, she could guess the tune within a handful of notes. If the song was "Another Me," she could tell even before it began, with the halting half-strum of Vaughn's guitar that Scarlett had kept in the video for *authenticity*.

Of course it was all *authentic*—the arrangements simple, the sound tinny. He'd been making the recordings in his room with his phone instead of real recording equipment. But the fans didn't care.

The hundreds of thousands of fans.

She sat up and glanced at her phone, wondering if it was autoplaying one of the recordings. But it was silent. She swiped over to the music account.

Nothing. Well, unless you counted the fifty thousand new views since this morning. Today's top track was "Off on Another Great Adventure." Not one of Orchid's favorites, to be honest.

Vaughn hadn't gotten to go on any great adventures. He'd died in a car at the bottom of Rocky Point Ravine.

But what was this song? She couldn't make out any words, but she knew it was Vaughn. His style, his voice. Where was it coming from? She opened the door to the hall. The music went on, still faint as ever. Now, she could hear words.

And when this heart, this body, this shore, this dawn breaks
There'll be another addition to my list of mistakes.
Because I never told you all . . .
That morningfall.

Yeah, that was Vaughn all right. Half his songs were about secrets. Maybe that's why she liked his music so much.

But this song, too, was a secret. Because Orchid had never heard it.

"Hello?" she called into the quiet hall. Students didn't stick around Tudor House these days if they didn't have to. It was one of the reasons Orchid liked to study here. Being invisible was a luxury she'd lost in the past few months. If she had to hide out in the Murder House to get away from people's prying eyes, so be it.

There were a few rooms still unfilled with blood or memories.

She walked farther into the hall, listening for the ghostly strains of Vaughn's voice. It got louder as she moved toward the front of the house. The doors to the kitchen, ballroom, and conservatory were open, revealing nothing but the usual Tudor House furnishings. She listened at the billiards room door—recently repurposed as Peacock's ground-floor bedroom since the accident—and heard nothing. The library—Dr. Brown's office—was shut, as usual, but the sound wasn't coming from there, either.

"Hello?" she said again, more loudly. "Does anyone else hear that music?"

She heard a door open in the second-floor hall and then Violet Vandergraf was on the stairs, descending toward her. "Hey, Orchid. What's going on?"

"Listen," she said, shushing her.

The music stopped.

Violet cocked her head to the side. "What am I listening for?"

"It's gone! I could have sworn . . ." Orchid shook her head. "I thought I heard Vaughn singing."

Violet's eyes widened and she pulled out her phone. "Um . . . let me call Scarlett, okay?"

"That's not what I meant," Orchid said quickly. "Not for real." They didn't think she was that crazy, did they? "Just one of the songs."

Violet chuckled. "Um, I mean, yeah. Someone's always playing them now. Wasn't that your whole point in putting them online?"

Was it? Orchid couldn't quite recall what had possessed her to let Scarlett put Vaughn's recordings online. It was in the days right after his death, when everything in the world had been a gray blur. She'd been sobbing into her pillow about how everything was all her fault, and how his whole life had been stolen from him. Scarlett was trying to help. She had some experience, she'd said, with streaming video games and other content. She could help Orchid with the publicity. If everyone was going to learn the truth about Orchid anyway, they might as well take advantage of it.

Orchid's lawyer hadn't seen the harm in it, so they'd let Scarlett do whatever she wanted. Neither Orchid nor her lawyer, Bianca, thought it would go any further than their friends at school.

They'd underestimated Scarlett.

Five songs. Five hits. Scarlett was the one who kept track of the viral spread of each track, pinpointing the source and optimizing the synergy, and a whole host of other terms that made Orchid's skin crawl. Back in Hollywood, that was the sort of stuff her manager had taken care of, and Orchid had hated her manager.

A few months ago, she had killed him.

"They weren't playing one I'd ever heard," said Orchid now. She checked the lounge. Empty. That just left the study.

She wasn't going in the study.

Violet frowned. "Weird. Are you sure?"

Was she *sure*? "The recordings are *mine*, Violet. He made them for *me*."

She held her hands up. "I know that. Everyone knows it. I'm . . . I'm going to call Scarlett, okay?" She lifted her phone to her ear.

"I don't need a babysitter." Orchid turned in place, listening. "I heard it."

Violet, the phone still at her ear, also looked toward the study, then back at Orchid. "You want me to look in there for you?"

Orchid swallowed. She hadn't crossed that threshold in four months, ever since she'd found Keith inside.

They'd cleaned everything, she'd been told. New rugs, new curtains, new upholstery on the chairs. Apparently, she'd made quite a mess with that wrench. Who knew the human body could hold so much blood?

"Yes," she said softly.

They'd sealed up the secret passages, too. For real this time. No more sneaking around under this house. No more break-ins. No more secrets.

Violet looked in the study. "Empty. And Scarlett's phone went to voicemail. She must be in a meeting."

Scarlett was always in meetings these days. That's what happened when most of the student body left. All those committees with no chairperson, and Scarlett more than happy to take them on.

"I don't need Scarlett to tell me what I heard."

Violet came over and took Orchid's hand, patting it in what Orchid could only assume she thought was a comforting manner. "Vaughn's not making new music, honey. He's dead. But it's okay. My grandma still holds out hope for Elvis."

Orchid snatched her hand back. She crossed to the coatrack and grabbed her jacket. April evenings were cold in Maine.

"Orchid, I miss him, too," Violet said. "I had to do that history poster all by myself, remember?"

Orchid rolled her eyes as she zipped up her jacket. She couldn't imagine what a hardship that had been. A whole history poster. Meanwhile, Vaughn's entire life had been stolen.

"I'm going for a walk."

"Good!" exclaimed Violet, who was probably even now texting Scarlett. "Clear your head."

What went unsaid: *and stop acting crazy around me.*

Yeah, right. The problem wasn't in her head. That music had been coming from somewhere.

Outside the walls of Tudor House, though, all was still. Once upon a time, Orchid had relished the remote peacefulness on this little island at the end of the world. But then, at least, Blackbrook had been bustling, a hive of brilliant kids running around the campus, the rulers of their own dominion, constantly busy with sports and activities and whatever teenaged dramas powered student life.

The school was a shell of its former self now. First there'd been the storm, which destroyed half the dorms and flooded several classroom buildings. They would have recovered from that quickly, with no greater damage to the school's reputation than a report that the living quarters were a mite crowded for a year or so. But then there had been the murders. Even those still willing to send their precious youngsters back to a school where the headmaster had been stabbed to death by one of his own staff members had balked when, only a month after the reopening, a student had been stalked and nearly murdered in her own dorm. She'd only survived by fighting her attacker off.

In the end, she killed him, but his reign of terror had caused no fewer than three additional deaths, of staff and students both.

Orchid wondered how Blackbrook's admissions office related that story, or if they even needed to. After all, most people had already seen it on TV or in the papers. Usually with Orchid's picture attached.

Vanished Child Star's Secret Life at an Exclusive Boarding School

No Charges Filed Against Former Child Star Emily Pryce in Death of Ex-Manager

Murders in Maine: The Stalking of Former Child Star Emily Pryce

The Surprise Connection Between Emily Pryce and Viral Music Sensation Vaughn Green

Scarlett had jumped for joy over that last one. The impressions on Vaughn's channel had spiked, and never stopped.

Orchid had been dreading all the publicity, but when she saw how it helped Vaughn, she found she couldn't begrudge it as much as she'd thought. After all, the danger of people finding out where she was had always been about Keith. And Keith was dead.

Even at Blackbrook, people stared for a few days, then stopped. With the kind of money most Blackbrook kids had, celebrity wasn't all that weird. The rich and famous rubbed elbows wherever they went. A former child star? Meh, that was nothing. The fact that she'd killed a man proved more impressive. After four months, the skeleton of a student body that remained on campus had all but absorbed the shockwaves of each disaster. It was, perhaps, a self-selecting group. Those who had the stomach or the need to stay on at Blackbrook, despite the death and destruction, were those most equipped to handle it.

Like the Murder Crew. Orchid, Scarlett, Mustard, Finn Plum, and even Peacock. No one thought Beth "Peacock" Picach would be returning to campus after the accident. Blackbrook's star tennis player had been in the car with Vaughn and Keith when it plunged off the cliff into the Rocky Point Ravine. Unlike the others, she had survived the crash, but with enough damage to her body to make playing tennis this season or any other massively unlikely.

Still, she was here, on campus. Murder Crew forever.

Orchid walked across the green but heard nothing but the breeze in the budding trees, the crunch of gravel beneath her boots, and the distant crash of waves upon the rocks. Here and there, an occasional light shone from a window. There was a jogger across the quad, a knot of students reading beneath a maple, a couple kissing in the portico outside the boys' dorm.

But no more music.

She hadn't imagined it. People didn't hallucinate their dead boyfriends singing an entire verse of a brand-new song. At least, not without the benefit of heavier drugs than Orchid had ever done, even back in Hollywood.

She kept walking, out to the edge of campus, only half-aware of where she allowed her feet to take her. Oh, who was she kidding? She knew where she was going.

The cliff.

The sun had dipped below the horizon now, bathing the rocks in a reddish-purple glow. The sea rolled beneath a darkening sky, but Orchid couldn't make out any of the shimmers from the bits of glass and metal still embedded in the base of the cliff. Maybe it had all washed away by now. All traces of Vaughn.

Except his songs.

Orchid hadn't been imagining it. She couldn't have been.

Movement caught her eye on the far side of the divide. At low tide, the ravine ran dry, and clamdiggers often picked their way across the rocks in search of shellfish. This one was just completing a climb back up to the summit of the ravine on the village side. He turned to look back at Blackbrook, and the last slivers of daylight illuminated his face.

Orchid's jaw dropped.

Vaughn.

2

Scarlett

I'm telling you, I saw him." Orchid's eyes were wide, her skin paler than usual.

Scarlett Mistry bit her lip. "And I believe that you saw . . . something." At sunset. Across the whole ravine. And in her current . . . fragile state. Scarlett wasn't about to call the school counselor about this, because Perry Winkle was kind of a jerk, but she had to nip this in the bud. "But . . . Orchid, there are always clamdiggers out at low tide. There used to be a whole club for them on campus." It had been one of the few clubs Scarlett hadn't joined, given her vegetarianism.

"It was Vaughn. I know it was."

They were sitting in the dining room of Tudor House, waiting for the other girls to join them. Although now Scarlett didn't know how good of an idea it was, given Orchid's state of mind. She'd already gotten some disquieting texts from Violet about Orchid's earlier insistence that she'd heard Vaughn singing a new song from somewhere in Tudor House. And now this?

Maybe she should encourage Orchid to call her therapist. This might be above Scarlett's pay grade.

"Violet told me what you heard—"

"Yeah, and how do you explain that?" Orchid announced, as if presenting the coup de grâce.

"I can't," Scarlett admitted. "I don't know what you heard, and no one else heard it. Maybe someone was listening to one of his songs outside, and it just sounded unfamiliar because of the way the sound traveled through the stones of the house."

Take that, Dr. Gadsden. The physics teacher had had the temerity to give Scarlett a B in physics last year. And, as she just proved, she'd learned plenty.

"It was new *words*, Scar. A whole new song."

Wouldn't *that* be nice? Scarlett had no complaints about their current levels of engagement, but a new Vaughn Green track would be just the thing to catapult the channel to insane heights. But it was unlikely. The music teacher had none, and Vaughn's cell phone, retrieved from the crash site, was toast. His teachers had told her he used the computer banks at school for all his papers, and Finn's dip into his Blackbrook cloud drive only turned up two additional recordings to add to the three he'd sent Orchid. They'd been popular, but the numbers would not be sustained without new content. It was the law of the internet.

"I know grief makes us think weird things—I know that," Orchid was saying now. "But it didn't turn me into a songwriter."

Ooh, next best thing. Emily Pryce, former child actress, now a singer-songwriter. One party Demi, another part Ariana . . .

"Okay," Scarlett said. "Let's do a thought experiment. Let's say you heard some music—some kind of music. And you went out walking at sunset to . . . well, chase it down. And out by the cliffs, you saw someone on the other side of the ravine that looked like Vaughn."

"*Was* Vaughn, " Orchid corrected.

Whatever. "What did you do? When you saw him?"

"I screamed, of course!" Orchid was gripping the edge of the carved wooden table with her hands. "I screamed his name."

Scarlett's brow furrowed. Yeah, that was going to have to stop. The tabloid stories about Orchid had been mainly sympathetic toward everyone at Blackbrook. They'd been good for Orchid's business, good for Vaughn's music. The last thing anyone needed was an article about Orchid standing on clifftops, beating her breast and screaming out her dead boyfriend's name. There was suitable mourning, and then there was certifiable.

Especially since they'd only dated for, like, a day . . . which was not a thing that Scarlett would *ever* say out loud. Orchid had a right to her feelings. As long as those feelings were good for page views. Scarlett had encouraged her to record an introduction to each song. As it was the first time Emily Pryce had been seen on-screen in years, it was enormously popular. But she hadn't been able to convince Orchid to do any more.

And maybe that was a good thing, if she was going to start ranting about ghosts.

"Then what happened?" Scarlett asked carefully.

"What do you mean?"

"Well—whoever it was, did they hear you? Did they turn around?"

"He stopped moving for a second," Orchid said. "I . . . I thought he heard me."

Sure. Ghosts are known for their excellent hearing. "And then?"

"Well, he kept going up the embankment, and then he disappeared into the trees."

"When you say 'disappeared,' you mean like, walked into the trees and then you couldn't see him anymore?"

Orchid narrowed her eyes. "Yes. I don't mean like he vanished in a puff of smoke."

"Good!" Scarlett exclaimed. "I'm just trying to figure out what we're working with here. Because you aren't talking about a real person, Orchid. Vaughn is dead."

Orchid's big, expressive, movie-star eyes filled with tears.

Scarlett sighed. "And I'm just saying that, you know, you were out there, where he died. It was dark. You were thinking about him"—obsessing about him—"and then you saw someone."

"I saw *him*."

"And when you called out, whoever it was very reasonably stopped and listened because they heard someone calling, but then when they didn't hear anything else, they just kept walking home with their bucket of quahogs."

"He didn't have a bucket," Orchid grumbled.

Gee, she sure saw that person very well all the way across the ravine at twilight. "Then what was he doing out there?"

"*Haunting me,* of course!"

Of course. Scarlett took a deep breath. "Why?"

"Because I'm responsible for his death. Because he has unfinished business. All the usual reasons. Geez, you've seen movies."

She had. And Orchid had been in them. But there was no such thing as ghosts. "Well, you're not responsible for his death, and you have probably done the most to help him with his unfinished business of anyone, so . . ."

"Anyone but you," said Orchid.

"Yes," Scarlett agreed. "I produced all his music, and I have been the architect behind all its marketing and monetization and even the images we chose for the videos. I worked my butt off for that boy and we weren't even friends." She shrugged. "And he hasn't been haunting me, so there."

Orchid groaned and put her head down on the table. "I know. I know how I sound. But I also know what I saw. What I heard. It doesn't make any sense."

It didn't make the kind of sense that Orchid would be interested in right now, anyway. Scarlett patted Orchid's head in what she hoped was a comforting manner. Her hair was a disaster, even by Orchid standards. The muddy brown dye had almost completely washed out, and the blond roots were growing in, but not in any cool, reverse-balayage kind of way. Plus, it needed to be washed.

"We should color your hair," Scarlett said.

"I don't care," Orchid mumbled into the tabletop.

That's the whole problem, Scarlett thought. Add it to the list of things she wasn't saying out loud. "Well, if you don't care, then I decree we're going to color your hair. Maybe some fun color. You know, for prom. You don't have to blend in anymore."

"I don't have to go to prom, either."

"Blasphemy." But Orchid was clearly not in the mood to discuss school dances. "Why don't you go upstairs and take a long, hot shower, or do a face mask or something? You don't have to come to the meeting."

Orchid rolled her eyes. "Oh, I'm released from Prom Committee duties because I saw my dead boyfriend's ghost? How magnanimous of you."

"You're welcome," said Scarlett, not taking the bait. It was probably better to go without Orchid anyway. Scarlett was attempting to convince Dr. Brown that, reduced student population or not, they still needed to hire a band for prom. If Orchid was there she might go nuts and lobby to just play Vaughn's maudlin tunes on a loop.

Not happening. Scarlett had her eye on a hot band from Portland called the Singing Telegrams. Upbeat, peppy, and you could dance to it. She'd listened to enough of Vaughn's ballads to last a lifetime.

The mysteries at Blackbrook come to a
thrilling conclusion in:

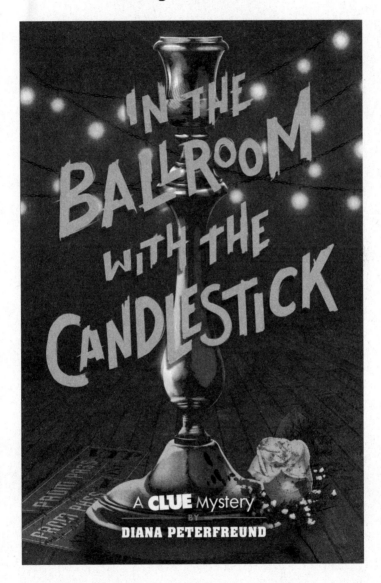